Chicago 1871

A Science Fiction Thriller

Chicago 1871

ISBN: 978-1731363220

ISBN-10: 1731363222

Contents

To my wife Patricia, for all the hard work

In Memory of

Gary J. Curley

Thomas E. Warren

The greatest distance between two worlds,

is time—*John Kirk, time-traveler*

ACT 1

As I light my pipe and stare into the cornfields, I think how ironic it is that I'll be dead in a week, killed by an infection that'll be curable in a few short years with the discovery of penicillin. But that's fate, isn't it?

My wife steps out of the house and walks over and hands me a cup of coffee. As I look up at her, it breaks my heart to see tears in her eyes. She smiles and ask, "Are you ready, dear?"

I nod and take a draw from my pipe. She walks back to the door and hollers through the screen. "Come on, children. Grandpa's ready!"

The door explodes open, and the kids come running out. They stampede across the porch and spread their quilts in front of me. I grin as I watch my sons walk out with their wives. There's my oldest boy, John Jr., then there's George, Paul, and my youngest who often asks how I came up with a name like Ringo. They sit behind the children against the railing.

Sissy, my youngest great-granddaughter, walks over to me and I lean forward to greet her. As she often does, she puts her little hands on my cheeks and stares into my eyes. She smiles and with her soft voice says, "I wuvs you, Grandpapa."

"Oh, aren't you the sweetest thing? Grandpapa wuvs you too."

I pick her up and put her on my lap. She wraps her arms around me the best she can and looks up at me. For a four-year-old, she's the most loving child I'd ever met.

"C'mon, Grandpapa. tell us your story."

"Hold your horses, Timmy. I'ma gettin' there." I sip my coffee, and then look back at my wife and think how she's just as beautiful today as she was fifty-nine years ago, the first time I laid eyes on her in Lincoln Park.

My boys, their wives, and my grandchildren sit quietly staring at me, impatiently waiting for me to tell my story—a story that only a handful of people have ever heard, and only half of them believe. I clear my throat and spit into the old coffee can I keep next to me.

"My name is John Kirk, and today is September 24, 1930. The best that I can figure is that I am eighty-three years old. I have lived a life without regret, and if I had a chance to do it all over again, I wouldn't change a thing.

"No matter your way of life, whether you're a man, woman, black or white, we all share a common dream—a dream of doing something great that impacts the lives of others. For reasons I can't explain, I have not only been blessed with doing great things, but I have also had a part in altering history. You see, I was born on Friday, June 4, 1994."

ACT 2

I was born in Sacramento, California, and grew up in a modest section of town. My father, Allen Kirk, worked as a firefighter for the city, and my mother, Kathy, worked at a local hospital as a nurse. I had a good childhood, and no matter how hard I tried doing the right thing, I would often find myself in trouble. My rear end was no stranger to spankings. As far back as I can recall, I remember having one ambition, and that ambition was to follow in my father's footsteps.

On the morning of September 24, 2018, precisely eighty-eight years from today, I'll wake up to the smell of bacon that found its way into my bedroom and kindled my belly to stir. I'll get out of bed, and after I've eaten, I'll stand in front of a mirror admiring my new uniform. It was a significant day for me, my first day as a career firefighter. The day I achieved my ambition.

Before that day, I had worked as a seasonal firefighter for the State of California and spent four years fighting wildfires. Although it was exciting and a great experience, I needed a full-time career and decided to switch over to the structural side of firefighting.

I applied at different departments, but they all wanted more experience than what I had, so I attended a college in Weed, California, and attended their fire academy and got my degree in fire science and became a certified EMT.

Soon after I finished school, I landed a job in a small Northern California city called Pine Valley. It was a beautiful town surrounded by towering mountains with two nearby lakes, Shasta and Whiskeytown

As I brushed out the wrinkles from my uniform, I felt arms wrap around me from behind. I glanced up and saw my mother's reflection in the mirror. She pressed her head against mine and whispered in my ear, "I'm so proud of you, I know your father would be too."

After my dad had died, my mother moved from Sacramento to be near me. She was forty-two, beautiful, and had long blonde hair to her waist. She was the best roommate you could ask for. After I got hired, we found a small two-bedroom house with a fenced yard and moved from Dunsmuir to Pine Valley, which is located just north of Redding.

"Put your things in the truck, I'll drive you to work."

"Mom, it's walking distance."

"I know, but it's your first day and I wanna drive you," she said and pinched my cheek.

"There's something else, isn't there?"

"Well, kinda. I have a nine o'clock interview at Mercy."

"Mercy Medical Center?"

"Yep." She said and smiled.

"Wow! When did that happen? And why haven't you said anything before now?"

"I wanted to make sure I got the job first. I wanted it to be a surprise."

"How cool is that?"

"Pretty cool," she said. "My boss at Shasta said they needed two mobile intensive care nurses, and with my experience I shouldn't have a problem filling one of the positions."

I smiled and grabbed my bags and took them out to her pickup. I looked up and the sky was mostly clear with a few scattered clouds in the west. Although it was light out, the sun still hadn't made its way up over the Cascades.

After we got to the fire station, I kissed my mother on the cheek and got out. As I was grabbing my bags from the back, I looked up and she took a picture of me. Then she kept taking them, one right after the other. I smiled and began posing for her. I held my arms out, made a few funny faces, and then pointed at the station behind me. She had a way about her that made me feel like a kid again, and I loved her for that.

As she stood there, she smiled and said, "Go rescue your queen."

That was something she often said, she wanted me to find someone to marry because she looked forward to having grandchildren. Under her smile, I could see the loneliness and pain that haunted her. She really missed my dad. I walked over and put my arms around her and said, "Mom, it's been over a year. Maybe it's time you started looking for someone too, you deserve to be happy."

She grinned and then got in her truck and waved as she drove off. At the front of the parking lot near the street was a 9/11 memorial wall that stood about five feet high and fifteen feet wide and had a flagpole at each end. One pole flew the American flag, and the other, the California state flag. Since I was a few minutes early, I slung my bags over my shoulders and walked over to the wall.

On the side facing the street, there was a picture of several firefighters raising the flag over the rubble of the Twin Towers. It reminded me of the Marines at Iwo Jima during the Second World War, and as I stood there, I thought about the firefighters and police officers that died that day and how they gave so much trying to save so many.

I looked at the front of the station, which was a tan two-story building with a high front. Above the second-floor windows was a large decorative relief of three horses pulling a steam fire engine. Behind the department pickup parked next to the station was a section of building that extended out with a door and two windows. I walked over there and tried the door, but it was locked. A firefighter walked up to the window on the right and looked out. He saw me and pointed to the rear of the building.

ACT 3

I walked around the corner and into the door where I met two firefighters face to face. One man was tall and burly and looked to be in his fifties. The other in his thirties. I looked around and the engine bay took up the entire down stairs with the offices to my left. There were three engines parked inside. Behind them, a fire pole and a stairway going up to the second floor.

"You must be John Kirk?" the older man asked.

"Yes, sir," I said and shook his hand.

"I'm Captain Mike Miller, you'll be on my crew." He introduced me to Gary Curley, he was Native American and before coming to Pine Valley he worked as a hotshot for an Indian tribe in Arizona. He was the off-going captain, and after we shook hands, Gary grabbed his bags and walked out.

Mike told me to put my bags over by the workbench and he'd introduce me to the guys. As I sat my bags down, I looked up and saw a face mask and helmet sitting there. The lens was discolored to a dark yellow and sucked inward, and the regulator melted to it. The top of the helmet was black and blistered and its brim warped. It sent chills down my spine. I couldn't imagine the horror the firefighter who was wearing it, felt.

I must've been in deep thought because when Mike walked up and put his hand on my shoulder, it scared the shit out of me. Mike laughed and said that the mask belonged to a firefighter named Roger who panicked in a house fire. He said Roger survived, but there wouldn't be any girls sucking on his ears anytime soon. That made me laugh, but it's a shame he couldn't hang, because once you panic you lose everyone's trust. It's a career-changer.

I walked over to the pole and looked up, it reminded me of when I was a kid. I used to climb on the back of our couch and slide down the lamp pole pretending to be a firefighter, pretending to be just like my dad.

"You like trivia?" Mike asked.

"Sure."

"Since you're fascinated with the pole, who invented it?"

I had no clue, so I took a wild guess, "San Francisco?"

Mike laughed. "Boston, 1880."

"I guess I should read up on my history." I said.

"It's like I always say, you can never learn too much," Mike said as we walked toward the engines. Mike reminded me a lot of my grandfather. He was smart and liked history too. Mike told me the engine in the middle was Engine 342, our assigned first-out engine. The volunteers manned the other two.

We walked up to a firefighter checking equipment in a side compartment of Engine 342. Mike cleared his throat, "Don, meet your new partner."

Don closed the compartment and looked at me. He was about five ten and had brown hair and olive skin.

"You John Kirk?" he said.

"Yeah."

"Nice to meet you. I'm Don, Don Elkins."

I shook his hand while looking at his name tag: 'Donald Elkins Firefighter/EMT.'

"Don's my nozzleman," Mike said. "You'll be working with him. After you get your things squared away upstairs, he'll show you the equipment."

I nodded. "Sounds good."

That's when I heard a voice holler from across the room, "John Kirk!"

I glanced over my shoulder and couldn't believe my eyes, it was a good friend of mine named Tom Warren. He walked up, and we gave each other a bro hug.

"How long's it been?"

"A while," I said.

"You two know each other?" Mike asked.

"Hell yeah! We worked together on the same engine crew with Cal Fire a few years ago," Tom said. "The last fire we fought together, we were part of a strike team that went to Washington state. They sent us to a fire that was thirty thousand acres with only had six volunteers fighting it. They had so many fires burning up north they couldn't fight them all!"

"I think I read about that in the paper," Don said. "Wasn't it called the Carpenter Fire or something like that?"

"Yeah, the Carpenter Road Fire. We camped in a small-town north of Spokane called Chewelah. Then they moved us west to the Columbia River," Tom said. "It was cool because we got to cross the river on a ferry and ended up on an Indian reservation."

"Man, it's great seeing you again." Tom said. We shook hands, and then Mike and I walked away.

Tom and I had worked together at Hornbrook, a small town in Northern California near the Oregon border. After our second season there, he transferred to the San Bernardino ranger unit. He said he was after the ultimate rush—he wanted to fight a Southern California wildfire pushed by the Santa Ana winds. I told him he was crazy. We stayed in contact for a while but eventually lost track. I often wondered what had happened to him, and here we are. Isn't life a trip?

I grabbed my bags and followed Mike upstairs. He showed me to the bunkroom. It had six beds in there, three were made. Mike told me to choose an empty bunk and put my things in the locker next to it, then he stepped out.

After I finished, I walked into the kitchen where Mike was dicing vegetables.

"Just getting the stew ready for dinner. Did you get everything squared away?"

"Yeah, I didn't have much." I said, and then I walked out of the kitchen to the front room. It was large and had six recliners, a wide-screen TV, pool table and a weight bench in the corner. Under the three front windows was a long couch, and a bookshelf full of books against the west wall. I walked over and checked out some of the titles while I waited for Mike.

After returning downstairs, we spent about a half hour going over the equipment and making sure the engines were ready to roll. At nine o'clock, we left and conducted fire inspections and did preplanning on local businesses. Tom and I caught up during the morning. He said Pine Valley had hired him about a year ago as an engineer. That's what he did for Cal Fire, and he was good at it.

Don on the other hand was a lot like me, very cocky with a sarcastic humor. All morning we went back and forth trying to get the best of each other. He reminded me so much of a friend I grew up with in Sacramento. I was going to enjoy working with my new crew.

ACT 4

Around eleven thirty, we stopped at Subway and picked up some sandwiches for lunch. I got my favorite, sweet onion chicken teriyaki, and then we returned to the station to eat.

Tom and I sat on one side of the table, Mike, and Don on the other. It seemed like every time I looked up; Don was staring at me. He was making me feel uneasy, like I had something hanging from my nose. I tried ignoring him, but the more I tried, the more he made it obvious. I couldn't take it any longer, so I said, "What?"

"How tall are you?" Don said

"What?"

"How tall are you?"

"I don't know, five seven. Why?"

"Because it has becometh evident that if you weren't so short, you'd look like Josh Hartnett," Don said.

I took a deep breath and smiled. His choice of words was funny, but I couldn't believe he just went there. Mike and Tom looked at me with blank faces, waiting for me to say something back, so I did. "That's funny, because it also becometh evident to me that you'd look like James Franco if your face didn't screw it up!"

"Oh, you're a real funny guy," Don said.

Mike and Tom laughed. "Looks like Don has met his match," Mike said.

"Whatever . . . So, who was that blonde babe that dropped you off?" Don said.

I shook my head. “She’d be my mother. Why?”

“Oops!” Tom said as he looked down at his food.

“Is she married?”

“Damn, don’t you ever give up?” Mike said. “You’ll have to excuse Don, that’s all he thinks about, women and fires. Not necessarily in that order.”

“If I were you, I’d hide my mother, my sister, and my grandmother from him. Hell, I’d even hide my brother,” Tom said.

“Dude, that’s cold-blooded,” Don said as he wadded up his sandwich wrapper and took a shot at the trash can. He missed.

“At least we know why you don’t play basketball,” Mike said.

Don grinned and looked at me. “Do you have any sisters?”

“Sorry, dude. I don’t have any brothers either.”

Mike took the last bite of his sandwich and said, “Well, Don can be an ass, but I keep him around because he’s a good firefighter.”

“He’s only good because fire excites him,” Tom said. “Hell, if he weren’t fighting them, he’d be setting ‘em. He’s what you’d call a pyro under control.”

Mike smiled. “His last girlfriend said the only way she could get him excited in bed was to yell, ‘Fire!’”

Don shook his head. “Go to hell!”

“In all honesty, I wouldn’t say this about many,” Mike said. “But I wouldn’t hesitate following Don through the gates of hell, because I know he’d get me there and back safely.”

Tom agreed, then said, “I think you guys will be a good fit.”

“Hey, Tom. You should try talking with your mouth closed.”

Now that made me laugh. I gotta say, Don’s witty.

Mike took a sip of his soda. "Don has firefighting in his blood. He comes from a long line of firefighters. Hell, his fourth great-grandfather helped fight the Great Chicago Fire back in the 1800s."

I looked over at Don, he was sitting there gloating, acting all proud. I couldn't help it. His face made me laugh.

"Something funny?" He asked.

"The Great Chicago Fire? I hate popping your bubble, but I don't think that's anything to be boasting about."

"And why not?"

"Think about it, they let the whole damn city burn. If you ask me, they were more like glorified window washers fighting fires from the streets. They didn't know shit about fighting fires. Now, if you wanna see what real bravery looks like, go outside and look at the memorial. Now those guys were real heroes."

"Fuck off," Don said.

"You asked."

After lunch, we drove to an undeveloped subdivision south of town. We stopped at a hydrant next to a cul-de-sac and did what we call a forward hose lay. That's where we pulled a section of hose off the engine and then the engine continued down the street dumping the hose off the back. We laid hose to the next block, connected it, and flowed water. Then we broke the hose down, reloaded it, and drove back and did it again. It was a trip seeing the five-inch hose lying in the street filled with water. It was as thick as a telephone pole.

Just when I thought we were finished, Mike made us hand-jack the hose. That's where we stopped the engine a block away from the hydrant and pulled the hose by hand from the engine and ran it to the hydrant. Now that was a workout. I was hot, sweaty, and thought I was gonna die.

The final time we connected it, Mike let me work the deck gun. It flowed an impressive 1,000 gallons per minute. Even though I worked my ass off, I enjoyed working with the guys. Don told jokes, some were funny, and others were downright nasty.

We got back to the station around 4:30 p.m. Mike headed upstairs to check his stew while we stayed downstairs and cleaned the engine.

"How's the cooking work around here?" I asked.

Don smiled. "First, you turn on the fire, and then put the food in a pan!"

I shook my head and asked Tom, "Is he always a smart ass?"

"Nah. Sometimes he's worse. To answer your question, we rotate shifts, and whoever isn't cooking, cleans."

"That's cool."

At six o'clock we had beef stew and cornbread. For dessert, we ate cherry pie and ice cream. Either I was hungry, or Mike was an excellent cook. All I know is that his stew rocked. After dinner, we cleaned the kitchen while Don kept us laughing with his jokes.

After I showered, I planted myself in a recliner in the living room. The guys were watching *Cops*, and then they turned the channel to a singing show called the *Voice*. Two of the male judges were ragging on each other; it was funny.

I went to the bunkroom and grabbed my laptop and sat on the couch under the front window. While I waited for it to power up, I looked outside the window. The sun had set, and the remaining light was dwindling. When the internet connected, I laugh, an ad for the TV show, *Chicago Fire* popped up. How ironic. I knew the end result of the fire, but there was probably a lot about the Great Chicago Fire I didn't know so I searched it on Google.

I couldn't believe how much information they had on it. There was story after story, and the stories never seemed to end. I read one about a man named David Kenyon, a black firefighter who worked for Engine Company 5. After the Great Fire, Chicago formed an all-black engine company as an experiment. They needed firefighters and wanted to help assimilate ex-slaves into the urban lifestyle. Kenyon got promoted to captain and was put in charge of the then new company, they were called Engine Company 21. After a few years, they were disbanded because their response times didn't meet department standards.

I stood up and stretched, and that's when I noticed that everyone had gone to bed. My eyes were heavy, so I sat down and turned off my laptop. As I waited, I looked out the window. The street was quiet with no cars and then a strange sensation came over me. I felt unbalanced, like I was having an episode of vertigo.

I closed my eyes and tried refocusing. That's when I noticed a line of darkness moving across the ground from the west. It looked like an eclipse. I pressed my face against the window and looked up as high as I could. I saw clouds moving across the sky and they were starting to block the moon. In the horizon to the north, I saw the partial snowcaps of Mount Shasta glowing in the moonlight. As I stared, I thought about when my mom and I used to live there, and then the mountains faded into the darkness. I looked up again and the moon was gone. As I looked down the road, leaves were blowing under the streetlights. The sign in front of the bank flashed, "11:24," and then "59°F."

I couldn't believe how late it had gotten, I was tired and couldn't stop yawning. I got up and went to bed.

ACT 5

I was jolted from a dead sleep by what sounded like a foghorn. I sat up as the lights came on, and I looked around, trying to regain my senses. Somebody was sitting on the bed next to mine, and as I focused, I realized it was Don.

"Station 342, Station 42 with Battalion 242, respond to a reported structure fire, 590 Walton Avenue . . . 590 Walton Avenue, cross street Page Court. Time out at zero-one-thirty-five."

"Get your lazy ass up. I may need you on this one," Don said as he pulled up his pants and walked by the foot of my bed. I jumped into my turnouts and followed them into the hallway. Mike and Tom took the stairs. Don and I went down the pole.

I climbed into the engine and put on my coat. My seat was behind Mike. Don sat to my right, in the jump seat behind Tom. Our air packs were mounted to the backs of our seats, which made donning them easy. I had only to sit back and put my arms through the shoulder straps, lean forward, and pull the tank from its bracket. Then I stood and tightened the straps before sitting back down.

The truck started, and then I heard the bay door rolling up. The red lights came on and rotated around the walls. Being in the state I was, it was kinda hypnotizing. As we pulled out of the station, Don stood and cinched his straps and then looked over at me. "Damn. You already got yours on?"

"Yep."

"Next time if you wait, I'll show you how a pro does it."

"That's okay. I've been watching, and I think I'll stick to my way."

"Oh, you're a real funny guy," he said and gave me the finger.

Mike gripped the microphone. "Pine Valley, Engine 342 responding."

"Copy. Engine 342 responding at zero-one-thirty-seven," the dispatcher said.

One-thirty-seven? No wonder I was tired. I yawned and leaned my head against the window and watched the lights reflect off the houses and trees. The trees were swaying, and the leaves were still flying in the air like earlier.

I jerked away from the window as a bolt of lightning ripped through the sky and came right at us. As it passed over our heads, it branched into several tentacles, and then the sky cracked. I was now officially awake!

"Where'd that come from?" Don asked.

I searched out my window, then squinted to see past the flashing lights. That's when I saw lightning behind the mountains. It was nonstop and looked like a combat zone. "From the west," I said. Don lowered his head and tried looking out my window, but by his expression, I could tell he couldn't see anything.

I gazed back at the mountains and thought about the only time I'd ever seen that much lightning. It was when I was fourteen and visiting my grandpa James in Joplin, Missouri. Every few seconds another streak of lightning would zigzag across the sky, and the booming thunder followed. The storm was heading toward us fast.

Tom slammed on the brakes as a trash can bounced in front of us and flew across the street, scattering garbage all over.

"Damn. That was close," Tom said.

Mike nodded.

The night had an eerie feel. It had all the right makings for a good Stephen King movie.

"Hey, Tom!" Don yelled over his shoulder,

"Hey what?"

"Hey, Tom. It just occurred to me that if this engine were made by Peterbilt, you'd be a peter pumper!"

"Don, I'm gonna wait until you get inside and get real hot, then I'm shutting off your fucking water!"

"I love you too, bro!" Don said and laughed. Then he looked over at me. "Two guys are walking down the street. One of them gets hit in the shoulder with bird shit. His buddy says, 'You want me to run in the gas station and get some toilet paper?'

"The guy looks up at the sky and says, 'Nah, that's okay. He's probably miles away by now!'"

"Don, act your age for once," Mike said as he glanced back at us.

"Okay, Pops," Don said and then leaned over and whispered, "how do you put out a fire?"

"Remove the heat, fuel, or oxygen?" I whispered back.

"Remove the captain!" Don said.

I leaned back and thought how funny it was that we were responding to a fire where people could be trapped or dying, and Don was telling first-grade jokes. At first, I thought maybe it was his way of coping with the situation. You know, trying to keep calm and collected. Nah. He was just an ass!

"Engine 342, Pine Valley," the dispatcher said.

"Engine 342, go ahead," Mike said.

"Engine 342 and all units responding to the structure fire on Walton, be advised that we've had numerous reports. We're assigning the Walton fire incident command to channel three."

"Engine 342 copies. Walton IC on channel 3," Mike replied.

"What's up?" Don hollered.

Mike looked back at Don and held up three fingers. "Sounds like we have a working fire. IC on channel three."

Don nodded and looked over at me. "Turn your HT to channel 3 and put it in your pocket."

"Okay," I said and reached over my shoulder and got the radio from its charger. The atmosphere inside the engine had changed to a sober one. I could see the tension building on Don's face. Playtime was over! We slowed down and turned left then made a right on Walton Street. I could hear Mike and Tom talking but couldn't make out what they were saying.

The frequent lightning made it appear that the night was being x-rayed. I turned and looked out the front window. Ahead, the road curved to the left. Thick smoke was drifting under the streetlight. It was coming from a house on the right.

"Pine Valley Engine 342 going on scene. We have a single-story residential dwelling with heavy smoke showing. We're gonna be making an interior attack," Mike said.

"Copy, Engine 342 on the scene reporting heavy smoke showing at zero-one-thirty-nine. All units and Battalion 242, Engine 342 will be making an interior attack."

An interior attack meant we'd be bypassing the hydrant and going directly inside to fight the fire. We'd be tanking it, using the water off the engine which was only about a three-minute supply. When Engine 42 arrives, they'll lay a supply line from the hydrant to our engine. This tactic will save valuable time and get water on the fire quicker.

Don glanced over at me. "You good?"

I gave him a thumbs-up.

As we got closer, Mike turned on the spotlight and lit the rear of the house, then he moved the light to the porch. The wind was blowing smoke over the house and into the front yard where it then drifted across the street. I looked, but I could see no flames, which meant the beast hadn't been let out of its cage yet.

"Don, you and John pull a preconnect and get inside!" Mike said.

Don looked at me. "You pull the hose, and I'll grab some entry tools and meet you on the porch."

I nodded.

When the engine stopped, I jumped off and went to the hose compartment behind the cab. The hose was stacked with two loops strategically placed in it for easy pulling. I put my arm through them, grabbed the nozzle off the top, and pulled the entire 150-foot bundle from the engine. As I walked toward the house, the hose unraveled behind me. When I got to the porch, I flung the remaining hose in the front yard and flaked it out, so it wouldn't kink when it got charged. Don ran over and hurled tools on the porch and then helped me position the hose for entry.

As I climbed the steps, I stumbled and fell to my palms. The deck was hard and covered with outdoor carpeting. The porch was about fifteen feet across and as wide as the house. It was enclosed by a railing and had a porch swing hanging to my left. I was taking mental notes, looking for potential hazards and planning an escape route if one was needed.

We dropped to our knees and scooted under the smoke to the front door. Don went to the left side, and I took the right. We were using the wall for protection because we knew once we opened the door, we'd be releasing a wave of superheated smoke, and if a backdraft were to occur, the wall would shield us from the explosion.

Mike came up on the porch and scooted behind Don. "Everyone's out. Give me a minute, and I'll kill the power and find the fire."

Don nodded.

Mike went to the side of the house and shut off the utilities. He then made his way to the rear of the house and located the fire, which was seated in a corner bedroom. He stood against the wall and used an ax to break the window.

Fire is like a living monster and is always in search of two things: oxygen and fuel. Once Mike got it open, he gave the beast the oxygen it was starving for. The fire instantly shifted inside and came roaring out the window. It was like baiting a hungry lion with a juicy steak, distracting it long enough so Don and I could slip in for the kill.

As we waited for Mike's signal, Don looked at me and said, "Black or brown!"

"Huh?"

"Black or brown, that's the color we're watching for. If the smoke turns black, it's hot and full of unburned gases and is getting ready to roll over. If the smoke's brown, the fire has transitioned from a contents fire to a structural fire and is compromising the integrity of the building.

"Keep a grip on my leg. That way we don't get separated. Remember to stay low because it's gonna be hot. I don't wanna have to drag your singed ass out."

I nodded.

Another bolt of lightning lit the porch as it ripped through the sky, and a deafening clap of thunder followed. It was so close I felt the porch and house vibrate. Deep breaths, deep breaths, I told myself. Deep breaths. I was trying to get the hair on my arms to lie back down, then I laughed. Here I am on the porch of a burning house, almost struck by lightning, the thunder so loud it busted my eardrums, and I was doing Lamaze.

"Don, you're clear. Utilities are off. The fire's seated in the northwest corner bedroom," Mike said over the radio.

"Copy that, Mike."

I reached down to my waist belt and turned on my PASS. It's an alarm that sounds if we stop moving. It alerts other firefighters that we may be in trouble.

I removed my helmet and put on my face mask then connected the regulator. As I breathed, I could feel the one-way valve open and close inside the mask. I picked up the Halligan bar, a forcible entry tool Don had thrown on the porch.

Don turned around and lifted his fist into the air. "Water!"

Tom saw the signal and opened a discharge valve, and water shot from the engine and into the hose. The line stiffened as the water rushed through the yard and up to the nozzle.

Don turned on his helmet light and searched around the door. He was looking for puffing smoke coming out of the cracks, a sign that a backdraft hazard could exist.

When a fire burns up the oxygen in a house, it creates a pressure imbalance, and without oxygen, the fire can't properly burn and releases unburned gases into the smoke. As the inside and outside pressures try to equalize, air is sucked in and smoke pushed out, giving it the appearance that the house is breathing through the cracks. Opening a door would cause oxygen to be sucked in, somewhat like a person who's been underwater for a while, gasping for air when they resurface. This rapid reintroduction of oxygen causes the vapors to violently ignite, creating a powerful and often deadly explosion called a backdraft.

"Looks good," Don said as he turned off his light. He removed his left glove and touched the door with the back of his hand, then the knob. He was checking to see how hot it was on the other side of the door before opening it. "You ready to get hot?"

"Born ready," I said.

Don connected his regulator and took a deep breath. It was getting intense. I almost felt like we were soldiers getting ready to jump out of a foxhole and charge an enemy machine gun.

"Try the door," Don said.

I tested the knob, and it turned. Perfect. Now we didn't have to force it. "Hey, Don. Before we go in, I just wanted to say something."

"What's that?"

"I hope I didn't offend you today at lunch."

"About what?"

"You know, about what I said about your ancestors fighting the Great Chicago Fire."

"No. We're cool."

I smiled. "Good . . . because I meant every word."

Don lifted his gloved hand and gave me the finger. "Let's get hot!"

ACT 6

I turned the knob. Then eased the door open. Thick smoke and heat rushed out and enveloped us. It was like opening a hot oven door and getting hit in the face.

Don went down on his belly and crawled into the smoke. I gripped his leg and followed. We continued forward, heading toward a glow in the distance. The floor was hot; the heat penetrated my turnouts. Every few seconds, I had to roll from my right side to my left, trying to stay cool. I felt like a chicken on a rotisserie.

The farther we progressed, the dimmer the glow seemed to get, as if it was moving away from us, but that didn't make any sense. We continued moving until it finally vanished, then we paused.

We were now in complete darkness, and we had lost all references to our surroundings. I closed my eyes and tried to refocus then lowered my head until my mask hit the floor. It was so dark, I couldn't even see my hand in front of my face. I thought about the hose and how it had become our lifeline. If everything went to shit and we needed to get out in a hurry, it would provide us the only true way to safety.

As we lay there, Don's PASS chirped. "You okay up there?"

"Yeah. Just trying to figure out where the hell we are!" he said and then shook his alarm, silencing it.

I heard banging on the roof. As I lay there in the dark, it was kinda spooky as the sound slowly passed over us. It was the ventilation crew working their way across the roof, checking its stability before taking a step. Their job is to cut a hole in the roof to create a chimney, allowing the heat and smoke to escape. Once that happens, we'd see and feel a difference in seconds and we'd be able to get off our stomachs. Then I thought how quickly this job can change. Just minutes ago, I was in a warm bed, sound asleep. Now I was on my belly in a burning house, hotter than hell, and I couldn't see shit!

Don reached up and turned his light on. The beam passed through the smoke about five inches before it vanished. The smoke was getting darker. The hair on my arms raised, then I quivered as adrenaline rushed through my body, or at least that's what I thought it was.

I was growing apprehensive and slightly claustrophobic. My thoughts drifted to my childhood, to a time when I was playing with a friend in my garage. He shoved an empty tent box over my head that covered me to my knees. It was tight, and I couldn't move. I tried getting out but couldn't. As I struggled, I fell over and freaked out. He stood there laughing the whole time.

Don pressed forward. We went a couple feet and then stopped. I could tell he was feeling around, making sure he wouldn't crawl into something like a couch or wall. We advanced again and then stopped. He turned on his light, but that time, the beam didn't penetrate. The smoke was so thick, it looked like he was shining his light on a black wall.

"Keep your eyes open and watch."

"Watch what?"

"The fire. It's getting ready to roll on us. Just keep watching. It'll be awesome!" he said with a sinister laugh.

"Hey, Don. I've been thinking about it all day, and it finally occurred to me. You're fucking crazy!"

A flicker came from the back room. As it intensified, I felt like I was lying in wait for a monster to come out and show itself.

The windows lit up, and a loud clap of thunder shook the house. I was so focused on the fire that the lightning and thunder were the last things I was expecting. My heart pounded so hard that I could feel it in my feet. I took a deep breath and thought maybe I should have stuck to wildfires.

"You okay back there?" Don said. He was still laughing.

"Yeah. But when we get out of here, I'm gonna tell Mike you need psychiatric help."

The rear room lit up, and the whole back of the house turned orange, bringing the outline of the hall into focus. We picked up the pace and made it across the living room floor. I looked up and saw pictures hanging on the wall. The plastic frames were beading up and dripping to the floor like candle wax. The temperature was rising and rising fast. As I watched it drip, the pictures inside the frames released thin layers of black smoke, emulating dark spirits as they floated effortlessly around the hall.

When a house heats to a point where it can no longer absorb the temperature, it starts off-gassing, releasing flammable vapors into the room. It's just like water, which evaporates when it reaches the point where it can no longer absorb heat. The black smoke was a sign that off-gassing was occurring.

The smoke in the back room ignited and rolled under the door header and into the hall. Finally, the beast was coming out to play. Once in the hallway, the flames worked across the ceiling and over our heads, and then out into the living room in a slow-moving wave.

"That was freaking incredible!" I said. I was mesmerized by the millions of tiny individual flames floating over our heads. I felt like a moth being drawn to a bug light.

Don raised the nozzle and shot a quick stream across the ceiling and then shut it off. The short burst of water was enough to cool the smoke and put out the fire. We had to use as little water as possible because the temperature near the ceiling was around 1000 degrees, and if he used too much water, it would turn to steam and disrupt the thermal balance. The temperature of steam doesn't rise. If it's 1000 degrees near the ceiling, it'll be 1000 degrees on the floor, and it would cook us like lobsters.

Now we had to move fast. Since the fire had rolled once, it wouldn't take long before it would do it again. We had to get to the base of the fire to stop the threat. It's kinda like holding a popsicle stick above a candle.

Once the stick ignites, you can put it out repeatedly, but the fire won't stop until you remove the heat source.

A chainsaw revved above us, and then cut into the roof. That was music to our ears. I wanted to lie there and wait for them to get the hole open, so we could see, but Don was relentless. Like a hunting dog going after its prey, he wanted the fire.

Suddenly, a white flash blinded me; it was like a nuclear bomb had detonated and spread throughout the house. The next thing I knew, I was lying flat on the floor with my ears ringing.

I lifted my head and looked around, trying to regain my senses. As the ringing lessened, I heard my PASS alarm chirping and tried reaching down to shake it, but I was having a hard time controlling my arm.

"Don, you there?" He didn't answer, so I assumed the worst and felt around for him. A few feet to my right, I found the hose. I called out again and still got no answer. I tried piecing together what had happened then remembered the flash. Did Mike not get the gas off? Was there a propane tank stored in the back room that exploded? Many theories flooded my mind, but that wasn't what was important now.

I thought about following the hose and getting out, but I couldn't abandon Don. Then I thought he continued to the fire. Yes, that made the most sense, so I followed the hose forward. After about seven feet, I found the nozzle lying there, and Don wasn't there. I called out again and still got no reply.

I turned on my light and realized the smoke had changed to a brownish-yellow. My skin crawled as I thought about what Don had said before we came in, black or brown. The fire had transitioned. I had to decide and do it quickly. Either charge the fire or get out. Not knowing Don's fate, I went after the fire.

I picked up the nozzle and crawled as fast as I could, using the base of the wall as a guide. When I got to the room, everything inside it was on fire. The flames were climbing the walls and burning across the ceiling; again, it wanted out.

I pulled my head back and took a deep breath then reached for my radio. "Engine 342, HT 342, do you copy?"

There was no reply. I checked the volume then tried again. Still no answer!

I turned the squelch knob back and forth. There wasn't even static. I turned it off and then back on, and that's when I heard Morse code. It was faint and broken, but I recognized it. It was something I had learned in Boy Scouts, and something my friends and I used all the time. The message being sent had something to do with cattle and going out West; they were paying twenty dollars a head. Then the code faded. How strange was that?

I looked up and the flames were spreading from the room and over my head.

"It's now or never!" I said and moved away from the wall and shot a stream of water across the ceiling and into the room. When the water hit the fire, it sounded like a freight train hit the side of the house.

After a few seconds, a wall of steam and smoke surged at me. I rolled back behind the wall to let it pass, then went back on my stomach and continued knocking the fire down. When I didn't see anymore, I moved back and sat up against the wall.

The heat was overwhelming, and my stomach was weak. As I rested, I laid the nozzle down in front of me and pulled out my HT again. "Pine Valley HT 342, do you copy?"

I sat there and waited for a reply that never came. I looked back inside the room and saw no flames; it was just smoldering in there. My mask was fogging and sweat was rolling down my face and into my eyes and mouth. Why was it so damn hot and smoky in here? Why hadn't they opened the roof yet?

The heat was draining my energy, and I knew I had to get out while I still could. At least if I got out, I could send help in for Don.

I straddled the hose, and on my hands and knees, I followed it toward the front door. I continued calling for Don, but he never answered. It was like he had just vanished into thin air. Finally, I made it to the door and went far enough out on the porch to get away from the heat and smoke.

I raised up on my knees and ripped off my helmet and mask, then I fell on my palms and took several deep breaths, trying to cool down. Out of the corner of my eye, I could see steam coming off my clothes.

“Please, someone, help me. I’m burning up!” I could barely speak above a whisper. The last thing I remembered, I was staring down at the porch and saw smoke coming up through the wooden planks.

ACT 7

I wasn't sure how long I'd been out, but something hard hit me in the head and woke me. I opened my eyes and saw an old white-haired man with muttonchops staring at me. He was holding some sort of instrument that looked like something my doctor used to check my reflexes.

"Did you just hit me with that?"

"I sure did, laddie," he said with a strong Irish accent.

"Why?" I said and rubbed my forehead.

"I was saving your life."

"With that?"

"It worked, didn't it?"

"That's because I wasn't dead!" I propped myself up on my elbows and looked around. My head was throbbing the way it did if you slept too long.

Behind the old man stood seven other men that looked to be in their mid-twenties to early thirties. They had on blue double-breasted uniforms with two columns of silver buttons down the front and a C sewn on the left of their chests. Six had handlebar mustaches that twisted at the ends, and the seventh man was clean-shaven. I looked down, and I was in a bed and covered to my waist. I had no clue how I had gotten there.

The room was long and had beds lined against both walls with a walkway down the middle; it reminded me of army barracks.

I looked at the old man and asked, "Who are you?"

"I'm Doc Martyn. And who might you be, laddie?"

That made me laugh. I swung my legs over the side of the bed and sat up then looked down at the old man's worn-out shoes. "Sure, you are. And I'm sure you already know who I am." I looked at the other men and facetiously said, "And I suppose you're the 1920 Chicago Cubs!"

They just stood there and looked at each other in confusion.

"Doc, I think you hit 'im too hard," one man said. He had a lethargic speech pattern with a Southern accent.

"Why's that?"

"Because he says we look like cubs. Everyone in their right mind knows we don't have bears in Chicago."

"I was talking about the baseball team." I said.

"Like I said, Doc hit you too hard because the only team we have in these parts are the White Stockings."

Now why would he tell me that? The White Stockings was the name of the Cubs before they changed their name in the early 1900s. I thought he was challenging my knowledge, so being a smartass, I said, "You don't know shit about the White Stockings."

"I know that Mike Brannock played one hell of a season for a nineteen-year-old," one of the men said.

"Yeah, but he doesn't match up to Jimmy Wood. Now if Jimmy keeps managing and hitting the way he did last season, we're gonna win a championship next year."

As they stood there talking about Marshall King, Ed Pinkham, and Fred Treacey, I felt stupid because I had no clue who these people were. I thought about Google, but as I looked around the room, I didn't even see a phone.

The guy with the Southern accent stepped forward. He was tall and, well, just flat-out big. He looked like he could rip someone in half with little effort. He put his hand out. "I'm Joe Weant, company pipeman."

I wasn't sure what a pipeman was, but I knew one thing for sure, his grip was strong enough that I jerked my hand back. I thought he was gonna break it. "Damn, Joe, anyone ever call you Hoss?"

Joe curled his brows and looked at the other guys. I could tell by his expression he was wondering if I had just insulted him. Then he looked back at me and said, "Anyone ever call you runt?" The guys laughed, and I did too. After all, that was a good comeback. Joe put on the cap he had been holding, and on the front was an insignia that looked like a Maltese Cross with the number 205 engraved on it.

The man standing next to Joe shook my hand. "I'm Nicholas DuBach, the company captain." He had dark hair, a short beard, and a mustache. He looked somewhat French but spoke with a slight German accent. Nicholas put on his cap, and it had the same insignia, but with the number 67.

One by one they stepped forward and introduced themselves. There was John C. Cooney, engineer. He said to call him Charlie, his middle name.

Then there was Daniel Crabtree, company stoker; Billy Colbert and Dale Van Nornam were both hosemen.

The last guy kept trying to get by Joe, but Joe was clowning around with him and wouldn't let him pass. Finally, he shoved Joe to the side and said, "Get outta the way, big ox." Then he shook my hand. "I'm Wayne, company pipeman."

Wayne had dark hair and a thick mustache that stretched from one ear to the other. As I shook his hand, I noticed he looked kinda familiar. I knew I'd seen him before but couldn't place where.

They all seemed cool, but I was still trying to figure out who they were, what station they came from, and why I was being punked. That's right, rookies always get pranked. It's a long-standing tradition. This, however, was over-the-top.

Nicholas cleared his throat. "You have a name?"

I laughed. "Of course, I do, but like I told Mr. Shoes, I'm sure you already know it. But I'll play along. It's John."

"Do you have a last name?"

"Yeah. It's Kirk!"

Nicholas reached into his shirt pocket and pulled out a watch and flipped it open. "It's two o'clock, and you've been here all night. You must have kin worried about you. If you give us your house number and street name, I can send one of my boys over to notify them of your whereabouts."

Martyn reached over and felt my forehead with the back of his hand. Then he held up a finger and asked me to follow it with my eyes then put a stethoscope on my chest and told me to take a couple of deep breaths. It made me laugh because the stethoscope looked like something they used back in the 1930s. It looked like a small horn.

"Well, the laddie appears to be doing fine," Martyn said. "No fever, good eye movement, and his heart's still beating. I see no reason to keep him any longer. You're welcome to take him."

The doc and the rest of the guys went over to the end of the room and talked. Every so often, one of them would look at me. After a few minutes, they walked back to my bed and Nicholas said, "Okay, Doc. We appreciate your help," and shook Martyn's hand.

I laid back on my elbows and looked around. I smiled. "So, where are we?"

"Kinda looks like you're in a hospital," Wayne said.

"You guys are nuts if you think I'm gonna believe this is a hospital. It's too damn dirty. The germs alone would kill you." I looked around for my turnouts. "Has anyone seen my stuff?"

"Yeah. We took them back to the firehouse," Daniel said. "The smell was making the ill, iller."

"You guys aren't gonna give up, are you?"

"Whaddya mean?"

"The gag."

"I'm not sure what you're implying, but I need to get answers from you about the fire last night," Nicholas said.

"About what?"

"Let's put it this way. I'll fill you in on what we know, and then you can fill us in on what we don't know," Nicholas said.

"Okay. I'll try."

"Last night we arrived at a burning house on Twenty-Fourth Street, not too far from the firehouse. We didn't arrive as timely as usual because it was off-hours. After we got to the fire, we set up our hoses, and that's when we heard a loud whirly noise coming from inside. It scared most of the men, and after it stopped, we heard a loud kaboom in the back of the house. After we investigated it, which was only seconds, we returned to the porch and found you. You were there, asking for help."

"Yeah. Your clothes were smoking," Wayne said.

"That was the damnedest thing I've ever witnessed," Nicholas said. "You were nearly on fire, and you're still alive to tell the tale!"

"And that yellow outfit, what type of ugly burlap is that?" Daniel asked.

"And why would any man wear yellow?" Wayne said.

"And who's Scott?" asked Charlie.

"Scott?"

"Yeah. The name on that iron contraption I cut off your back. And how the hell did you get that thing harnessed like that?" Dale said.

"Whoa! Stop with the questions. You're making my head spin!" I fell back on the bed and closed my eyes. I lay there until I couldn't hear anything. I hoped that when I opened my eyes, I would be in my bed and all this would have been just a bad dream.

Slowly, I opened my right eye, and Joe was right there staring back at me. We both jumped.

"Damn it, Joe!" I said as I got up. "Why are you guys still here? Where's Mike, Tom, and Don?"

Nicholas raised his brows and looked over at Charlie. "Let's continue. Somehow our hose got pulled into the house, and the fire put out. Is that of your doing?"

Nicholas's tone was getting serious, and I was confused. I thought about the time when I was younger and a friend spent the night at my house. Just to mess with me, he woke me up out of a dead sleep and said, "Where is it?"

I looked at him, dazed and unable to focus, trying to figure out who he was. And then he repeated it. "Where is it? Whaddya do with it? Come on. Where is it?"

"Where's what?"

"You know, where is it?"

I lay there staring at him. It was one of those "the lights are on, but nobody's home" moments. Then after a minute or two, he laughed. Yes, I too have wondered about the sanity of my friends, and no, it wasn't the same friend who put me in the tent box!

Anyway, they were asking me questions I had no clue to, so until I figured this out, I thought the safest answer would be "I don't remember."

"The boys and I are going down to tend to the horses," Charlie said. Nicholas nodded, and they left. Joe and Wayne stayed.

"Did he say horses?"

"Yep," Joe answered. "A man's gotta be able to get around."

"What?" I said, then looked to my right. At the end of the room were five windows. Each was about two feet wide and six feet tall and arched at the tops.

I uncovered myself and saw I still had on my gym shorts and a T-shirt. I got up and walked down the aisle. As I walked by, the people lying in beds turned their heads from me, avoiding eye contact. How strange was that?

I walked up to one window and glanced out. I was expecting to see mountains and a city with cars traveling down the streets. But I didn't. What I saw sucked the air right out of me.

ACT 8

As I struggled to catch my breath, Nicholas walked up. "You okay?"

"This can't be real," I said, my breath stuttering as if I'd been crying. The mountains and cars I expected to see weren't there. Instead, I saw horses pulling wagons, wooden sidewalks, and buildings constructed of wood and brick that lined the streets in both directions. Behind the buildings across the street were more buildings that went on for miles until they formed a skyline against what looked like the ocean.

I put my palms on the window and took a deep breath. I felt like Alan Grant when he first saw the dinosaurs in the movie Jurassic Park. Glued to the window, I couldn't look away.

After a few minutes, I closed my eyes and prayed that when I opened them, everything would change back to the way it was supposed to be. It didn't.

I looked down to the street and saw Daniel and the rest of the guys standing around two shiny red wagons parked at the edge of the road. I looked closer and couldn't believe my eyes. The one in front was a steam fire engine with two black horses hitched to it. The one behind it was a buckboard loaded with hose. It had one horse.

I had to take a double look at the people walking down the street. The women wore long dresses and fancy hats, and the men wore clothes that reminded me of Gold Rush Days in Old Sacramento where everyone dresses like they're in the 1850s.

I looked over at Nicholas and asked, "Where are we?"

"It's like Wayne said. You're in the hospital."

I looked back out the window and still couldn't believe what I was seeing. I knew I was gonna regret asking but did anyway. "What's the date today?"

Nicholas laughed. "It's the twenty-fifth day of September."

I watched the wagons pass on the street, then looked at the people, then the buildings, and asked, "Of what year?"

"You're kidding, right?" Wayne said.

"I wish I were, but I need to know what year it is."

"It's good ol' 1871!" Joe answered.

I don't know why I did it. I guess I was still trying to prove all it was, was a hoax. But I walked up at Wayne and looked him straight in the eye and said, "You know, I've seen you somewhere before, and I just can't remember where. Just maybe, if you weren't wearing this stupid-looking mustache, I'd remember!" I grabbed his mustache and yanked as hard as I could. I thought it would pull right off. Boy, was I wrong.

Wayne flinched and grabbed his face. His eyes watered, and if looks could kill he had that look!

"I'm sorry. I thought it was fake," I said. Nicholas and Joe just stood there smiling.

Behind me was a stairway, and I decided I had to get outside and see what was there. I walked over and bolted down them. I skipped every other step and could hear them yelling at me that I couldn't go outside.

They're crazy if they thought I was gonna believe it was 1871. I ran down two flights of stairs to the lobby. The front entrance was on my left and the receptionist to my right. I looked around, and there were pictures of priests and nuns hanging on the walls, none in color except the painting of Jesus.

The lady sitting behind the desk was around thirty; she had brown hair and wore a white cap. She glanced up at me and quickly looked away. What the hell was wrong with these people? Why were they so rude?

They were coming down the stairs and getting closer. I don't know why, but I was scared. It was like I was in a bad dream, being chased by a monster. I couldn't let them catch me.

I opened the door and leaped out onto the landing. There were about fifteen steps in front of me that led down to a walkway that went out to the street. They were getting closer, and my adrenaline was flowing and my heart pounding.

I ran down the steps and across the walkway, past the trees and out into the street. I tried stopping but couldn't and ran into the side of a horse pulling a buggy. I bounced off and spun around a few times before landing on my butt.

As the buggy continued by, the driver stood up and yelled at me. "Are you mad?"

Joe and Wayne came running toward me, and behind them, I saw Nicholas and Doc Martyn at the top of the stairs, talking. I looked around, and the crew was near the wagons laughing and pointing at me. But the people on the sidewalks were rushing away from me, like I had a bomb and it was getting ready to go off. That's weird, I thought. I almost felt like I was in the Twilight Zone.

As I sat there and looked between my legs and noticed a small line had formed in the sand. Curious, I reached down and brushed the dirt to the side, then a little more until I saw wood. I'll be damned, the streets were constructed of tightly fitted planks.

I looked over at Nicholas, and he was still standing there with Martyn. On the building above their heads, the sign read, "Sisters of Mercy Hospital." The building was massive and took up most of the block. There were three floors above the lobby and one below it with its windows at ground level. The place almost looked like a university.

"Are you okay?" Joe said as he and Wayne walked up.

"Yeah. My mother always told me to look both ways before running into the street because I might get hit by a car. She never said anything about a horse and buggy!

ACT 9

"So, where am I?"

"Looks like you're sitting on your ass in the middle of the street!" Wayne said.

I shook my head and gave him the finger.

"What the hell's that supposed to mean?"

"It means your number one!"

Wayne looked at his middle finger and said, "Why thank you. I've always wondered what that meant." He reached down and gave me a hand. "Let's get you outta the street before you really get run over. Besides, you're scaring the fine folks of Chicago."

"Did you say Chicago?"

"No . . . I said the fine folks of Chicago."

Joe looked at Wayne. "See? It's just like the doc said. He's got that amnesia."

"He ain't got no damn amnesia."

"Then why can't he remember where he's at?"

"I don't know. Maybe the doc hit 'im too hard!"

"Seriously, are we in Chicago?" I asked.

"Yes, Chicago!" Wayne said and then continued arguing with Joe.

"This can't be Chicago!"

They stopped arguing and looked at me. “And why not?” Joe said.

I was starting to feel nauseated and confused.

Across the street and directly in front of me was a shop called Boles Western and Victorian Fashions. After I brushed the dust off my shorts, I headed over there. I looked around, and the women were herding their children down the sidewalks like I had the plague or something.

The sidewalk was elevated about a foot off the ground, so I stepped up and walked over to the door. Before I opened it, I looked at my reflection in the window. I wanted to see if something was wrong with my face.

I remembered a show I once saw about a woman that everyone was afraid to look at because they thought she was a freak. But it turns out that she was beautiful, and everyone else was ugly. My face looked okay, so I opened the door and walked in.

I took about five seconds to realize this wasn’t the place I wanted to be. There were racks and racks of beautiful dresses, and one shelf had a sign on it that said, “Dolly Varden Fashions.”

I backpedaled and got behind a rack, hoping to get out before anyone saw me, but I looked to my right and saw three women behind the counter staring at me, giggling. I was so embarrassed, I could feel my face turning red.

“You do know that this is a ladies’ shop?” the eldest of the three said.

“Yes . . . I just found that out.”

“Normally, women come in and choose their own clothes, but I guess there’s a first time for everything,” she said. “Are you looking for something special. Perhaps for your wife?”

“No, ma’am, I’m not married,” I said and walked out from behind the rack. The other two women turned their heads, and the woman I had been talking with reached down behind the counter and pulled out a blanket. She unfolded it and brought it over to me.

“Here. Put this around you. It’s not every day a naked man walks into our store!”

Now it made sense why everybody was avoiding me. I was lucky I didn't end up in jail for indecent exposure.

"When you find some clothes, you can bring back the blanket." She had a warm personality and looked a little older than my mother.

"Thank you for the blanket."

"You're very welcome. I'm Ruth," she said and introduced me to the other two women, Rebecca and Terry. Rebecca had long dark hair and seemed to have a fun personality, the type you could go have a few drinks with, while Terry was more serious.

"I'm John Kirk. It's a real pleasure to meet you all. Your dresses are beautiful. I saw a show once about pirates, and the women wore dresses like these. One girl wore hers so tight, she passed out."

Ruth laughed and put her finger on her lip. "Hmmm, I don't think I've ever seen that show, but we'll have to watch for it. We're always looking for new styles."

"Ma'am, I appreciate the blanket, but I was wondering if I could ask one more thing?"

"Sure."

"Could you tell me what the date is?"

Ruth smiled. "It's Monday, the twenty-fifth day of September."

"What year?"

She looked surprised by the question. "Are you okay?"

I carefully thought for a second on how I would answer that and said, "Yes, ma'am. It's just that I was hit in the head earlier, and now I'm having a hard time remembering things."

"Oh dear," she said. "It's 1871. Were you robbed? Is that why you don't have any clothes?"

"Not exactly."

"Would you like for one of my girls to go fetch Doc Martyn?"

"No, ma'am," I said. "He's the one that hit me."

Ruth sharply turned her head toward Rebecca and Terry and said, "Now why would he do that?"

As I walked out of the shop, Joe and Wayne were leaning against the hitching rail. Joe smiled as he looked over my head at the sign and said, "Did you find somethin' purdy?"

"Yeah, lots of purdy things. Only one problem, they didn't have your size."

Wayne laughed. "I'm taking a liking to this guy."

Joe handed me my yellow turnout pants and my boots. "Here, put these on. We're tired, and we wanna get back to the firehouse. It's been a long night."

"Thanks," I said, and after I put them on, I went back into the shop to return the blanket to Ruth.

When I got outside, Wayne and Joe were crossing the street, heading toward the wagons. I stood there on the sidewalk, watching them, my stomach knotted. I was all alone, lost in an unfamiliar place with nowhere to go.

ACT 10

About halfway across the street, Wayne stopped, then turned around. He took a couple of steps toward me and hollered, "You just gonna stand there or are you coming?"

"You want me to come with you?" I yelled back.

"What else you gonna do? Nicholas says we already have too many vagrants around town, and since you don't know where you live, he doesn't want you sleeping under a sidewalk somewhere."

Not only was I relieved, but I was excited. Now I know how a homeless dog feels when he gets tossed a bone. I ran over to them. "Contrary to popular belief, I do know where I live."

"Oh yeah? Where's that?"

"California."

"California? What the hell are you doing here?" Joe asked.

"That's the part I haven't figured out yet."

Joe had a long stride, and I had to double step just to keep up. As we crossed the street and neared the steam engine, I couldn't take my eyes off the horses. They were big and looked powerful. I wasn't sure of their breed, but they reminded me of Clydesdales. They were black and had long manes with feathering around their hooves. The horse on the left had a white spot on his forehead, and the other had a white ankle.

They watched me as I walked by. I wanted to pet them, but their size was intimidating. To be honest, they scared me a little.

The steam engine was a lot bigger than I imagined. The boiler must have stood ten feet high, and it was nickel-plated and had a black base. I couldn't believe how shiny the valves and pipes were. I could see my reflection in them. It had wooden spoked wheels that were painted red with black bands around them.

Daniel stood behind the steamer next to the furnace. I couldn't believe that without fire, that whole thing wouldn't work.

"Whaddya think?" Nicholas asked.

"It's beautiful," I said as I dragged my fingers across the fender. I had a new appreciation for something that only a few days ago I would have laughed at. Then from my periphery, I saw Nicholas look over and give Charlie a nod then a wink. That was odd, but I didn't give it much thought because the steamer had my undivided attention.

"Once we get to the firehouse, I think it'd be proper for you to show John his way around the engine," Nicholas told Charlie.

"I reckon so," Charlie said and climbed up on the seat.

"Go hop on the wagon with Joe and Wayne, so we can get outta here," Nicholas said and then climbed up next to Charlie.

I ran to the other wagon. Dale and Billy were sitting on the front seat, and Joe and Wayne were sitting in the back, on the hose. They were facing backward with their feet planted on the tailboard.

The wagon was full of hose, and in the front, there was a wooden box painted red that went from one side of the wagon to the other. It reminded me of the toolbox in the back of my mother's pickup. I climbed up and sat next to Joe and smiled at him and Wayne. I was excited.

When the wagon moved, I looked over my shoulder and saw the horse's head bobbing up and down as he began pulling. This was fun, like being on a hayride. The horse looked to be the same breed as the others, but this one was gray with white spots.

Between Billy and Dale, a copper bell hung from a pole. I laughed, thinking that must be their version of a siren. The wagon bed was enclosed by three sidewalls about a foot high and mounted on the left wall were shovels and axes. On the right was an assortment of different-sized nozzles. I couldn't get the smile off my face as I looked at all this stuff. I felt like I was in an antique store.

I looked over at Joe and Wayne and said, "I guess this is a hose wagon?"

"Yep." Wayne grinned. "Did the hose give it away?" I didn't know what it was about Wayne, but he sure was a smartass.

"It's brand-new," Joe said. "We used to have a cart we pulled everywhere by hand. When we got this wagon and Jack, it made our lives a whole lot simpler."

"Jack?"

Joe glanced up front. "Yeah, Jack, the horse!"

I nodded. "What's in the box?"

"Fuel for the steamer."

"What type of fuel does it use?"

Joe shook his head. "Wood and co. Don't you folks have steamers in California?"

"We do, but not many. What's co?"

"Co. You know, that black shit they dig out of the ground."

"Oh, you mean coal."

"That's what I said, co."

Wayne lay back on the hose and looked at me. "Yep. If I were you, I'd watch out for that Nicholas."

"Huh?"

"You gotta be careful when you're around Nicholas," Joe said.

"Whaddya mean?" I asked, and then I thought about that awkward wink and nod Nicholas gave Charlie. Joe and Wayne were starting to worry me.

"He's tricky," Wayne said.

"Yep. There's only one reason he brought your things back to the firehouse," Joe said.

"I thought they were making people sick?"

"He needed a reason to lure you back. Besides, them people are in a hospital . . . They're already sick!" Wayne said.

"Come on, guys. You're scaring the crap outta me. What's he gonna do, pull a Hannibal Lecter on me?"

"Just remember," Joe said, "when Nicholas talks to you, you better pay close attention. If not, he'll have you obligated to the company before you're any wiser."

"That's it? You're scaring the hell out of me because he wants me to join the company?"

"Yep," Wayne said.

"What's wrong with that?"

"Let's just say it ain't easy work and leave it at that," Joe said.

"You noticed there's only seven of us. We're supposed to have a crew of eight. Since July, we've been a man short," Wayne said and gave me a once-over. "No offense intended."

"None taken. Trust me, I'm used to the short jokes."

"We lost Robert back in June to a back injury. After that, he decided this job wasn't a good fit and never came back."

"You're forgettin' Joshua," Joe said.

"Yeah, but he only amounted to a 1!"

"A one?"

"Yeah, a 1" Wayne said. "When we get a new man on the crew, we like to wager on whether they're gonna be a 1 or a 2."

"How's that?"

"There's not many real men left in Chicago, and out of the ones that are, few can handle the job we do. Nicholas is a hard foreman to work for.

He loves to train. If you weren't a man before, you'll be one by the time he gets through with you. That's if you last!"

"We've had guys lose their breakfast in the streets," Joe said.

"Lose their breakfast?"

"Yeah, you know," Wayne said, then put his finger in his mouth. "And the ones who get past the training, we bet on how many fires it'll take to chase them off. You know . . . before they turn yellow," he said while looking at my pants. "No offense intended."

I rolled my eyes and grinned. "None taken. Just so you know, these yellow pants will outperform your polyesters any day of the week. And as far as training goes, you guys don't know the first thing about it. No offense intended!"

Wayne laughed. "What're polyesters?"

Joe looked at me, and I could tell by his face he was puzzled, and then he asked, "What's a Hannibal Lecter?"

I laughed. "Where I come from, Hannibal Lecter is someone who likes to eat people."

Wayne nudged Joe. "See, that's why I didn't go to California on that cattle drive with my brother. Those people out there are lunatics. No offense intended."

"Cattle drive to California?"

"Hell, you're from there. Don't you know anything? They're paying twenty bucks a head."

Shit! Twenty-bucks a head? That Morse code I heard on the radio must have been a telegraph I picked up. But how? That means when I was in the hall, calling for help, I was already in 1871.

As we traveled down the street, I looked around at the buildings and their construction, wondering how it was possible to have gone 147 years into the past, and then the bigger question: why?

As we passed each block, the buildings changed from businesses to tenements and then to houses. At first, the houses were so close to one another that they almost looked connected. Then a few blocks farther, the houses got sparser and the yards bigger. There were outbuildings and barns. I saw cows and horses in a few yards, and in one yard I even saw a goat. Then I noticed how dry everything was. The grass was tall and yellow, and everything was built of wood.

At the next block, we turned east. Ahead, on the left were more businesses, and on the right, the farms continued. The sun was beating down, and I wiped the sweat from my forehead and looked up. The sky was clear. Not even a puffy cloud in sight.

A breeze blew from the south, and it felt good on my face. I closed my eyes and tilted my head back, and that's when I got the most ungodly whiff of methane, better known as cow shit. It was so pungent that I almost gagged and had to pull my shirt up over my face to breathe.

"Yep. Those southern winds are mighty tasty," Joe said. I couldn't believe he stuck his nose in the air and took in a deep breath as if he enjoyed it. After a few blocks, the smell either dissipated or I got used to it.

"That's Porkopolis," Wayne said. "The stockyards south of here are the largest in the country."

"Porkopolis?"

"Yeah. It's because they have more pigs here than anywhere, even more than Cincinnati," Joe said.

As we came into the business district, I was surprised to see all the people waving at us. Wayne and Joe waved back and then Joe nudged me. "Where're your manners?" I sat up and waved too. It made me feel good that Joe included me as one of them. Small children ran from the sidewalks and chase us, shouting, "Ding . . . ding . . . ding."

Billy reached up and rang the wagon's bell, and the children cheered. It reminded me of when I was young and would gesture to truck drivers to blow their horns, and how excited I got when they did. "When's the last time it rained?" I asked.

"Oh, I don't know, other than a few sprinkles earlier this month, I think the last decent rain was back in the early part of July. Right, Wayne?"

"Yeah, July."

Joe kept waving to the children, and by the look on his face, I could tell he loved this job.

ACT 11

The firehouse was on the north side of Twenty-Second Street, near Wentworth. Joe said Lake Michigan was only about a mile to the east.

"That was Lake Michigan I saw from the hospital?"

"Yep."

"It's big. I thought it was the ocean!"

We pulled into an alleyway next to the firehouse and drove around to the rear. It was a two-story brick building with four bay doors, two in the front and two in the back. The doors were painted red, and each had two halves that opened from the center outward. Above the doors was a sign that read, "Engine Company No 8." In the back was a horse corral with several horses in it and a couple of wagons parked alongside it. Joe said the horses and wagons belonged to the crew. He, Wayne, and Dale jumped off the wagon and opened the doors. The bays were pull-through.

"Come. We'll show you how we do this," Joe said.

I jumped down and followed him and Wayne to the front. The room was large, and to my right, a wooden ladder went up to a loft full of hay. On the other side of the steamer, four horse stalls had Dutch doors, you know, the type with an upper and lower half. Next to the stalls, a staircase spiraled up to the second floor. It reminded me of the stairs they have in lighthouses. At the top of the stairs was a large landing with a door that I figured went to the living quarters.

It was cool, watching them unhitch the horse. First, Wayne attached a cable to the harness and then loosened two straps around Jack's belly. Joe opened the collar, and then Wayne lifted the harness into the air, using the cable where the harness stayed suspended. It took all but twenty seconds to do.

"That's it?" I asked.

"Yep. This is our new quick-hitch system, easy on, easy off," Wayne said. After Jack was freed, the horse walked around the steamer and stood waiting in front of his stall. I thought it was cool he did that without being led. Joe told me when we got an alarm, the horses went straight to their wagons and stood underneath their harnesses, waiting to be hitched. Then he told me that they would be outta the barn in less than a minute. I laughed. Personally, I thought he was full of shit.

As Wayne put Jack in his stall, he said the horses were Percherons, and each weighed around 2,000 pounds and were very intelligent. When they first got them, the horses had to be kept at the city stables while we had the firehouses fitted with horse pens. Wayne said that one day, the stable master hitched a fire horse to pull his wagon so he could make deliveries. While he was inside the general mercantile, the fire bell rang. When he got outside, the horse and his wagon were gone.

Joe laughed. "Damn horse took off with the man's wagon and all his supplies."

"Once these animals get trained," Wayne said, "they live for one thing, and one thing only, and that's pulling these wagons to a fire."

Jack stuck his head out and Joe rubbed it, then Joe stepped back and told me to pet him, that Jack wanted it. Joe and Wayne walked away and left me there staring at Jack. It took a minute, but I finally built up enough courage to reach up and touch him. He flinched, and I jumped back. Jack stood there and looked at me. I was almost afraid to move. We stared at each other for a minute or two, then Jack stuck his head back over the door, then he sniffed at my hair. I slowly reached up and touched him, and when he didn't move, I petted him. When he didn't back away, I put both of my hands on him and rubbed his face and neck. He moved closer and put his head next to mine. It was exhilarating to be standing so near to such a big and powerful animal. He blew air down my neck and gave me the chills. It tickled so much I almost wanted to curl up into a ball.

Joe came back with two buckets of water and gave me one. Then Joe went into each stall and topped off the troughs. I was still somewhat leery, so I stayed outside the pens, and when Joe needed a bucket, I handed it to him. After he finished, we went upstairs.

When he was about halfway up, something Joe said earlier jarred my mind. He called this a barn. Usually, I wouldn't have given it much thought because that's what we often called the engine room in the future, but the fact they had horses and hay inside, made me wonder if this was where the term originated from.

I walked in the door and peered into the spacious room beyond. In the middle was a large round table, and the guys were sitting there playing cards. Dale was dealing and glanced up at us. "You boys want in?"

"Nah, I'll let one of you win for once. I'm gonna show John around."

They all laughed.

At the front of the room two large windows overlooked Twenty-Second Street, and against the far wall was a counter with an odd-looking machine sitting on it. It had two reels with ticker tape stretched between them, and on the wall behind it was a silver bell. I walked over to get a better look.

Joe walked with me. "This is where we receive our alarms. When someone pulls a firebox, the signal goes to the watchman at the courthouse, telling him which box number was pulled. He'll check the box number and find its location on his chart. After that, he'll let the telegraph operator know, and then the watchman will ring the city bell eight times, letting everyone know there's a fire. Then he'll ring it for the ward number. We're in Ward 5, so if the bell rings eight times and then five more times, it's our fire. While that's going on, the telegraph operator sends a citywide telegraph to all the firehouses to let us know the box number. When the telegraph arrives, it sets off the gong and the stock ticker punches holes in the tape. Charlie, who is also our company watchman, will then check the box number against his chart to find out its location. It's his responsibility to record the locations of all active fires."

"What's a gong? And why does the company watchman need to know where all the fires are?" I asked.

“The gong is the silver bell on the wall. And Charlie needs to keep track of fires because . . . well, let’s say Ward 6 receives an alarm at Box 300 at Canal and Fifteenth, then a short spell later another alarm sounds in the same ward at Box 312, located at Randolph and Clinton. Charlie checks the tape and knows that Ward 6 is already on a fire, then he’ll self-dispatch to the second alarm.”

“Man, I gotta give it to you guys. You’ve got this figured out. But I got one question—”

“What’s that?”

“Let’s say you get to a fire and need more help. How do you let the watchman know that?”

“That’s simple. The chief or his driver resets the box and then resends the alarm. Then he’ll pause a few seconds and send two rings and then eleven rings. That’s what we call a two-eleven. That lets the watchman know we require additional help at Box 300. Then if we desire more help, which is highly unlikely due to our skills and training, he’ll send a three-eleven and so on. How do they do it in California?”

“The dispatcher calls and tell us.”

Joe’s shook his head. “Man, that must take a bunch of time.”

“Whaddya mean?”

“I mean, it must take a bunch of time for the dispatcher to ride all the way to the firehouses and tell you there’s a fire!”

I laughed. Their technology was limited, but for what they had, they were more advanced than I could have ever imagined. I hated to admit it, but I was impressed.

“Come on. I’ll show you the rest of the firehouse.” As we walked across toward the hall on the other side of the room, we passed a doorway on my right, so I stuck my head in there to see where it went. Inside was a stairway leading down to the street.

I followed Joe into the hallway. On the right was the bunk room, which had eight beds. On the left side of the hall were two rooms. Joe called them water closets. To me, they looked like ordinary bathrooms, old-fashioned but they had a toilet, sink, and a bathtub.

At the end of the hall, a flight of stairs went to the roof. On either side of the stairs were windows overlooking the city to the north. On the roof were several cots, chairs, and a large picnic table. On the far side was a boxed-in area that looked like a garden. I walked over to it and scooped up a handful of dirt then released it through my fingers. A garden on top of a roof; how cool was that?

Joe said they grew vegetables up there, like tomatoes, greens, and carrots. Then he told me that a couple of years back, a guy named Porter brought fruit to Chicago from a place called Darien or something like that. Joe said they were long and yellow, and wished he could grow some in the garden. I guess he didn't know that bananas grew on trees, so I told him. The edge of the roof had a three-foot-high parapet surrounding it, just the right height for me to lean on and look around the city.

I walked over to a cot and sat. It had a stuffed mattress, and I wasn't sure what it was stuffed with, but it wasn't bad. The back was slightly raised. It reminded me of a lawn chair my grandfather had in his yard. Then Joe came over and lay on the cot next to mine. After lying there and talking for a while, we went downstairs. Nicholas and the guys were still playing cards, yelling, and making all sorts of noises, then it went quiet. Most had their cards lying face down on the table while Nicolas and Dale were the only ones holding. They sat there staring at each other without blinking. It reminded me of a movie I once saw about a gambler.

Nicholas maintained eye contact with Dale as he slowly reached down for a card off the deck. He folded the corner up so he could see it, and then said, "I'll raise you two." Then he picked up the card and put it in his hand. Dale looked at his hand and then drew a card. He eyed Nicholas then looked back at his hand. It was so quiet; you could've heard a pin drop. Then Dale said, "Sum-bitch," and threw his cards on the table.

Nicholas grinned and put his cards down. He had a two of spades, seven of diamonds, jack of hearts, nine of diamonds, and a five of spades. I've never played cards before, so I wasn't sure of what happened, but Nicholas clearly had a losing hand and bluffed Dale into giving up.

Daniel, Charlie, and Wayne got up and told me to follow them downstairs. On the way down, the thought crossed my mind, The Charlie Daniels band. I wanted to ask Charlie and Daniel if they could sing, but I knew they wouldn't get the joke, so I didn't.

"By the way, why are these stairs spiraled?" I asked.

"It keeps the horses from climbing them when we let 'em loose in the barn," Charlie said.

ACT 12

When we got down to the steamer, Charlie showed me the engine and said it could pump 800 gallons per minute. Then Daniel gave me a quick lesson on the furnace. He said that while the guys hitched the horses, he would start the fire, and his job as a stoker was to get the steam pressure to 60 pounds by the time they arrived at the fire.

"If a stoker stokes the fire, what does a pipeman do?"

"Pipemen run the nozzles, and the hosemen lay and maintain the hoses. It's their job to keep the water flowing to the pipemen," Charlie said.

It was all making sense. I followed Daniel over to the hose wagon, and he lifted the lid to the wood box. He pulled out a bundle of wood, and each stick was about two inches in diameter and ten inches long. There were eight sticks in a bundle. The box had a separator in it, and on the other side were chunks of coal, each about the size of a fist.

"If I yell for fuel, grab this bucket and fill it with coal," he said as he held up a red two-gallon bucket. "If I say wood, grab me a full bundle. You got that?"

"Coal, one bucket. Wood, a full bundle. Got it!"

Joe walked up with two pitchforks. "Here, give me a hand," he said and handed me one.

"Okay." I didn't know what he expected me to do with it, so I looked at it for a few seconds, held it up, and said, "Look, Joe, I'm Farmer John!"

Joe stood there and stared at me with a blank face. I guess you must need to be from the West Coast to understand that one.

We walked around the steamer to the stalls. All three horses were standing there watching us. Charlie and Daniel headed upstairs and I'm not sure where Wayne went, but we stopped at Jack's stall, which was the last one near the back.

"Wait here, and I'll climb up and throw you down the hay. When I do, give each horse a flake," Joe said.

I leaned the pitchfork against the wall and walked over to the black horses. When I slowly reached over and touched them, they flinched and stepped back and watched me.

"Go ahead. Pet 'em. They won't bite," Joe shouted from the loft.

"I want to, but I don't think they like me."

"Percherons are curious horses. You'll need to spend time with them so they get to know you. You may have to command them at a fire, and if they don't know you, they won't listen."

Both horses walked up to me and stuck their heads out of their stalls. I reached up, and this time they let me pet them. I rubbed their faces and talked to them. It was so cool.

I got closer to them and wrapped my arms around their necks, and that's when I felt the sheer power of these horses. I think if I hung on, they could fling me around like a rag doll.

"Man, these guys are stout," I shouted up to Joe.

"They are!"

"What's their names?"

"The horse with the white face is Fast, and the other one is Faster."

"Nuh-uh." I laughed.

"That's their names," Joe said.

"Why would you guys name 'em that?"

"Because one's faster than the other."

I laughed and thought he was joking, but he shook his head and walked away from the edge.

As I reached up to pet Fast, a loud thud made me jump. Joe had thrown down a half bale of hay, and it hit right next to me. He told me to break it in half and fork one to Jack and the other to Faster. Then he threw more down for Fast and climbed down while I fed the horses.

"So, whaddya think?" Joe asked.

"What do I think about what?"

"About all this."

"I think it's cool."

"Cool?" Joe said as he wiped the sweat from his forehead. "You've been saying cool all day. I don't get it. It's hotter than hell!"

I smiled. "Where I come from it means it's neat."

"Why don't you just say neat?"

"I guess it's a California thing." We stood there and watched the horses eat. "You know, where I come from, you'd only see this stuff in books."

"What stuff?"

"You know, the horses, wagons, and buggies. I mean we have them, but not like this. Steam engines are a whole new story. Let's just say we don't have many."

"I figured California would have all this. Sounds like you guys need to catch up to modern times," Joe said.

Jack put his head out, and I walked over and pet him. It was cool he was getting to know me. As I pet him, I remembered the last time I had seen a steam fire engine. I was around ten. My father took my mother and me to Seattle, and they had a fire museum there with all types of old fire stuff. They had a couple of steam engines too, but I didn't appreciate them like I did now.

I thought about the hay and looked at Joe and said, "You guys have bailed hay?"

"Yeah. Our supplier bought one of them Mormon Beater Hay Presses last year. Now we get it in 300-pound bales. Cool, huh?" He said. "Don't you have baled hay in California?"

"Not sure. We don't have horses."

Joe gave me a funny look and then walked away. I was really starting to like it here, then I realized Joe used the word "cool," and I had to laugh. My slang was rubbing off.

***

When Charlie and Daniel got upstairs, they sat down at the table across from Nicholas. Nicholas peered over his cards at them and asked, "What do you think?"

"Other than being fifteen hands tall, he's got the spirit," Charlie said.

Nicholas laughed. "You measure him like a horse?"

"Hell, I bet he could walk under Jack without bending down." Daniel laughed.

Nicholas laid his cards on the table leaned back in his chair and interlocked his fingers behind his head. "What about his mental state? Does he seem right in the head? Doc said the amnesia only affects the memory. As far as working and talking, Doc says he's in good shape."

"I'm not sure what this amnesia is, but he doesn't seem ill, and he's sharp as a tack," Dale said.

"I say we give 'im a go-around and see what he's made of. After all, he says he has experience, and we're a man short," Billy said.

"I agree, but we know nothing about him. Don't you find it odd him just showing up on that porch? Besides, that sum-bitch yanked my mustache!"

Nicholas laughed. "Now that was the funniest damn thing I've witnessed. I'd keep him around just for the laughs. But I suppose there are a few things we can learn about him. I'll stop by the Western Union in the morning and have Sam send a telegraph to California. If nothing else, maybe we can find his kinfolk."

"I agree. Besides, that contraption he had mounted on his back has me bamboozled. I'd like to learn a little about it," Dale said as he picked his tooth with his dagger.

"Dale, if you don't quit picking your teeth with that Arkansas toothpick, you're gonna end up stabbing yourself in the throat!" Charlie said.

***

Joe went back up to the loft to move hay around and told me I should stay down and spend time with the horses. After a couple minutes, I took a few steps back and yelled up, "Hey, Joe, have you ever heard of virtual reality?"

Joe looked over the edge. "Doesn't it have somethin' to do with women and marriage?"

"That's virtues—never mind," I said and walked back over to the horse stalls and folded my arms across Faster's door. I rested my chin on my hands and watched him eat. I thought about the fire on Walton Street and the storm. Then I remembered the black smoke and the rollover and how awesome it looked, and then there was that flash. That's when everything seemed to have changed. Don was gone, the smoke had turned brown, and then I remembered tripping on the porch and how it was concrete and covered with carpeting. When I came out of the house, the smoke was coming up through wooden planks, not concrete. It wasn't the same house!

Faster looked up and saw me standing there, and he came over and put his face over the door. I reached up and put my arms around him. Then Fast came up, and I put my other arm around him.

"Can you guys keep a secret?" I whispered. "I think I just figured this all out. Everyone who has ever claimed to die, says they all see the same thing, that they saw a white light . . . I think I died last night!" When I said that, Fast and Faster jerked their heads back like they understood what I had just said, and it spooked them.

But why would God send me here? Is this my heaven? Why wouldn't he have sent me to be with my father? I had so many questions, but no way of answering them.

I thought for a minute and then looked at the horses. "I got it! Just watch, and I'll prove it to you." I gave Fast and Faster a quick rub on the forehead, took a few steps back, and yelled up, "Joe, come here. Come here!"

Joe must've thought something was wrong because he came down that ladder like his life depended on it. I couldn't believe how someone so big could move so fast. It almost made me laugh.

"What's wrong?" he said, half outta breath.

"I need you to do something."

He took a breath and said, "What?"

I pointed at my shoulder. "Take your best shot!"

"Huh?"

"You heard me, take your best shot."

"Are you crazy?"

"Earlier, Wayne told me you hit like a little girl! I wanna see if he's right."

"Maybe I should go hit him," Joe said.

"Come on. Just hit me. Wayne tells me you're a big sissy, and to be honest, I think I believe him."

Joe's face changed, and he looked at me with a subtle grin and said, "No problem."

I figured if I was dead, he could hit me, and it wouldn't hurt. I mean if I were dead, I shouldn't be able to feel anything, right? He cocked back, and his facial expression changed to that of a raging bull. The second his fist came at me; I got the most disturbing thought. I remembered how bad it hurt when I ran into that horse earlier. Before I could say stop or move out of the way, I was on the ground, grabbing my shoulder. Joe hit me so hard, my ass went numb.

As I sat there on the verge of crying, I looked over at the horses and said, "Well . . . that blows that theory all to hell!"

ACT 13

I looked up and saw Daniel at the top of the stairs. He turned and yelled, "Joe just knocked the shit outta John!"

It only took seconds before everyone came scrambling through the door and down the stairs. "What in tarnation's going on down here?" Nicholas shouted as he came off the stairs.

"He wanted me to hit 'im, so I hit 'im!" Joe said.

"Why would you want him to hit you? Joe has enough strength to knock a cow off its feet!" Nicholas said.

"I know. I just found that out," I said as Nicholas helped me to my feet. I walked over and sat on the tailboard of the hose wagon.

Nicholas sat next to me. "Have you been able to remember anything yet?"

"I know it's gonna sound bizarre, but I remember fighting a fire last night. The only problem, it wasn't the one you think it was. The one I was fighting was in Pine Valley."

"Pine Valley. I don't recall a town by that name around here. Do any of you, boys?"

They all shook their heads.

"That's because Pine Valley isn't around here. It's in California."

"California? You're telling us you came all the way from California to Chicago in one night? You're full of shit!" Daniel said.

Joe was standing in front of me and asked, "Are you okay?"

"Yeah. Other than my broken shoulder and numb ass, I'm fine."

"Did you say you're a dumb ass?" Wayne said.

"I said numb ass!"

I couldn't believe my eyes. As I was talking to Wayne, he was standing there one second and gone the next. Joe hit him so hard, it looked like he had vanished. Joe looked down at Wayne and said, "That's for saying I hit like a girl!"

"Have you lost your damn mind?" Wayne said as he struggled to get up. I felt terrible but couldn't stop laughing.

"Joe, will you quit hitting people?" Nicholas said and then looked at me. "Doc seems to think you have something called amnesia. He says it has something to do with not being able to remember things. So, you say you have experience in fighting fires?"

"Yeah, I've been doing it since I was eighteen. My father was a firefighter too."

Nicholas raised a brow and glanced over at Charlie and grinned, then Daniel sat down on my other side. "That iron contraption we cut off your back, what is it?"

"You cut it off?"

Billy brought it over and handed me the tank. The regulator was still attached to the mask. I flipped it over and checked the gauge. It was over half full. Then I looked at the straps, and like Daniel said, the waist belt was cut a few inches from the buckle.

"Watch this," I said. I squeezed the buckle and separated the two ends, then I put them back together and then separated them again so they could see how it worked.

"I'll be damned. If I'd known that, I wouldn't have cut it." Dale said as they crowded around staring at it. Both Billy and Daniel had to try it.

Wayne nudged Dale. "You're a big dummy!"

"Hell! You're the one that told me to cut it."

Then they wanted to know what the tank was and why I had it harnessed to my back. I told the guys it was full of air, and it allowed us to go inside burning buildings without breathing smoke. We wore it on our backs so our hands could do other things.

"Bullshit!" Dale said.

Nicholas picked up the tank and knuckled it a few times, and then held it next to his ear and shook it. "I can't hear anything," he said, looking surprised. They all had funny looks on their faces, and I don't think they quite knew what to believe.

Then I asked Joe if he wanted to try it. Joe stared at me for a few seconds and then finally said, "Sure, I'll try it."

I laid the tank on the hose, disconnected the face mask from the regulator, and handed him the mask. I could see the mess on the inside of the lens. "You should wipe it out before putting it on. It's got dried sweat on the glass."

"No problem," Joe said, and then spat on the lens and wiped it out with his sleeve. I laughed. I couldn't believe he just did that.

I helped Joe put on the mask and connected the regulator, then I turned it on. When Joe took his first breath, his eyes got big as he looked around like he was trying to see where the air came from. He looked like a fish inside a fishbowl.

Charlie pointed at the red nob on the side of the regulator. "What's that for?"

"That's called a purge valve. If you need more air inside the mask, you turn it."

"Can I try?" Charlie asked Joe.

Joe nodded.

Charlie touched the valve, and when I told him to twist it, he did. The sudden flow of air scared the hell outta Joe because he jumped and ripped off the mask. It was the funniest thing I'd ever seen. I looked over at Nicholas. He seemed in deep thought and was staring at me, which made me feel a little uneasy. I disconnected the mask and turned off the tank.

"Why don't you boys go upstairs and let me and John have a little chat," Nicholas said.

When they'd left, Nicholas and I sat back down on the tailboard, and he looked at me for a minute and said nothing, as if still lost in thought.

"Is something wrong?" I asked.

"No, not exactly. I have a proposal for you."

"You do?"

"Yeah, I know Doc says you have the amnesia. I'm not sure what that means in detail, but otherwise, he says you're in good shape. By what the boys and I have seen, and the experience you say you have, maybe we could help each other. I need to fill a position, and you could use a place to put your head at night. Until such time that you remember where you live, just maybe we could come to some sort of agreement."

I took a deep breath and Nicholas continued. He said the position paid a modest wage of one dollar per day, and I'd have a place to stay, a uniform, and a sense of pride. I had little choice, and even if I had, I could not have turned down the opportunity. "When do I start?"

"Then it's settled. You can start as of right now. You'll be my new pipeman and work with Wayne and Joe. They'll show you what to do."

I felt God was watching over me. I was now a member of Engine Company 8, but I still couldn't shake my curiosity about how and why this had all happened.

I followed Nicholas upstairs, and he told me duty hours start at eight o'clock in the morning and lasted until six at night. After that I could do whatever. If I stayed at the firehouse and answered alarms during off-hours, there was extra pay involved.

After we got upstairs, Charlie found me some uniforms that fit perfectly in the waist but were three inches too long. We went across the street to a shop called Sally's, but she was on vacation and wasn't due back for another week. Then I thought about Boles. I was sure they'd do it for me. They were happy to see me and glad I was doing good. Joe and the other guys were too embarrassed to come inside, so they stayed with the wagon.

After we left Boles, we went to a shoe store where I got fitted for boots. By the time we returned to the firehouse, the sun was setting behind a brown haze of blowing dust.

When we got upstairs, Nicholas was standing on a small stool, lighting a lamp fixed to the wall. There were six in the main room and two in the hall. After lighting the lamp, he shook the match, and it left a smoke trail in the air, reminding me of the burning pictures I saw the night before.

Nicholas stepped down from the stool. "Don't you look spiffy? Boys, I think John's gonna raise some brows at the shindig tomorrow. Welcome to the company."

I couldn't say how good that made me feel. It gave me a sense of belonging, like I was now part of the family. And for that, I would be forever grateful to Nicholas.

Charlie walked out of the back room and tossed me a duty hat. It was dark blue and looked like a conductor's hat. It had a short bill in front, and above it was a silver Maltese Cross with the number 245 engraved on it. "A uniform isn't complete without one," Charlie said. "Wear it with pride!"

"I will," I proudly said. I put it on and looked up at Nicholas, who had moved to the next lamp and was lighting it. "So, what type of shindig?"

Nicholas stepped down from the stool and then scooted it to the next light. "During the spring and fall, the fine folks of Chicago put on a potluck at Lincoln Park. It's their way of showing their appreciation for the firefighters, and it gives us a chance to mingle with the people we protect. There's lots of food, music, and dancing. We even have a tournament of horseshoes."

As I watched Nicholas light the next lamp, I saw no place to put kerosene, so I asked. Nicholas said they burned manufactured gas; a gas processed through the gasification of coal. He explained that the gas company heated coal in oxygen-deprived ovens and then piped the gas throughout the city for lighting and cooking. That surprised me;

gasification was basically the same thing as off-gassing. They figured a way to harness it and use it as a utility. Man, these people were brilliant!

ACT 14

The next morning, we were about a half hour into training when I ran to the hose wagon and puked my guts out. The crew stood there laughing.

"I thought you were gonna run circles around us?" Wayne hollered.

"He did. Didn't you see that circle he ran around us to get to the wagon?" Daniel said.

Joe walked over and handed me a tin cup of water. It had a six-inch handle and looked more like a giant ladle. I wiped my mouth with my sleeve and took a swig, then poured the rest over my head and took a deep breath. I may have been embarrassed, but I was no quitter. I pulled my shirt off and said, "You guys are gonna have to do better than that!" I got up and walked over to the steamer for a second dip of water and drank from it.

"Are you going to live?" Nicholas asked.

"Yeah, but it's too damn hot to be wearing a long-sleeved shirt!"

Nicholas smiled, and before you knew it, the whole crew had their shirts off. I'm not ashamed to admit it, but Nicholas was working the piss out of us, and these guys enjoyed it. Every hose pull was a hand-jack, and to make things worse, the damn hose was leather and put together with rivets. It was five times heavier and twice as hard to drag as a modern hose. On top of that, Nicholas was timing and yelling at us the whole time, acting like a drill sergeant in the Marines. I felt like I was training for the damn Olympics.

After what seemed like the fiftieth hose pull, Nicholas told us to have fun and cool off. Wayne and Joe smiled at me, opened their nozzles, and knocked me on my ass. They kept spraying me until I got up and ran over to the horses. They were all laughing.

"Let's go clean up, so we can make an appearance at the shindig," Nicholas said.

We left the firehouse around twelve thirty and traveled up State Street. Wayne said the shindig was on the north side of Chicago in Lincoln Park. He said it would be cooler there because the park was on the shores of Lake Michigan.

"If everybody comes to the shindig, what happens if there's a fire?" I asked.

"Not all companies are coming today. They'll have another one tomorrow," Joe said.

"That makes sense."

The temperature seemed to drop, and the smell of moisture was in the air, the smell you get when you're near the ocean. We turned right and went down a dirt road that led through a grove of trees that lined the beach. On the other side of the trees was a wide sandy area where several engines, wagons, and buggies had parked. There were hitching rails with horses tied to them, and lots of people wandering all over. The trees created a canopy that provided shade over the grassy area where most people were sitting on blankets. Several fire pits were burning, and the smell of food was in the air. The overwhelming aroma made my stomach growl.

The shoreline was sandy and about a hundred feet wide from the grassy area to the waterline. The waves that rolled in were choppy, and the water went out as far as the eye could see. As we were getting down from the wagon, Wayne said, "Don't be surprised if you see colored folk here."

That was off the wall, I thought. Joe sat there and didn't say anything, like he didn't want to be having this conversation. "Whaddya mean?" I said.

"In other words, I'm letting you know that Company 5 has a Negro on their crew. His family will probably be here as well. Just don't be offended if he and his kind are here."

"What kind is that?"

"You know, colored folks."

"Why would that offend me? Aren't they people just like us?" I said.

Joe grinned and looked away.

Charlie threw me two wood blocks and told me to chock the rear wheels. After I did that, we walked toward the park area. Joe pointed out some of the steam engines and said that all the engines had names, like our engine was called Old Economy and Engine 5 was The Chicago.

The Chicago, Engine 5, that was the engine company that the black firefighter belonged to that I had read about on Google the other night! Could this really be happening? Could I be about to meet David Kenyon, a real emancipated slave? Bouncing on my heels, I scanned the crowd, hoping to spot him. It was as if I was trying to get a glimpse of a movie star.

There were people all over, a lot of them. Most were eating while others stood around, talking and laughing. The younger children ran around and played while the older kids were down the beach, diving off a wooden pier.

Joe and I went over and stood in a line for the food. There were several tables placed end to end, and they had more food on them than I'd ever seen in one place. There were steaks, potatoes, greens, and the list went on. At the other end was a whole section of homemade pies and cakes. The food made my mouth water.

"Sure looks good and smells mighty tasty," Joe said as he handed me a plate. I laughed because I was skeptical of Joe's definition of tasty.

"Be sure to fill your plate. There's no shame here. We eat till our guts bust!"

"Sounds good," I said as I followed him in line. I couldn't believe how much food he was loading on his plate. He was stacking food on top of food on top of food. "Damn, Joe. You gonna eat all that?"

He chuckled. "Are you kidding? It's my first plate. I'm just gettin' started!"

We were about halfway down when I glanced toward the end of the table and froze in place as my mind went stupid. A young woman walked around the end and put down a pie next to the others. She looked up and made eye contact with me and smiled. She was the most beautiful girl I had ever seen. She was around twenty, had long dark hair, and was part Native American or Mexican.

As I stood there in la-la land, some dorky-looking dude walked over and put his arm around her, then pulled her tight against him. Then he glared at me. Wow! Just got busted staring at someone else's girl, I thought as I looked away.

After I returned to my senses, we finished loading our plates and went over to where Nicholas and the rest of the crew were sitting. There were about fifteen other firemen there too.

"Hey, Nick. Who's the new kid?" one man said. "He sure looks a mite short!"

Nicholas took a bite of his food and said, "He's our new secret weapon."

"Secret weapon? How's that?"

"Well, William, it's like this. I hired him to get in places we're too fat to fit. His name's John Kirk, and he's from California. Me and the boys put him through one of our fail-or-succeed training sessions today, and I can say this with certainty, he's got balls of steel," Nicholas said and smiled at me.

"At practice today, John told us that in California they have a new type of rubber hose with two cotton jackets covering it, and is lighter than ours," Nicholas said. "You did you say rubber, right?"

"Yeah, rubber," I said.

"Have any of you guys heard of such a thing?" Nicholas asked.

"James, don't you know someone who bought a rubber company in Ohio, that Goodrich fella? Isn't he trying to change vulcanized rubber by using something called petroleum or something like that?"

"Yeah, but I keep telling him he's wasting his time using petroleum. That petroleum rubber shit won't ever amount to anything useful," James said. "I'd just like to know how your boy heard about it."

ACT 15

After we finished eating, Joe went for more food while I went for pie. I couldn't believe how many pies there were, and they all looked delicious. A group of men standing a short distance away were laughing, and as I looked over at them, I noticed a group of blacks sitting near the tree line by themselves.

"Come on, Joe," I said and looked at his plate. I couldn't believe it was just as full as the first time.

"Where're we going?" he said as he shoveled food into his mouth.

"Just come on." My heart was racing, I didn't know if I was nervous, excited, or both. Two men and three women, one of the women was elderly. They were sitting there on a blanket, and several children were playing at the tree line. As we got closer, the men stood, and one of them was wearing a fire uniform. The other stood slightly behind him

That had to be him. I looked back at Joe, and he was lagging, more concerned with stuffing his face than keeping up. He was a prime example of someone who couldn't walk and chew at the same time.

I walked up to the man and put my hand out. "You must be David Kenyon?"

He stepped back a foot and looked at my hand then made eye contact with me; his brow crinkled in confusion.

Joe leaned over and whispered in my ear, "I don't think this is a good idea. Folks are watching."

I'd taken a history class or two, so I understood what was going on. It was just after the Civil War, so racism was still a huge problem everywhere. But coming from the twenty-first century, I didn't see why it had to be that way, so I ignored him. "You're David Kenyon, aren't you?"

"Yes, sir. I'm David Kenyon."

"I'm John Kirk, and it's an honor to meet you. You know, where I come from, it's polite when two people meet, they shake hands."

"You want me to shake your hand, Mista John?" he asked and looked down at my hand and then back at me. I saw surprise, fear, and confusion at the same time in his expression.

I smiled. "Yes."

After studying my hand for a few seconds, he reached over and gripped it. A smile slowly grew on his face as his shake got faster and harder. "Mista John, it's a pleasure to meet you."

"How'd you know his name?" Joe asked.

"Let's just say I've heard of him." I walked over to the woman he was sitting with and said, "Ma'am, you should be proud of David because he's gonna do great things for the fire service, and he'll be remembered throughout history."

Her brows raised in surprise, then she looked at David, and then back at me. "Thank you, Mista John. I sure do appreciates it."

David introduced me to his friend, George Reid. The name George Reid caused me to pause because he was another fireman I had read about on the internet.

I looked at George, "Nice to meet you. Are you a fireman too?"

"No, sir, Mista John, but someday I hopes I is."

I looked back at David, "Just one thing, next year they're gonna promote you to captain and put you in charge of Engine Company 21, and George, next year you will be a fireman and work for David. Just remember this because the survival of your company will depend on it.

Where I come from, we have poles to slide down to get to the engines quicker."

"Are they really gonna make you captain?" George said.

"I don't know. We'll just have to wait and see. But if they do, I promise I'll get you a job with the company," David answered.

After a few more minutes chatting, we walked away, and Joe asked, "What the hell is that supposed to mean?"

"What?"

"Saying all that about him being captain?"

"Because it's gonna happen!"

"By the way, we don't have an Engine Company 21," Joe said.

"You don't now, but next year you will."

Joe shook his head. "Where's your proof?"

I don't think he believed me, but that was okay. We walked over and sat down on two tree stumps next to Nicholas and the rest of the firemen.

James Enright, who turned out to be the captain of the Little Giant, looked at me and said, "I don't know how y'all do it in California, but you're in Chicago now, and around here, we don't shake hands with the coloreds."

"Why not? Isn't he a man like you and me? Aren't we trying to accomplish the same goal?"

"I don't know your upbringing, but it's not wise for a half-pint to be sassing his elders!"

"I didn't mean it in a sassy way. All I'm saying is that we're all men trying to do the same job. I know there's a division, but answer one question. If you were trapped in a fire and facing certain death, and then an arm reached through the smoke to save you, would it matter at that point if it was black or white?"

“That’s an interesting perspective your boy has. He’d fit right in with those bureaucrats at city hall. I think the change the city’s kicking around falls right in line with his thinking,” William said before he took a bite of the chicken leg he was holding. I don’t think he had good teeth because, when he bit the chicken, he ripped the meat from the bone and part of it was hanging out his mouth. Then he reached up and shoved it in.

“First of all, you need to quit calling them black before you offend one of them,” Dale said as he shooed a fly off his food. “Oh yeah, what change is that?”

“Well, it’s not supposed to be known yet, but the city council’s been kicking around this notion to create an all-colored fire company and name it Company 21. They say it’s supposed to help them adjust to our ways of life,” William said.

Joe’s eyes got big, and he about fell off his stump. “How the hell did you know that?” he asked me.

I smiled.

“Shit! That’ll never happen!” Wayne said.

“I wouldn’t count on it. They’ve already got the chief considering it.”

“Hell, they got their freedom. What more do they need?” one of William’s men said.

“How about a chance at life?” Joe said.

“Let me ask you this,” Nicholas said. “What freedom does a man have if he’s not given the opportunity to provide for himself and his family? Look at Kenyon. Hasn’t he served the department well? If the chief hires a colored engine company, it’s gonna be his decision and his decision alone. We’ll just have to come to grips with it.”

They all sat there quietly. I guess none of them wanted to challenge his logic. I shooed a couple flies off my arm and took a bite of my pie. Damn flies were everywhere. I looked at Wayne’s plate, and they were crawling all over his food, and he forked a bite into his mouth, paying no attention to them. I think if they didn’t fly away, he would have eaten them.

ACT 16

Damn! This pie's delicious," I said before I shoved another bite into my mouth.

"Whaddya think of the chicken?" Joe asked.

"I think it's the best chicken I've ever had. Who cooked it?"

"Gladys cooked it."

"Who's Gladys?"

"She's the cook at Quinn's, the restaurant across the street from the firehouse."

"Our firehouse?"

"Yep. The same place we get our food every day."

"She sure is a good cook! All this talking about food made me hungry. I'm gonna get me some more chicken," I said and got up.

I went over to the tables and took a drumstick. I couldn't believe how big they were. They were the size of turkey legs. I turned as something brushed against me, and my heart stopped. It was her!

"Pardon me, sir. I'm so sorry."

Her beauty was spellbinding, and after standing there for a few seconds in a stupor, I squeaked out, "That's fine, it didn't hurt that much. I'm John Kirk, the firefighter." I closed my eyes and thought, how stupid was that?

"Why sure you are. It's nice to make your acquaintance. I'm Lindsay," she said and extended her hand with the palm facing down. I looked at it and wasn't sure what to do, so I held her fingers and kissed the back of her hand like I'd seen them do it in movies. She giggled.

"You're quite the gentleman, Mr. John Kirk," she said, smiling. Then that dorky-looking dude she was with earlier stepped up, grabbed her by the wrist, and pulled her away from the table. He tried staring me down, but the punk didn't scare me.

"You're coming with me," he said to her. "I'm not having my girl acting like a two-bit whore around another man,"

"Stop, Luther. You're hurting my arm," she said, trying to yank it back, but he just held on tighter.

Why do I always find myself in these predicaments? All I wanted was some of Gladys's fine chicken! I know it's not my place to interfere with a dude and his girl, but I couldn't just stand by and let this bastard manhandle her like that, so I grabbed Luther's arm. "Come on, man. That's no way to treat a lady."

Luther, who stood about four inches taller than me and exceeded me by about fifty pounds, turned and sucker-punched me. It knocked me to the ground, and I was lying there, counting stars. Then a warmth covered my face, and I wiped it. That son of a bitch broke my nose, and blood was gushing out all over the place. I sat up and leaned forward and squeezed my nostrils, trying to control the bleeding. The parts of my face that weren't going numb hurt like hell.

"Next time, mind your own damn business!" Luther yelled.

I looked up just in time to see Joe grab Luther by the throat. He cocked his fist back and said, "You see my fist, Luther? Unlike my little buddy, I want you to see this coming." Then Joe punched him, and Luther landed a few feet from me. Joe hit him so hard it made my face hurt even more. We were both sitting there bleeding.

David rushed up and handed Lindsay a wet cloth, then she placed it over my nose and held it there. She had this mesmerizing effect about her. I couldn't take my eyes off her; she was an absolute goddess.

"Are you okay, John Kirk?" she softly said as she applied the rag to my nose.

"Ouch!" I moved away from the rag. It didn't really hurt as much as I played off, but I was enjoying her affection and didn't want it to end.

"I'm so sorry," she said as she moved the cloth to the left. "How's that?"

"Better."

"What about me?" Luther said. It made me laugh because Joe knocked his attitude right out of him.

Lindsay glanced at Luther and said, "What about you?" She stood and kicked him. "What about you? You got what you deserved!" She kicked him again. "And another thing, don't you ever speak to or come near me again, you beef-headed barrel boarder. I'm sick of you treating me like I am your horse. You don't own me!"

If looks could kill, I'd be running for the hills if I were Luther. She searched around as if to see if anybody was watching, and the entire park was. She then threw her umbrella at him. "Here's the only piece of junk you've ever given me. Keep it! I would rather stand in the hottest sun or the wettest rain for all eternity than to use your eighteenth-century hand-me-down!" she screamed and then stormed off.

I looked up at Joe. "Damn! I don't know what she just called him, but it didn't sound good."

Joe chuckled. "She just called him a stupid, dull bum."

I don't know why I tried helping Luther, but he was sitting there with his head tilted back and holding his nose. "If I were you, Luther, I'd lean my head forward and squeeze my nose. Otherwise, if you swallow that blood, it's gonna make you sick."

"Go to hell!"

Oh well, I tried. Then Lindsay came rushing back through the crowd and kicked Luther again. "And most of all, you're a chucklehead!" she said, and stalked off again.

The crowd burst out laughing.

"Joe, what's a chucklehead?"

"She just called him stupid."

Joe reached down and helped me to my feet. I thanked David for the towel, and as I walked back to where the crew was, Joe made a detour for more food. The guys asked me if I was okay and said I should try and stay out of trouble.

The crowd drifted away and left Luther sitting on the ground by himself. I don't think many people liked him. By that time, my nose had quit bleeding, but my eyes were still watering. Although my nose was messed up, I could still smell the food. Then Joe walked up and handed me a chicken leg. I smiled and took it.

Joe and I turned when we heard an ungodly sound coming from behind us. In fact, I'd say the whole park turned. It was Luther. He climbed to his feet and tried to make it to the woods but didn't quite get there. He stooped over and puked his guts out so hard, it looked like he was struggling to drive out a demon.

I shrugged my shoulders, and told Joe, "I tried warning him."

Joe laughed. "Kinda reminds me of you this morning at training."

After eating, we got up and walked around, trying to work off how full we were. Most of the firemen were over in an area, playing horseshoes. Nicholas asked if we wanted to play, but I didn't want to make sudden movements and take the chance of making my nose bleed again, so I declined.

A while later, we got back to the firehouse; everyone went home at six except Joe. After it got dark, Joe asked if I wanted to go to the roof and enjoy some fresh air. It sounded good, so I agreed.

Joe plopped down on a cot, and I wandered around the roof and stared at all the lights. It was crazy that there were so many, and yet there was no electricity. It's kinda funny how I envisioned the 1800s as being dark and primitive, yet they had most of what we have in the future.

I went from the back side of the firehouse to the front. Across the street was a four-story apartment building. Most windows had curtains except for a few. A window on the third floor was open, and inside I saw a naked woman. She was standing in front of a mirror, massaging her breast. I didn't wanna seem like a perv, so I walked over and laid back down on my cot next to Joe's.

I stared at the moon for a few minutes, and that's when I realized it looked the same as it did in 2018. That's 147 years, and it hasn't changed. "Hey, Joe, have you ever looked at the moon? I mean really looked at it?"

"Yep. I'm really looking at it right now."

"No. I mean have you ever looked at it and thought about all the people that have seen it? Just think. I bet Adam and Eve used to lie in the garden and stare at the same moon, just like we're doing."

"I've never thought about it, but that's some heavy thinking."

We lay there for a few minutes, then I glanced over at Joe. "So, what's your story?"

"I don't have any, just the ones I've heard and read."

"No, I meant tell me about yourself. Do you have a family, are you married, and where're you from? Your Southern accent tells me you're not from around here."

Joe sighed. "I was born in Northeast Texas in a spread called Troup, about a half day's ride south of Tyler. I was born the year Texas joined the United States, and then we left in 1861 after Texas's secession from the United States. When Mr. Houston refused to join the Confederates and was removed from the governorship, our part of Texas went to hell. My dad was gonna help build the Palestine-Troup rail line, but that was put off till 1872. My father decided it would be best to get away from the Civil War and go North to find work. We ended up here in Chicago."

"Are you married?"

"No. For now, my love is my mother and my job."

"What about your dad?"

As Joe looked at the moon, a tear sparkled as it rolled from his eye and toward his ear. "We buried him in July. He was killed when his delivery wagon flipped over west of town."

“Man, I’m sorry to hear that. I lost my father too. He died fighting a warehouse fire in Sacramento last year.”

Joe wiped the tear from his face. “Were you close?"

“My dad and I did everything together. He was my hero,” I said and wiped my own tear.

“My father and I were close too. Sure seems that me and you have a lot in common.”

Joe sat up and faced me. He then pulled out his eight-inch bowie knife. “You know, I’ve always wanted a little brother, but after I was born, my mother wasn’t able to bear any more children.”

“Why’s that?”

“Look at me. Look how big I am. My mother’s a tiny woman. I was thinking, maybe you’d like to be my brother.”

“Well, we kinda are, aren’t we?”

“No, I mean blood brothers, like how the Indians do it. You do have Indians in California, don’t you?”

“Shoot, yeah. We have casinos everywhere!”

“Casinos?”

“Gambling halls,” I said and stared at the knife. It was big. “What about the other guys?”

“Wayne’s got Daniel. They grew up together, and they’ve always considered themselves brothers, and the other guys have families. I just thought it would be cool if we could be brothers.”

“Yeah, it’d be cool,” I said and held my hand out. “Just don’t cut my hand off!”

Joe sliced his palm and squeezed his fist shut. I could see blood drip from the bottom of his fist, and then he handed me the knife. “You want me to cut my own hand?” I said.

“I did mine. It shows courage!”

For cutting my own hand, I was having a hard time finding the courage he was talking about. I put the blade in my hand and squeezed it and felt a pinch. I opened my hand and couldn't believe it. My hand was bleeding. That damn knife was sharper than hell. That wasn't so bad, I thought and held my palm open for him to see. He gripped it and squeezed. With his other hand, he took the knife from me and wiped the blade on his pants and then put it back in its sheath.

Oh my god. I just violated every protocol on blood-borne pathogens. Who knows where that knife's been, and now I would probably catch some type of disease.

I lay down and looked back at the moon. "Joe, I just wanted to say thanks for what you did at the park. It really means a lot knowing you have my back!"

"You don't have to thank me. Besides, I've been looking for a reason to hit that sum-bitch for a long time!"

I laughed.

"Luther's the biggest jackass in town, and he's been nothing but problems for Ms. Lindsay."

"She certainly is a gorgeous girl," I said.

"You should ask if you can court her."

"Court her?"

"Yeah, become your girl."

I laughed. "Where I come from, they call that dating. Besides, I couldn't do that. She's Luther's girl."

"Are you deaf? She told that piece of shit not to come around her again."

"Yeah, but that's because she was upset."

"Let me fill you in on something. Around these parts, when a woman tells you to stay away from her, you'd better stay away from her."

“Really?” Now I’m not one to go chasing after another guy’s girl, but if it’s over, well, let’s just say the wheels in my head were turning. “But I don’t know anything about her."

Joe laughed. “I can tell you ain’t from around here. She’s only the biggest star in Chicago.”

“Huh?”

“She’s an actress and stars in the show Dolly Varden at McVicker’s!”

“Whateverrr!”

Joe wrinkled his nose. “What’s that supposed to mean?”

“Where I come from, that’s what we call Valley talk. We say that when somebody says something unbelievable. You know, whateverrr!”

“You calling me a liar?”

“No.” I laughed. “Not at all. It’s like saying horseshit. We say whateverrr!”

“Oh.”

“So… where’s McVicker’s?”

“On Madison between Dearborn and State. We should go to the play. It’ll be fun,” Joe said.

“But I’m flat broke.”

“Ask Nicholas. He’ll give you some money against your pay. If not, I’ll pay.”

I lay there fixated on the moon and thought about Apollo 11. “That’s one small step for a man and one giant leap for mankind.”

“What’s that supposed to mean?”

“That’s what the first man on the moon said. You see the dark spot on the upper right side that looks like a scorpion’s claw?”

“I never noticed it before, but yeah, I see it,” Joe said.

“The round spot that looks like the hand of the claw is called the Sea of Tranquility. That’s where Neil Armstrong landed on July 21, 1969.”

Joe stared at the moon for a few seconds and then laughed. “Jules Verne. Did he write that?”

“Huh?”

“You know, the fella who wrote 20,000 Leagues Under the Sea.”

“I know who he is. I read the book when I was ten.”

“Whateverrr! You couldn’t have read it when you were ten. The book just came out in print last year!” Joe said.

I laughed. Joe was learning Valley talk.

ACT 17

The next morning was Wednesday, September 27. I stretched, and as I rolled over, I bumped my nose. Damn that hurt! I never knew my nose was so big until it got broken; seems I was constantly hitting it.

I walked out to the main room, and everyone except Nicholas was sitting there, talking. I walked over and looked out the window and noticed that the sky was overcast. It was surreal; kinda like the feeling you get after waking up in a new house. I was still trying to adjust. The guys were hoping the clouds would bring rain, but I knew differently. I walked over and sat with them.

I heard someone coming up the stairs; it was Nicholas. When he walked into the room, all the guys held up their middle fingers. Nicholas curled his brows and said, "What the hell is that supposed to mean?"

"It means you're number 1," Wayne said and smiled.

Shit—I put my hands over my face and wanted to deflate in the chair. It was the same feeling I got when I was growing up and we made friends with a kid from South Korea named Dong-Hyun Kim. Yeah, Dong Kim. Don't think we didn't have fun with that name. Anyway, he was always asking about American slang words. He wanted to fit in. One day, he wanted to know the slang word for friend. Being smart asses, or being flat-out mean, we told him it was pussy. It was all fun until one day we were at Walmart with our parents, and from a couple of aisles away, he started yelling, "Hey, pussy, come here. I wanna show you something!" I think everyone in the store was looking, and yes, that was one of the times I found myself in trouble.

Nicholas walked over and set a paper on the table and asked for me to fill it out. It was a simple work application that only asked a few questions, such as name, birthplace, address, and next of kin. Then Nicholas left for city hall and to stop by the Western Union office.

***

"Good morning, Sam," Nicholas said to the older man sitting behind the counter.

"Mornin', Nicholas."

"Sam, I need to send a telegraph to California. Sacramento to be exact."

"California. What in tarnation you got going on out there?"

"We took on a fireman who claims he's from Sacramento. We'd like to see if we can't find out a little about him, and maybe locate his kinfolk and let them know of his whereabouts."

"Completely understand," Sam said and then took out a piece of paper. "You want it sent to Sacramento?"

"That's where he listed his birthplace. I figure that's a good place to start."

"Now I've heard of Sacramento. The last folks who sent a telegraph to California, sent it to some post office in a place called Bishop Creek. I don't even think California knew where that place was."

Nicholas smiled and handed Sam another piece of paper. "This is where I need it sent. What's that gonna run me?"

Sam read the paper and then looked at the chart on the wall. "Well, looks like Chicago to Sacramento is charged at 2,000 miles, five cents per hundred miles. I'm gonna have to get you for eight bits."

"Sounds fair," Nicholas said as he reached into his pocket and pulled out a dollar bill. "Here you go, Sam. How long's that gonna take?"

"I'll send it right off. I should have an answer for you, oh, I imagine in a day or two."

"Fair enough. I'll check back day after tomorrow."

"Now that your grandfathers talked awhile, let me take over a bit. You all know my maiden name is Lindsay Smith and probably don't know, but I was born December 15, 1851, at Fort Yuma, California. When I met John, I lived in a small cottage in the southern part of Chicago, just west of the Chicago River near Mather and Canal Streets.

It was the day after the shindig. I heard a knock on my front door. At first, I would not answer it, because I thought it was Luther. But as the knocks continued, they got softer instead of meaner. I knew if it had been Luther, he would have knocked the door off its hinges, so I cautiously opened it. To my relief, it was my older sister Melanie. I stepped back to let her in.

"Is that buffoon giving you problems?" she asked.

"Not today, but I didn't wanna take any chances." I locked the door and walked over and sat on the bed. I was facing the looking glass on the dresser and picked up the brush and brushed my hair.

"So, what was all the ruckus at the park yesterday?"

"You didn't hear?"

"Just that there was a little fighting and a lot of blood."

"Oh my! Luther punched a fireman in the face and broke his nose, and then Joe Weant punched Luther. Luther embarrassed me so much that I kicked him and told him never to come around me again. That's why I was afraid to answer the door."

"Are you all right?"

"If that jerk doesn't come around, I'll be fine," I said.

"Who's the fireman Luther hit?"

"He must be new. I've never seen him before. His name is John Kirk."

Melanie studied my face. "I know that look," she said. "He caught your eye, didn't he?"

I smiled and moved closer to the looking glass. I was trying to avoid her question.

"That's what I thought," she said and scooted closer. "So, tell me about him. What does he look like?"

I spun around on the bed. I couldn't get the smile off my face, and she saw that. "Oh, he's so handsome and such a gentleman," I said. "When Luther grabbed me by the arm and was hurting me, John came to my rescue. That's when Luther turned and hit him. Poor John never saw it coming. I felt so sorry for him. That's when I told Luther we were finished."

"Oh my," Melanie said.

"You should have been there!"

"Which firehouse does this John work at?"

"He was with Joe Weant, so I guess Firehouse 8."

"Did he make eyes at you?"

"When I went to talk to him, he was so nervous, he couldn't talk straight. Then he smiled at me with his gorgeous eyes, and I thought my heart was going to stop. Yes, we made eyes!"

"I'm so glad to see that sparkle in your eyes. We should go find out where he works and invite him and Joe to your show."

"I thought about it, but it wouldn't be proper, would it?"

"Proper? It's not like you're spoken for in marriage. Personally, I feel you should have been done with Luther long ago, and everyone seems to know it but you," Melanie said. "If nothing else, look at it as a gesture of gratitude for their help."

I turned back to the glass and ran the brush through my hair and thought about what she had just said. I wanted to so badly that my stomach felt nauseous, and I was thinking of what people might say. "I don't know."

“What if I invited them? I can see it in your eyes that you fancy him,” Melanie said.

***

Joe and I went up to the roof and lay on the cots, waiting for Nicholas to return. The cloud cover blocked the sun, and the temperatures were at least five degrees cooler than yesterday. My eyes were looking at the buildings, but the only thing I could see was Lindsay’s face. “So, are we going to the show tonight?”

“If you want,” Joe said.

“Sure, is nice up here,” Wayne said as he walked over and lay down on the cot next to mine. “Sure, would be nice if these clouds would drop some rain.”

I rolled my head toward Wayne and said, “Yeah, it’d be nice, but it ain’t gonna happen.”

“You sound mighty sure of yourself.”

“I am,” I said and closed my eyes for a few seconds. “Wayne, can I ask you something?”

“Sure.”

“If you knew something bad was gonna happen and knew if you said something that no one would believe you, would you say anything?”

Wayne laughed. “Hell, I say shit all the time that no one believes. What sort of stupid-ass question is that?”

“Seriously. What if you knew something was gonna happen and it was going to kill a lot of people, would you try warning them?”

Wayne sat up and swung his legs over the cot. “Now that’s a horse of a different color. If I seriously knew that something bad was gonna happen, of course, I’d say something. That’s my job, saving lives. And if they didn’t believe me, then that’s their choice. At least I’d know I did everything possible to warn them.”

"What if I told you something was gonna happen in a few days, and I know it because I'm from 147 years in the future? Would you believe me?"

Wayne and Joe sat there in silence for a few seconds, and Wayne said, "No!" And then they burst out laughing. "John . . . second thought, I wouldn't say anything. I think you've been hit too many times in the head."

I stared at the clouds and thought about what Wayne said. Even if I told everyone, I still wouldn't have done everything possible. What about preventing it? I knew exactly where and when the fire would start, so why not just stop it from happening?

"Are we practicing today?" Joe asked.

"Yeah, as soon as Nicholas gets back from city hall. He said there's something different he wants to try with the hoses."

ACT 18

Melanie and I were having a good visit. We were laughing, brushing each other's hair, and just teased each other like sisters do until we heard a loud knock.

"You get in the closet! I'll get the door," Melanie said. I trembled because I knew that knock. Luther was a very unpredictable person and had a mean streak. If things didn't go his way, who knows what he would do.

As Melanie open the door, I heard Luther say, "Where's Lindsay? I need to talk to her!" I peeked out through the crack between the door and door frame and saw Luther try and push his way in, but Melanie put her foot down and blocked the door. He tried looking around the room, but he didn't see me. "Where is she?" he demanded.

"Go away. She doesn't want to speak to you!" And then she slammed the door in his face and locked it. Melanie wasn't the slightest bit afraid of him. She was married to Brian Flynn, a bounty hunter whom everyone knew and no one wanted any trouble from.

Luther kept knocking. "You know if it weren't for Brian, I'd kick this door right in and flatten you!"

"I'll be sure and relay that to Brian!" Melanie yelled back, then the knocking stopped. "He's gone," she said. I walked out, and she was laughing.

"What's so funny?" I asked.

"Joe must've walloped him really hard because both of Luther's eyes were black and blue. He looked like a raccoon!" she said.

"Is Brian in town?"

"He's on a cavalry expedition near the Border. They're having problems with fur smugglers crossing in from Canada. He'll be gone for about a week."

I reached into my dresser drawer, pulled out two show tickets, and handed them to Melanie. "Here. If by some chance you happen to run into Joe or John, would you please give these to them?"

Melanie took the tickets and winked at me. "How will I know who John is?"

I smiled. "He's probably the only fireman that looks like Luther!"

***

It was a little after nine when Daniel came up to the roof. "Nicholas just got back and wants us to go over and get breakfast. It's ready."

"I'll go," I said and then got up. Joe came too. We walked across the street to the restaurant, which was on the southeast corner of Twenty-Second and Wentworth. I hopped on the sidewalk and walked past several large windows with several panes connected by mullions running both vertically and horizontally. Inside, people were enjoying their breakfast.

Before we walked in, Joe walked over to the hitching post in front of Quinn's and took down a red flag. "This is how we know the food's ready," he said.

We walked in through swinging doors—the type of doors saloons had in the old West. Then I realized, I was in that period.

A man was sitting with his family at a table to our right. "Mornin', Joe. They keeping you boys busy?"

"Morning, Mr. Henry. We had a house that caught fire the other night. Other than that, they had one in Ward 11 yesterday, but that's about it."

"That's good to hear. I sure hope these clouds bring a good rain with them. Lord knows we could use it," he said and then looked at me. "What on God's green earth happened to you?"

I didn't know what to say, and then Daniel came to my rescue. "He was helping someone, and that's the thanks he got."

"What's this world coming to when you can't help your fellow man? You boys have a fine day and keep up the good work."

"Will do," Joe said.

In the rear of the restaurant, there was a counter with eight chairs. We walked back there and sat down. Behind the bar stood a seasoned woman with gray hair past her shoulders, and a large silver necklace around her neck.

"Good morning, Joe, Daniel," she said with a raspy voice, and then glanced at me. "Haven't seen you before. Are you new around these parts?"

"Mornin' to you, Ms. Mollie," Joe said. "This is John Kirk. He's from California. He joined our company yesterday."

"I sure hope you ain't yella like that last guy who joined. He was afraid of his own shadow. We could sure use a few good men, and he whudn't one of 'em," she said as she stared at my face. I knew Mollie wanted to say something but didn't. She made me laugh. For an older lady, she was sure blunt.

"Gladys, the boys are here for their breakfast!" Mollie shouted as she walked to the kitchen.

Joe nudged me. "That's Mollie. She owns the restaurant." He stared past me into the dining room. I turned to see what he was staring at and saw a young colored girl cleaning tables. She looked up, and when she saw Joe, she smiled. Joe cleared his throat and in a loud, but pleasant voice said, "Good mornin', Ms. Sharon."

"Mornin', Mista Joe," she said and continued cleaning. She never lost that gorgeous smile. Hmmm, not once did she look at Daniel or me.

A middle-aged colored woman walked out from the back. She was carrying several paper bags of food. "Mornin', Mista Joe, Mista Daniel." Then she looked at me. "Good Lord, child! What happened to you?"

"Ms. Gladys, this is our newest fireman, John Kirk," Daniel said.

"Well, it sure is a pleasure a-meeting you, Mista John."

"The pleasure's all mine," I said.

"I heard there was a ruckus at the park yesterday," Mollie said and then looked at my face. "And judging by your face, you look like you were part of it!"

"Yes, ma'am. I was a big part of it."

"You just let me tell you one thing. That Luther has never been right for that girl, and the whole damn town knows it," Mollie said. "And if he were to get trampled tomorrow by a herd of cows, it wouldn't be soon enough."

Mollie seemed to already know the whole story. Man, word sure gets around.

Joe handed me two bags and gave Daniel a couple. "Thank you, Ms. Mollie, Ms. Gladys," he said. "Sure do appreciate the kind words and the fine food."

"You boys have a wonderful day," Mollie said.

As we walked toward the door, Joe looked back at Sharon, and they both smiled at each other. As we crossed the street, I kept looking at Joe, but I said nothing. When we got to the sidewalk in front of the firehouse, he stopped and said, "Okay, why are you giving me that look?"

"What look?" I asked.

"That look!"

I smiled. "Okay. You can't fool me. I know that look."

"What look?" Joe said.

"That look. The way you and Sharon looked at each other."

Joe grinned. "Can't two people smile and say hello?"

"Yeah, okay," I said and grinned right back.

"Besides, that wouldn't be proper." Joe said and smiled. I could tell he liked Sharon, and by the look she gave him, the feeling was mutual.

"It's about damn time you got here," Wayne said as we walked in.

"If Ms. Sherry would fix somethin' for you to eat before coming to work, you wouldn't be so damn hungry all the time," Joe said.

When I heard the name Sherry, it triggered something. It was like I had heard the name recently but couldn't remember where.

"Let's eat. Afterward, I have some good training planned for the day," Nicholas said.

A few minutes into breakfast, there was a knock on the stairway door. Dale jumped up and answered it. "Come in," he said.

I turned around and saw a young woman walk in, and she came over to the table.

"Mornin', Ms. Melanie," Nicholas said.

"Good morning, Nicholas, gentlemen. I'm sorry for barging in and interrupting your meal," she said, "but the reason for my visit was to bring these by and give them to Joe and . . ." She paused when she saw my face. "You must be John Kirk?"

"Was it the nose, or the eyes that gave it away?" I said.

"Well, kinda both." She laughed. "Lindsay wanted me to bring these by and give them to you and Joe as gratitude for aiding her in the park yesterday," she said as she handed the tickets to Joe and me.

I looked at it as my heart started pounding. It was a ticket to the Dolly Varden show.

"I'm so rude," she said. "I'm Melanie, Lindsay's older sister."

I stood up and said, "Why, of course, you are. There's no shortage of beauty in your family." She held her hand out, and like I did with Lindsay's, I bent over and kissed it.

"Such a gentleman you are, Mr. Kirk." She giggled.

"Call me John. Mr. Kirk makes me feel old."

I walked Melanie downstairs and to the front door and asked her to thank Lindsay for me. Then I went back up to finish my breakfast. We had scrambled eggs, fried potatoes, biscuits and gravy, and bacon. I'm a biscuits-and-gravy person, and I can honestly say it was the best I'd ever eaten.

"Looks like Johnny boy has a secret admirer," Daniel said.

"Suuuch a gentleman!" Wayne said. "You're overdoing it! When a lady holds her hand out, you let her rest it on yours, and then you gently shake it. You don't kiss it, dumbass!"

"Yeah. That's the shit they do in England," Billy said.

"Oh well," I said, and yes, I felt like an idiot. Joe winked at me and held up his ticket. The crew was still cracking jokes, so I just tuned them out while I ate. I thought about Lindsay, and how this worked out without me having to come up with any money. As far as them laughing at me, it didn't bother me; it made me feel like I was part of the family.

***

After Melanie delivered the tickets to Joe and John, she came back to my house. She looked at me and said, "Oh my gosh, I saw him. He's charming!"

"Isn't he handsome?" I said.

"Oh, beyond my imagination!"

"How is he? Does he look bad?"

"His nose is swollen, and he has bruises under his eyes, but he doesn't look anywhere near as bad as Luther."

"What about the tickets? Did they take them? Are they coming?"

"Yes, they took them, and yes, they'll be coming tonight!" Melanie said. "He's such a gentleman. I held my hand out to shake, and he kissed it. Don't you let this one get away."

I giggled. "He kissed my hand too. I thought I was gonna faint!" I said and gave Melanie a hug. "Thank you."

ACT 19

After breakfast, we drew up some water and formed a line in front of the sink. We cleaned the dishes in a couple of minutes; that's what you call teamwork.

The crew suddenly stopped and stood quietly. I looked at them, trying to figure out what was happening. Dale raised his finger and held it over his lips so I'd be quiet, and that's when I heard the deep tones of a bell ringing outside. Each bong echoed; it was almost scary. Nicholas and Charlie walked over to the window, counting each ring on their fingers.

Once the bell hit its eighth ring, everyone ran to the front windows to look out. They were looking for smoke. The bell paused and then rang again. That was exciting; I wanted to jump out of my skin. The bell rang five more times before stopping.

"That's us!" Nicholas shouted. The guys ran out the door while he and Charlie went to the teletype. I stayed because I wanted to see it in action. Nicholas smiled at me, then the bell on the wall rang, and the tape turned. Charlie pulled out a sheet of paper from the drawer as the bell continued ringing. When it was finished, it was Box 514. Charlie checked the sheet and said, "Twelfth and Michigan."

Again, Nicholas ran back to the window and checked for smoke, but still couldn't see any. Then we ran down the stairs, and the front doors were already open, and the horses hitched. I couldn't believe how fast they were. Smoke was already coming from the steamer and filling the barn. It smelled like chimney smoke.

"Twelfth and Michigan!" Nicholas yelled to Billy.

I jumped on the wagon next to Joe and Wayne, then we were off. Michigan was a few blocks east of the firehouse, and we turned north there. After we made that turn, that's when Charlie and Billy put the horses in a full gallop.

I closed my eyes and felt the cold wind blow across my face, thinking how nice it was that the sun wasn't beating down on us.

Wayne looked at my turnouts and laughed. "I got a new nickname for you. Corncob."

"Huh?"

"Corncob. Wearing all that yellow makes you look like a damn ear of corn."

"Hahaha," I said. I inhaled a breath of choking smoke. It had a strong stench of sulfur. I turned around and saw black smoke coming from the steamer.

"Daniel's putting coal in the furnace. He's got pressure," Joe said.

The smoke was pouring from the smokestack and coming right at us. It surprised me that Jack kept running right through it, completely unfazed.

I coughed. "Damn. We ain't even there yet, and I'm getting exhausted!"

Joe and Wayne just stared at me, then Wayne laughed. "Oh, I get it. Smoke, exhaust, you're getting exhausted. Hahaha! You're a funny guy."

When he said that, it reminded me of Don; that's something he always said. Then I thought about home and how none of it exists yet. Everyone I knew, like my mother, hadn't even been born yet.

As we sped down the road, Dale rang the bell, and Nicholas blew the steamer's whistle. People were all over, waving at us as we drove by.

The farther we went; I noticed the people were only giving us quick glances as we passed by. Their attention was focused on what was in front of us.

I turned and looked. Two blocks ahead of us, smoke was drifting across the road. I knew that color and knew it well: it was the color of vegetation burning.

We stopped at the corner of Twelfth and Michigan. The vacant lot on the northwest corner was burning. The fire was at a point we often referred to as "taking off." The flames had spread out far enough that they were pulling cool air down to replace the air the heat was displacing. The fire was creating its own wind, and quickly spreading through the foot-high grass right toward two buildings on the north side of the field.

"Make your fight from the south and move in behind the north flank before it reaches those buildings!" Nicholas yelled.

Charlie jumped down from the engine and threw chock blocks under the wheels. Joe and Wayne grabbed two hoses off the back and ran toward the fire. Billy and Dale pulled a supply hose from the wagon, then ran it to the hydrant at the corner of Twelfth and Michigan. When they got the hose to the corner, Daniel pulled off an extra section and uncoupled it. He ran the end over to Charlie, who connected it to the steamer intake and yelled for Billy to open the hydrant. Daniel ran back and pulled off a couple more sections of the hoses Wayne and Joe were pulling and uncoupled them. He ran those ends over and coupled them to the steamer's discharge pipes.

If you think all that sounds confusing, I stood there like an idiot and watched. I wasn't about to get in their way. Everything they did was methodical, and the speed in which they did it was mind-boggling. By the time I figured out what they were doing, they had water flowing.

"John, help Joe with the hose!" Nicholas yelled.

I ran over and grabbed the hose behind Joe and helped him pull it. Joe charged across the smoldering burn like he was a tank. We were now racing the flames to catch them before they reached the buildings.

The fire was moving fast, and we were fighting a losing battle. Then Joe made a brilliant move. He yelled to Charlie to increase the pressure, then shot a stream over the flames and onto the building. He drenched the walls, and when the fire reached them, it went out. I was impressed. Once Joe set his sights on the fire, it didn't stand a chance.

After we got the fire knocked down, Engine 10 pulled up and stopped next to our engine. They looked at the smoldering field, and one man sitting in the front seat said, "You boys need to start saving us something to fight. This is becoming a waste of our time!"

"That's what happens when you go up against the finest crew in the department," Wayne said. "No offense intended!"

"We'll just have to find out this Sunday, won't we?" the man said and stuck his nose up in the air. "Let's get outta here. The shit's gettin' mighty deep!"

After Engine 10 pulled away, Charlie shut down the steamer, and we broke down the hose and loaded it back on the wagon. But it didn't make sense that we were loading the hose while the whole damn field was still smoking and pieces of wood burning.

"Joe, aren't we gonna put the fire out?"

"It is out."

"It's still smoking!"

"A little smoke never hurt anyone."

I shook my head. "Man, in California we'd make sure it was completely out and wouldn't call it contained until we cut a fire line all the way around it."

"I think you guys in California have too much time on your hands. Maybe you need to have some real fires out there!" Wayne said as he helped load the hose in the wagon. I almost wanted to laugh.

On the way back to the firehouse, Joe and Wayne told me how each company competed against each other. Wayne said it went back to the old days. That made me laugh, because, to me, these were the old days. He said fire crews used to get paid by insurance companies to be the first to arrive and put out the fire.

Joe said companies would even send men out to cover hydrants with wooden barrels so other crews couldn't find them. He said that, to that day, crews still race to fires, and that last year, the A. D. Titsworth and the Long John were racing to a fire on Canal Street, the Long John rolled over, and the driver almost died. The Long John crew swear up and down that the Titsworth purposely ran them off the road.

***

At six thirty that night, I was at the theater, getting ready for my seven o'clock show, when I heard someone jiggling the nob on my dressing room door. I jumped and then quietly walked over to it. Then there was a soft knock. Still cautious, I put my ear against the door to see if I could hear anything then asked, "Who is it?"

"It's me, Melanie."

Relief flooded me, and I opened the door. "Sorry, but I'm still a little nervous, knowing that scoundrel is running around," I said as I walked back to my vanity to finish my makeup.

"You look beautiful in that dress," Melanie said as she sat on the sofa.

"It's a new dress sent over from Boles." I sat there and moved closer to the mirror and colored in my eyebrows then brushed rouge on my cheeks. I had to wear it dark, so the audience in the rear of the theater could see I had rosy-red cheeks.

"Lindsay, I don't think you need to be concerned about Luther. I'm certain he got the message."

"I hope you're right, but I don't trust him."

Melanie grinned and stepped up behind me. She straightened the shawl around my shoulders and handed me my white gloves.

***

Joe and I got off the streetcar and stood on the sidewalk until it pulled away. Across the street is the theater. It was a four-story building with tall windows and a sign that said McVicker's Theatre on the upper side. On the roof was a sculpture of an eagle, and behind it was an enormous flag that flew above the building. Next door was a smaller two-story building with a sign that said, "Green Room—Sand's Pale Cream Ale."

People were walking all over, and buggies were passing by on the street. I even saw a group of Indians down the sidewalk. It was cool; three wore headdresses with feathers.

"We have a few minutes. Let's go to the Green Room," Joe said.

I did not understand what cream ale was, but I assumed it was like cream soda. I was kinda thirsty, so I said, "Okay, but since you're my big brother, you'll have to buy."

He smiled. "Okay."

We strolled across the street and went into the shop, and that's when I realized the Green Room was a bar. The barkeeper was at the end of the bar pouring drinks for two men, and behind the counter were shelves of bottled alcohol.

A man standing at the other end of the counter slurred, "You boys keeping us safe?"

"Trying our best," Joe said.

"Good to hear."

"Barkeep, pour us a base-burner," Joe said.

"Coming up," the man said then placed two glasses in front of us. He filled them about half full and said, "That'd be ten cents."

Joe flipped out a quarter. "We'll have one to follow and keep the change."

"I appreciate it," he said and picked it up.

Joe picked up his glass, said, "Bottoms up," and downed it in one gulp.

I thought I'd be like Joe, so I lifted my glass and repeated him. As soon as it hit my throat, I knew something was seriously wrong. The liquor felt like burning gasoline. I immediately coughed it out all over the countertop. I couldn't quit coughing. Joe and the guys at the bar couldn't stop laughing. My eyes were burning, and my face went numb. "What the hell was that?"

"Good ol' whiskey!" Joe said.

"Damn! This stuff would make tequila taste like water," I said.

"Drink up. We have a show to catch."

I looked at Joe. "It's okay to be drinking?"

"Why wouldn't it be?" he said and downed his last shot.

"Because we're in uniform!"

"So?"

I shook my head, picked up my glass, and said, "Here goes nothing." Then I gulped it. Although it burned like hell, I swallowed it. "At least I know why they call it a base-burner!"

"Let's go to the show," Joe said and picked up his cap.

We left the Green Room and walked over to McVicker's and got in line. The front door was huge, about twelve feet high and wide enough that six people standing side by side could walk in together. The top of the door was arched. It sure must've been a popular design. Eventually, we made it inside and gave our tickets to the usher. He used a map to show us the location of our seats. It was in the front row.

I was feeling the alcohol. I looked around the auditorium and almost lost my balance. Joe laughed at me. The theater was much larger inside than it looked outside. The seating went all the way to the stage with a proscenium arch, then there were three more balconies above us and two levels of viewing boxes on the left and right sides of the stage. I would say there must've been at least two thousand seats in there. A large curtain blocked the stage. It followed the contour of the seats.

"This is so cool, Joe. It makes you feel like you're in a different world. You know, maybe we should come back tomorrow night and invite Ms. Sharon."

Joe jerked his head back. "Huh?"

"You heard me!"

ACT 20

Joe laughed. "You must be liquored up talking like that."

"Why? Because she's colored?"

"Who says I even like her?"

I smiled. "The way you looked at each other does. I wasn't born yesterday."

The lights dimmed, and as the curtains opened, the band played. The music was loud and filled the theater. The atmosphere was full of excitement; it was like walking into the gates of Disney World for the first time. I melted into my seat as I saw Lindsay standing center stage. She was breathtaking. The dress she wore was astonishing. She took a bow with the other cast members, and as they cleared the stage, Lindsay broke out with a song. Her voice sounded like an angel's.

The show lasted for an hour, and it was unbelievable. I wished my mother could have been here to enjoy it with me. I looked at Lindsay as she performed her final song and I said, "That's the girl I'm gonna marry!"

"Whateverrr!" Joe said and smiled. I laughed.

At the end of the show, all the actors came on center stage and took another bow. The audience stood and applauded. I whistled. The clapping lasted several minutes, and the actors continued bowing.

"This is one of the best nights of my life," I told Joe.

We got up from our seats and waited for the theater to clear. I couldn't believe how many people were there. I was impressed!

"We have a few minutes before the streetcar gets here. You wanna go to the Green Room?" Joe said.

"You think it's a good idea?"

"Why wouldn't it be?"

"You know, dressed in department uniforms and drinking in public?"

"Where else we gonna drink? Don't you have whiskey in California?"

I nodded. "Of course, we do, but it's against policy to drink while on duty or while representing the department while in uniform."

"That's dumb."

We walked out of the theater and headed next door. Between McVicker's and the Green Room was an alley, and as we crossed it, we heard scuffling between the buildings. We stopped to look, but it was too dark to see. We continued, and that's when we heard the squeals of a woman. We stopped, and I looked at Joe, "Did you hear that?"

"It came from the alley," he said. We rushed back to the alley and walked in it a short way, and as my eyes focused, I could see Luther holding Lindsay by her throat against the wall.

Luther glanced at us and said, "This doesn't concern you. Mind our own business!" I don't think he could see well enough to recognize us, and he turned back to Lindsay. She looked my way, and from what I could make out, she was pleading for help.

I looked at Joe and said, "Fuck it!" Then I made a charge at Luther. By the time he realized that I was coming, it was too late. He let go of Lindsay and I tackled him. I ended up on top, and I just lost it. I hit him so many times, I thought I was gonna kill him. Joe grabbed my arm and pulled me off him.

"That's enough," Joe said. Now you must remember, that's coming from a guy who likes to hit people.

"Okay, okay," I said. "I've wanted to kick that motherfucker's ass since the day he sucker-punched me." I stood there overlooking him and trembling. The adrenaline was racing full force through my body.

Lindsay was crying and went back inside McVicker's through the side door. Luther lay there in a ball. Blood was everywhere, and if his nose wasn't broken before, it was now.

"If you ever come near her again, next time, I won't stop!"

Luther climbed to his feet and held his hand up and then staggered down the alley. I kinda felt bad for him, but he brought this on himself. He had the opportunity of a lifetime, and all he had to do was treat her decent. I noticed this time; he kept his head forward and was holding his nose.

The side door of the theater opened and Melanie ran out. "Are you okay?" she said.

"I'm fine. How's Lindsay?"

"She's okay but shaken."

"How's the hand?" Joe asked.

"It hurts worse than my nose now, but not as bad as the first time you shook hands with me," I joked.

Joe laughed.

Lindsay walked out and looked around then ran over and put her arms around me and hugged me tightly. "Thank you, John Kirk. You saved me again."

"I don't know about all that," I said. I wanted so bad to hug Lindsay back, but I didn't wanna get blood on her dress. Melanie asked if we could escort them to Lindsay's house. With Luther running around, they didn't feel safe.

"Sure," Joe said and then went next door to wait.

We walked into the Green Room and sat down, and Joe ordered us a round. At the end of the counter, I couldn't believe what I saw and had to take a double look. At the opposite end of the bar was a man with two boys. One looked about twelve and the other fourteen, and they had drinks sitting in front of them.

I nudged Joe. "Check that out."

"Check what out?" Joe said after looking.

"Those boys. They're drinking!"

Joe looked back at the boys and watched as they gulped their drinks and then slammed their glasses on the counter. "That's pretty bad," Joe said. "Them being so young and able to hold their liquor better than you!"

A while later, the girls walked up and stood outside the door, so Joe and I downed our drinks and went out to meet them. A minute later, the streetcar stopped.

We took it down State Street to Harrison and then caught another car going west on Harrison to Canal. After getting off at Canal, we walked a block south to Mather Street where Lindsay lived.

Lindsay's house was the third one from the corner and sat on the north side of the street. It was of average size for the neighborhood and had a porch and yard. The house next to hers sat on a larger parcel and had a barn in the backyard with horses and at least one cow.

We sat on the edge of the porch and talked, then Melanie saw a light come on next door.

"Who's out there?" an older man's voice hollered from the dark.

"Just us, Mr. Johnston!" Lindsay yelled back.

"Is that you, Ms. Lindsay? Is everything all right?"

"Yes, Mr. Johnston. Melanie and I just have a little company over. Everything is just fine!"

"Is that Brian I see over there?"

All four of us were holding our mouths to keep from laughing. The old man was nosy and persistent.

"No, Mr. Johnston," Lindsay hollered back. "Just me and Melanie and a couple of firemen that came to our aid tonight. They walked us home to make sure we made it okay."

"Did you say firemen? Well then, you're well cared for. I'm goin' back to bed."

"Thank you, Mr. Johnston. Good night and tell Mrs. Johnston hi for us," Melanie said, and then the door slammed and the lights turned off.

After visiting and having a little more to drink than I should have, Joe and I walked back to the firehouse. It seemed like a long way. Maybe if I wasn't seeing double, it would have been shorter. We stumbled up the stairs into the main room. It was about ten o'clock, and everyone was long gone. It was stuffy inside, so Joe and I went to the roof and laid on the cots.

"So, are you gonna ask her?" I said.

"Am I gonna ask who what?"

"Sharon?"

"Who says I even like her?"

"Your actions do. Listen, if you fancy her, that's cool. Don't make the mistake of letting other people's opinions affect what you feel in your heart. My mother always said that other people's opinions are cheap. They don't have to live with the consequences of your decision, you do! If you like her, go get her. We're brothers and I'll stand by you!"

Joe just sat there with a straight face. He seemed to be in deep thought for a moment and then asked, "What's a hoss?"

I busted out laughing. "Haven't you heard a word I've said?"

"So how do I ask her?"

"Hoss is a cowboy from Nevada. He's big and strong and never loses a fight. But on the inside, he's got a big heart and would give you the shirt off his back. As far as Sharon goes, I'm not gonna tell you what you should do. That's something you'll have to figure out on your own."

"Your mom sounds like a smart lady," Joe said.

"Yeah, she is." I lay there thinking about how much I missed her and hoped she was okay. I wished there was a way I could let her know I was okay.

***

The next morning, Nicholas stopped by the Western Union office to check on the telegraph he sent to California.

"Mornin', Nicholas," Sam said as he took a sip of coffee.

"Morning, Sam. Just thought I'd stop by to see if you got word back from California."

"Well, you're in luck there. Your telegraph came back about an hour ago. There seems to be a problem with your boy Kirk."

***

When I woke up, I was sweaty, and the sun was blazing down on me. I looked around, and I was still on the roof. My head hurt a little, and I thought what I wouldn't give for a few aspirins. I went downstairs, and the crew was sitting around the table, drinking coffee.

Wayne looked up and laughed. "Holy shit!" Then everyone else laughed.

"What the hell happened to you? Your face is the color of Old Economy," Daniel said.

That's when I felt the tightness of my cheeks and the soreness of the burn. "You guys are cold, letting me lie up there and burn."

"That doesn't make any sense," Joe said. "You think we're neat?"

"No, Joe, cool is neat. Cold is fucked up!"

Daniel laughed. "Man, y'all from California is strange."

Joe stood. "Come on. Let's go get breakfast."

"Is it ready?" Wayne asked.

Joe walked over to the window and looked over at Quinn's. "Not yet, but we'll go over and wait."

I followed Joe down the stairs, and on the way across the street, he asked, “You really think I should ask her?”

“No,” I said, “I’ll ask her!”

“You sure?” Joe said.

“Duh, you’re the one who wants to court her, not me!”

“I’m nervous.”

“Big guy like you, imagine how she feels.”

“Yeah, I guess you’re right. I should just forget it.”

“Joe, stand up and be a man. Do you want to be my big brother or big sister? Women respect men who know what they want. Besides, if everything we wanted in life were easy, it wouldn’t be worth having!”

Joe looked at me and smiled. “You know, you’re pretty smart for being such a runt!

ACT 21

"Any coffee left?" Nicholas said as he walked in the firehouse, returning from the Western Union office.

"Yeah, there's still half a pot," Daniel said. "It's fresh. Just made it."

"Where's John?"

"They went to Quinn's to pick up breakfast," Charlie said.

"That's funny. I didn't see the ribbon out front."

"It wasn't. They said they'd go wait for it."

"I think Joe wanted to show off John's new color," Wayne said.

"What do you mean his new color?"

"He fell asleep on the roof last night. Woke up sunbaked," Billy said. "Felt sorry for him because it looked like it hurt."

"Well," Nicholas said, "put your cards down. We need to have a little chat. Seems there's a little problem with John!"

***

We were standing at the counter when Mollie walked out. "Mornin', Ms. Mollie," Joe said.

She looked at me and shook her head. "What in Sam hill happened to you? First, you come in here with a busted-up face then a cut-up hand, and now your face all burned up. You keep this pace; Mr. Coffey will be planting you in the ground in no time at all."

"Who?"

"Mr. Coffey," Joe said, "the undertaker. And if you want an open box at your funeral, his wife Linda can fix you up good enough to attend Sunday services."

"Joe . . . would you shut up? I'm not dying!"

Joe smiled. "Ma'am, it's not exactly his doing."

"Joe, don't you give me no sass. You keep an eye on this boy and keep him out of trouble, you hear?"

"Good morning, boys," Gladys said as she walked out from the kitchen.

"Mornin', Ms. Gladys." Joe said.

"Good Lord, child. What happened to your face? Give me about ten more minutes, and I'll have your food ready."

"Yes, ma'am," Joe said. "Is Ms. Sharon here?"

"You need a word with her?" Mollie asked.

Joe looked at her and hesitated. "Yes, ma'am, we sure do."

After Mollie followed Gladys into the kitchen, I gave Joe a nudged. "What's this we stuff, you gotta mouse in your pocket?"

"I asked, didn't I?"

"No, you asked if we could talk to her. There's a difference, especially if you're chicken!" I said and flapped my arms teasing him. "Cock-a-doodle-doo."

Just then, Sharon and Mollie walked in and saw me. Mollie looked at me like I was crazy, but Sharon laughed. Talk about feeling like an ass. Then Gladys walked in and her face said it all; she was curious about why we wanted to speak to Sharon.

"Mornin', Ms. Sharon," Joe said.

Sharon lowered her head and with a soft voice said, "Good mornin', Mista Joe."

Joe cleared his throat. "Ms. Gladys, I was wondering if it would be all right if Sharon could take John to the theater tonight?"

"What?" Gladys said as they looked at me. Talk about being on the spot.

Joe shook his head. "No . . . I mean, would it be all right if Sharon accompanied John and me to the theater this evening?"

A smile grew on Sharon's face, but her mother stood there expressionless. "Let me get this straight. You wanna take my baby girl Sharon to the theater tonight?"

"Yes, ma'am!"

"Could I, Mama? I've never been to a theater before."

Gladys was silent for a minute, then said, "That wouldn't be proper, Mista Joe."

I felt bad for Sharon. She looked disappointed. "Ms. Gladys, what if you went too?" I said. "I went last night, and it was so incredible. I think you both would enjoy it!"

"Please, Mother? It would be so much fun!" Sharon pleaded.

"I don't think they'd take kindly to us showing up at one of their theaters," Gladys said, and then she looked at Sharon. "Now you go in back and get these gentlemen their food."

"Ms. Gladys, you would be my guest. If anyone wanted to take issue, they'd have to take it up with me," Joe said.

"I appreciate your offer, Mista Joe, but we don't means to be making any problems for no one . . . It's not our place to be there." Gladys walked toward the back then stopped and turned. "I'll tell you what. Come back in the afternoon and I'll think about it."

"Yes, ma'am," Joe said and smiled.

After we got the food, we headed back to the firehouse, and Joe had a smile that wouldn't quit. It made me feel good to see him so happy. As we walked up the stairs, he stopped and said, "You're the best brother a fella could have." That made me feel good. I smiled, and we walked inside. The crew was sitting at the table, waiting for us.

"Joe, where'd you find that damn smile?" Wayne said. Then they looked at me.

"Across the street," I said.

"After we eat, we need to have a meeting," Nicholas said.

We sat the food on the table, and everyone dug in. They acted like they hadn't eaten in weeks. Unlike the other times that we'd eaten, little was said. It was like something heavy was weighing on their minds.

Joe looked around. "Okay, what the hell's going on?"

"Let's eat, then we'll talk," Nicholas said in a severe tone.

***

I walked out on the porch and near the barn were two young boys squatted next to a man. The man, with his sleeves rolled up to his elbows, held the horse's hoof as he shoed it. The screen door slammed behind me, and one of the boys turned. "Momma!" Both boys bounced up and came running.

The man lowered the horse's leg and stood. He patted the horse on its side and led it to the corral.

"John, breakfast is ready!" I yelled.

"I'll be right there!"

The boys ran up and grabbed my legs and hugged me. "You boys go in and wash up so you can eat."

John came up on the porch and knelt in front of me. He put his head on my belly. "Have you felt the baby move today?"

"While I was fixing breakfast and singing, he kicked."

"You have a beautiful voice."

"It's either that or he likes the smell of bacon!" I said.

John stood up and put his hands on my face and gently kissed me on the lips then said, "We have two boys. This one will be a girl."

“Oh my god, I’m in love!” I shouted.

“What on earth’s going on?” Melanie said as she sat up in bed and shook me.

“Please, tell me you’re not real!” I said.

“What? What on earth are you talking about?”

“Why did I have to wake? I had the best dream ever. I was married to John Kirk, and we had two boys.”

***

After breakfast, we cleaned up and sat down at the table. I sat across from Nicholas, and he still had that odd look about him. The other guys sat with their arms crossed and looked on.

“I’m not gonna beat any dead horses here, so I’ll get right to the point. Are you wanted by the law?” Nicholas asked.

“What the hell are you talking about?” Joe said.

“I’m asking John if he is hiding from the law. This is something I need him to answer.”

“No, sir,” I said, surprised at the question too. “I’ve never had any problems with the police . . . at least not any bad ones.”

“You have bad police in California?” Joe asked.

“No, I meant bad encounters!”

“Oh.”

“Okay, let’s say I believe you,” Nicholas said.

“What’s this all about?” Joe said.

“The marshal in Sacramento could find no record of you. The only Kirks he found was a Mr. and Mrs. Rex Kirk. They had no knowledge of you, and I’m curious on why.”

Rex was the name of my dad's great-great-great-grandfather. I was shocked and didn't know how to react. I sat there for a minute, thinking of what I should say, and then decided I should just come right out and be honest. "Do you guys believe in God?"

"What type of ignorant question is that?" Charlie said. "Of course, we do. Doesn't everyone?"

"There's something I've wanted to tell you but didn't know how. I figured if I did, none of you would believe me and think I was crazy . . . but I think God sent me here."

They all laughed.

"What's that supposed to mean?" Wayne said. "Last I heard, we were all sent here by God. We're his children, dumbass!"

"You've all been so great to me, and I owe you the truth, so I'm just gonna come right out and tell you. The reason you didn't find any records of me in Sacramento is because they don't exist, or at least, not yet they don't."

"Why wouldn't they exist?" Dale said.

"Because I haven't been born yet!"

They sat silently while looking at me then busted out laughing. "What a bucket of hog shit!" Daniel said. "Just when I thought we were getting somewhere!"

"If you haven't been born yet, how come you're sitting here?" Nicholas asked.

"I don't know, but I was born on June 4, 1994. I was a firefighter in 2018, and while my partner and I were inside a burning house, there was a flash of light. After that, everything changed. When I woke up, I was in the hospital, looking at Doc Martyn. You guys were there, and at first, I thought you were playing some sort of prank on me, but it didn't take long to figure out that wasn't the case. I've been trying to come up with an explanation, but for the life of me, I can't figure this one out. I'd even resigned myself to the fact I must've died and this is my heaven, but Joe helped me prove that theory wrong. I wish I could explain it, but I can't, and for that, I'm sorry."

Nicholas shook his head and buried his face in his palms. I knew he didn't believe me, and I really couldn't blame him. If I were sitting here listening to someone else tell the same exact story, I'd probably bang my head on the damn table.

"I've always lived under the belief that a man is only as good as his word, and a man who cannot tell the truth is untrustworthy. And it's absurd that you expect any of us to believe that tale," Nicholas said.

"I think we should take him out back and string him up!" Wayne said.

I wanted to laugh but remembered that they hanged people in these days. I got knots in my stomach because I sensed the outcome of this wasn't going to be good.

"Personally, I think he's got what it takes, and with some proper training, I think he could serve the company well," Daniel said. "But whatever Nicholas decides, I'll stand by his decision."

Nicholas looked at Charlie. "What say you?"

Charlie leaned forward. "I was taking a liking to him, and I wish I could say yes, but I'm in the middle. I, too, will agree with your decision."

About then is when it sank in that they were deciding whether to keep me around. "Guys, you do realize that I'm sitting right here."

"That's the way we men do it if we got somethin' to say. We'll say it to your face," Billy said.

I sat back in my chair and felt like shrinking. I was getting nervous. I looked up and silently asked, God, why me? If this was a test to show how I should appreciate what I have, it's working.

Dale and Billy also agreed to go with the decision Nicholas made.

Then everyone looked at Joe. Joe looked at them one by one, and then at me.

"Well, Joe?" Nicholas said.

Joe's eyes went to the ceiling, and then he took a deep breath and said, "That's one small step for a man, and one big step for mankind!"

"That's one giant leap for mankind," I said.

"What?" Wayne asked.

"That's what John told me. He said that's what the first man on the moon said in 1969. How could he have known that if he didn't live during that time? Then he said he read 20,000 Leagues Under the Sea when he was ten."

I wanted to fall off my seat. I knew Joe was trying to help, but he was making me sound crazier than I already was. "Stop talking, Joe," I said under my breath.

"Just look at his fire coat, his pants, and that funny-looking fire hat. What about the iron container he has air trapped in? All this stuff we've never seen the likes of. Even if none of this is true, how could he remember where he's from? He's got that amnesia—"

"It's like I told you before, he ain't got no damn amnesia!"

"Wayne . . . if you don't shut up, I'm gonna hit you so hard that, when you wake up, we're all gonna have gray hair!"

Wayne sat back in his chair and didn't say another word. I guess he took Joe seriously.

"He's a hard worker and we need him. I say he should stay," Joe said. "If y'all vote him out, then I'm gonna go too, and I think the rest of you should also leave because I know we've all said things that weren't exactly true. I know I have!"

"Joe's right," Billy said. "I once told my mom I saved a cat from a pack of dogs, so I could keep it. I stole it from Old Lady Makowski's yard."

Everyone looked at Billy and laughed. "A cat? I could understand a dog, but a cat?" Dale said.

"Joe . . . you're dumb," Daniel said. "I can't believe you're buying into this nonsense."

Joe looked at him. "You call me dumb one more time, and I'm gonna knock the stupid right out of you!"

Nicholas appeared to be in in deep thought as he sat there and stared at me, "You do realize that I'm a devoted reader, and there's no way you read 20,000 Leagues Under the Sea when you were ten. It just published last year. Okay, then tell me the captain's name?"

I laughed. "That's it? That's all you wanna know? It's been fourteen years, but that's an easy one. Captain Nemo. Him and his crew lived in a submarine and took on three survivors from a navy ship. Would you like me to tell you about his next book?"

Nicholas's face looked surprised as he drew his head back and nodded. "Okay, I think Joe has a valid point with the things John says. Not so much about the moon or reading the book when he was ten, but there are things that need explaining."

"Are you're actually considering this?" Wayne said.

"You know, when we found him and he couldn't remember anything other than his name, the doc figured he had amnesia. Let's just say, for argument's sake, that he does and is saying he's from California because he needed a place to call home. Whether he read about California or heard about it, what's the harm in letting him be from there as long as he's not running from the law? As far as claiming to be a fireman, look who he's around, the finest the department has to offer. Can you blame him for wanting to be a part of our company? If we throw him out in the streets and he has nowhere to go, what type of men would that make us?" Nicholas said. "My parents were immigrants, and if they weren't given a chance, who knows where I'd be now."

They sat quietly around the table and nodded, seeming to agree with Nicholas. That made me feel relieved.

Charlie lifted his head. "I agree, and we ought to let 'im stay. If he says he's from California, then I'll accept that. Maybe with time, he'll remember."

Daniel looked over at me and then at Nicholas. "I agree."

Nicholas stood. "Well, I guess that's the way of it. If John keeps of sound mind and performs without faltering, he can stay."

Everyone stood. "Welcome to the family," Wayne said.

Joe gave me a man hug and almost pulled me off my feet.

ACT 22

After the meeting, Joe and I walked over to Quinn's and set the dishes on the counter near the kitchen. Gladys came out of the back and walked up to us. "Mista Joe, I wanted to say that I appreciates your invitation for the theater tonight, but I thought mighty long and hard, and the fact is we can't accept. It just wouldn't be proper."

Joe's face dropped to the floor. It was like the life had just drained from him. I felt bad for him.

"Ma'am, there's no way of changing your mind?"

"I'm sorry, Mista Joe. It just wouldn't be proper."

We left Quinn's, and as we walked down the sidewalk, Joe was quiet. Then we heard a female calling out, "Mista Joe, Mista Joe!"

We turned, and Sharon was running toward us. Joe's face lit up, and his frown was replaced by a goofy smile.

"Here's you go, Mista Joe, you forgot your biscuits," she said and handed him a paper bag.

Confused, Joe took it. "Thank you, Ms. Sharon, but we didn't ask for any biscuits. I don't think it's ours." He handed it back to her. I rolled my eyes. I couldn't believe him.

"Take the biscuits, Joe," I said.

"Take it?" Joe said as he looked at me. "It's not ours!"

"Joe, take the damn biscuits!"

"Yes, take it!" Sharon said.

"Okay. Thank you, Ms. Sharon."

"Peck and Wabash," she said in a low voice.

"Huh?"

"Peck and Wabash. I'll meet you there at six thirty," Sharon said and then ran back to Quinn's.

"Joe, I swear if I were any bigger, I'd kick you right in the ass! She said she'd meet you tonight at six thirty. She's gonna go to the theater with you."

"She said that?"

"Not in so many words but yes!"

Joe threw the bag up in the air and hollered then picked me up and shook me.

"Put me down!"

Joe shook me a few more times and then dropped me. "I'm sure glad God put your ears where he did."

"Why's that?" Joe said.

"Because if you didn't have ears to stop that smile, the top of your head would fall off!"

"This is the best day of my life. I just wanted to pick her up and give her a big ol' kiss!"

"Play your cards right . . . you'll get your opportunity."

"You don't think ill of me, do you?"

"For what?"

"Because I'm different than she is."

"Joe, you're not different. The way I see it, I see two people that like each other, and if it makes you feel any better, where I'm from, white and colored folks marry each other all the time."

"Really?"

"Yep!"

After we got upstairs, Joe walked over and put the bag of biscuits on the table. Like always, the crew sat playing cards. It's either train or play cards.

Wayne peeked over his hand. "What's in the bag?"

"Biscuits from Quinn's . . . For some reason, they thought we ordered them," Joe said.

Nicholas smacked his cards down on the table and stood. "Let's go train!"

***

After we left the fire station, we went to a burned house on Twenty-Fourth Street. Nicholas told me this is where they found me. I walked up on the porch and looked at the deck. It was made of wood planks. When I opened the front door, the overpowering stench of charred wood and burned household furnishings almost choked me. Inside, the upper walls and ceiling were black from smoke damage. I followed the smoke pattern down the hall to the back room, where I squatted down and had vivid flashbacks of flames rolling overhead and the inferno inside the room.

"Do you remember anything?" Nicholas asked.

"Yes . . . I put this fire out."

"You were inside here while it was burning?"

"Yes!" I said and then walked into the room. I followed the burn pattern—charring depths of the wood called alligatoring to the back wall where a table sat in the corner. I moved it away from the wall, and the charring wasn't as deep below it. "This is where it started, on the table."

"You're right," Nicholas said. "It started by means of a tipped-over lantern."

I think Nicholas brought me here to jog my memory. The only problem, there was nothing wrong with it. My problem was figuring out how I got here.

We left and went down the street and practiced. Nicholas pushed us harder than the last time. I got to where my legs were shaky and unstable. I had to sit and rest, but I didn't want to seem like a wimp, so I fought on. It made me laugh to think that I was in shape. Boy, was I wrong!

Charlie and Daniel fired up the steamer, and for the next hour, we laid hose and flowed water. Nicholas timed us from the point we pulled the hose off the wagon till the time we had water flowing. He marched back and forth, hands behind his back, barking orders. "Get your asses moving. Move it, move it, move it! You guys are as slow as my great-grandmother, bless her heart." I wanted to laugh and die at the same time; he was relentless. Finally, we took a much-needed break.

While I sat there resting with the guys, they explained that Nicholas was hard because he wanted us to be the best company in the department. At the end of each month, we had competitions, and the winning company received free meals for a month, thanks to the donations of the fine folks of Chicago and the insurance companies. Daniel said that since Nicholas had been training us, we'd won the last five competitions.

"The chief was so impressed that he promoted Nicholas to company captain at the beginning of the month," Dale said.

"When Nicholas first got transferred to our company in January, we were a bunch of misfits," Billy said. "At first, we thought that sum-bitch was gonna kill us, but to his credit, he made us the men we are today."

Nicholas looked at Billy and grinned. Wayne handed me the ladle of water, and it didn't even bother me it had shit floating in it. Wayne took a swig of his water and said, "You're doing good."

"Wait . . . Did you just say I was doing good?"

Wayne smiled.

"Thanks . . . That really means a lot," I said and poured the rest of the water over my head and then handed the cup to Joe. He still had that goofy smile on his face. I closed my eyes and shook the water outta my hair. "Aw, that feels good. You know, Joe, I was thinking about tonight."

"Oh yeah?"

"We should go by Lindsay's and ask Melanie if she'd go with us."

"I thought you liked Ms. Lindsay? Besides, Ms. Melanie's spoken for!"

"Joe, listen and try to understand what I'm saying. Two white boys escorting a colored girl to the theater, do you really think that's gonna look good? Now, if we invite Melanie, it would look more like a friendly gathering."

Joe sat there for a minute and then nodded. "Oh, I get it! People would be so focused on you and Melanie that they wouldn't even notice Sharon and me. Good plan!"

I couldn't help but laugh. He sure had an odd way of looking at things. I smiled and got up.

The clouds had burned off around noon, and the sun glared down as the temperature rose. Although I knew it wasn't gonna rain, the guys were disappointed. The rest of the afternoon was uneventful, and I sat around, impatiently waiting for six o'clock. I knew Joe was excited, but I was just as eager because I knew I'd see Lindsay perform again.

A few minutes before six, Joe and I went outside to hitch Joe's horse to his buckboard. Then the city bells rang and rang six times then once more. I was curious about why it stopped at six, and Joe told me it had something to do with the police. That they had some type of emergency in Ward 1."

"Hop on," Joe said. The wagon was slightly dilapidated, but if it rolled, I was game. I climbed up, and as we traveled down the street, Joe told me this was his hobby, fixing up broken-down wagons. He reminded me of a friend I knew who liked working on cars.

Lindsay's house was about twenty blocks away, and believe me, the trip seems a lot shorter in a wagon than walking it drunk. When we got there, Joe knocked on the door, and we waited. He knocked again with no answer.

"What now?" I asked.

"Hell, I don't know!" We walked away, and then he stopped at the top of the steps and then went back to the door. He lightly knocked, and said, "Ms. Lindsay, it's Joe and John. Is anyone home?"

"Is that you, Joe Weant?" a voice said.

"Yes, me and John!"

The door opened, and Melanie was standing there, and Lindsay was behind her, holding an iron poker.

"Sorry for keeping you waiting, but we thought it may be Luther." Melanie said.

Lindsay smiled at me, and I didn't know why, but she had this effect on me that made me stupid. I didn't know what to say. My mind was just blank!

After I got my senses back, we explained the situation to Melanie and asked if she wouldn't mind going to the show with us. She said she'd be happy too. Then a black one-horse carriage pulled up front and stopped. The driver, dressed in a black suit and top hat, got down and opened the side door and waited. The wagon was compact and had only one seat and room for two people.

"Lindsay, your ride's here!" Melanie yelled.

Lindsay ran to the door and looked out then grabbed her hat and walked out onto the porch. She stopped and held her hand out. This time, I was proper and just gently shook it. She moved a little closer and whispered, "I had a dream about you this morning," then she walked away.

I just stood there and watched her climb into the carriage. "What's that supposed to mean?" I yelled as her carriage pulled away.

On the way to Sharon's, we went over a wooden bridge that crossed the Chicago River. It was wide enough for four wagons. I looked down at the water and saw all types of stuff floating in it, and it smelled nasty.

The area was a residential neighborhood of small houses with porches and small yards. We pulled over on Peck Street, and as the sun finished setting, we saw a silhouette approaching from Wabash. It was Sharon. I jumped down and helped her into my seat, and then I into the back. I noticed she kept looking down the street. It reminded me of when I used to sneak out of the house to go hang out with my friends.

The theater was about a mile from Sharon's house. We had an excellent time at the show. I could tell Sharon enjoyed herself, and everyone seemed respectful of her. It surprised me, especially after all the stuff I'd heard growing up, you know, about the slaves and the prejudices of people, but it wasn't anything like that. I thought of Gladys and wished she would have come too.

When the show ended, Joe and I went to the Green Room and ordered up a shot of whiskey while Melanie and Sharon stayed behind to help Lindsay. After we finished our shot, Joe bought two bottles to go. I think he was planning on having a good time.

We met the girls out front, and then went to Lindsay's house and hung out on her porch. Joe opened a bottle of whiskey and took a drink then handed it to me. After I almost gagged, Melanie took the bottle from me, then she took a swig. Turns out, whiskey was no stranger to Melanie. She and a friend of hers, Kathya, enjoyed visiting the side door of a local saloon every Friday night. Lindsay was more reserved and at first didn't want to partake. I feel bad about saying this, but after we relentlessly egged Lindsay and Sharon on, they finally gave in and took a sip. Peer pressure's a bad thing! I felt terrible watching them cough, but that feeling didn't last long; before I knew it, Joe was opening the second bottle.

We were having so much fun and laughing that we must have gotten a little loud because Mr. Johnston came out to his porch holding a lantern. "Anyone out there?" he yelled out into the dark. We got quiet until he went back in, then we laughed again.

Around eleven, we left to take Sharon home. We sang songs and laughed the whole way. I think everyone we passed knew we were lit. I could tell Sharon was having more fun than she had probably ever had in her life. Poor girl. She was so hammered; she was having a hard time holding her head up and kept leaning against Joe.

I had so much fun, I forgot to ask Lindsay what she meant earlier about telling me I was in her dream. When we got near Sharon's, we parked about a half block away from her house. Joe got down so he could help Sharon. It was a good thing because she fell off the wagon and right into his arms. She looked up at Joe with the most seductive smile and said,

"Why thank you, Mista Joe." Talk about the most perfect moment for him to kiss her. Did he? No! I shook my head.

Joe said he'd be back and then walked Sharon to her house. It was dark. I couldn't see that well, but I climbed on the front seat and sat there and waited for him to return. My head was spinning, and I had to use my hands to prop myself up to keep from falling over.

"Oh my god," I said when Joe walked up and got on the seat. He had the biggest smile on his face. "You kissed her, huh?" I slurred.

Joe smiled, and that's the last thing I remembered.

ACT 23

It was still dark when I opened my eyes and looked around. My head was killing me, and I wished I had aspirin. My first thoughts were of the date, and if it was 1871, then tomorrow, Saturday the thirtieth, will be the start of a series of fires that will lead to one of the most devastating disasters in American history.

I put my hands behind my head and thought about the other night when I surfed the internet. All the stories I had read were still fresh on my mind. If history was set to unfold, then I knew where and when the fires would start. We could be at the O'Learys' house and change history forever. I had to figure out a way to tell them this without them thinking I was crazy.

"Hey, you awake?" Joe whispered from the doorway.

"Yeah, why?"

"You wanna come help me? I got the wagon hitched."

"Help you do what?"

"Go fix Gladys and Sharon's steps," Joe said.

"You're kidding right? What time is it?"

"It's five. I figure it should only take an hour or so."

I rolled over and lay there for a few seconds, hoping he'd just go away. I didn't wanna get up, but I knew how much it meant to him, so I sat up. "Awww, shit! My head is killing me," I said.

"Where. Chew on this." Joe handed me a handful of weeds.

"What's this? Foxtails?"

"No. Foxtails are hairy. It's barley. Chew on it. It'll help your head."

I put a few stems in my mouth and chewed on them. They didn't taste very good, but it seemed to work because, by the time we got to Sharon's, my headache was gone. In the back of the wagon Joe had precut boards and tools, and we took them over to the front porch.

"Joe, are you sure it's all right to be doing this at this time of morning?"

"Gee, haven't given it much thought, but they'll be grateful. My dad always said, if you don't get up before the chickens, you're wasting your life away." Right after he said that, I kid you not, the roosters in the neighborhood crowed. It was like they heard him.

Most of the steps were rotted and the only way up without falling through was walking up the very sides. We ripped the bad ones off with a pry bar and laid the new ones in place. They were a perfect fit, then Joe pulled a handful of nails from a paper sack.

"Joe, you're gonna wake up the neighborhood," I whispered. I don't know why I was whispering, because the banging was loud and echoing between the houses and down the street.

In the east, the sky was changing to a lighter blue, as the sun made its way toward daybreak. Out of the corner of my eye, I caught movement on the porch. The door cracked open, and Gladys stood there in the doorway, wearing a nightdress and a headscarf. I tapped Joe on the shoulder. "Dude, we're dead!"

"Lord, have mercy! What are you boys doing out here making all this noise at five thirty in the morning?"

"Ma'am, I saw that your porch needed repair, so I brought John over to fix it before work. Wasn't that mighty kind of him to volunteer?" Joe said as he grabbed my shoulder and shook me.

Gladys walked over to the edge of the porch and put her foot on the top step. She smiled. "Ooh, Lord, that does feel good."

"Mercy me!" someone yelled from across the street. "Two white boys choring for a colored woman. Just when I thinks I saw it all."

"Good morning, Mista Anderson," Gladys yelled back, then she walked over to the door and hollered inside. "Sharon, bring these boys some of that fresh coffee. They're doing us a fine service." She walked back to the step, put her foot on it again, and giggled.

When we got back to the firehouse, it was about six thirty, and I went straight to bed, hoping to get a little more rest before the guys showed up for work. I had to stop this volunteering shit, especially so early in the morning.

It only seemed like minutes until Wayne was kicking my bed. "Get up, you lazy shit! Breakfast is ready. Go help Joe fetch it!"

I opened one eye and looked at him. "Damn, you're an ass!"

Wayne laughed and walked into the other room. I got up and put my boots on and went into the kitchen, where I ran water over my head.

"Had a rough night, did ya?" Daniel said.

"Yeah, sort of."

"Hell. If I looked like that when I woke up, my wife would up and leave me," Dale said, and they laughed.

I ran down the stairs and caught up with Joe just before he walked into Quinn's.

"Finally wake up?" he said.

"Yeah. What time is it?"

"A few minutes after eight," Joe said as we walked into the restaurant and back to the counter where Mollie was sitting. "Mornin', Ms. Mollie."

"Good morning, boys."

Gladys walked out from the kitchen with our food and put it on the counter and turned around and walked back into the kitchen without saying a word. She didn't even smile. Joe and I looked at each other. I didn't know what he was thinking, but I was thinking how weird was that? Especially after I did all that volunteering this morning.

"I understand you boys took Sharon to the theater last night?" Mollie said. Oops. If Mollie knew, then Ms. Gladys probably knew too, and that was why she seemed so cold.

"Yes, ma'am, she went with me, John and Ms. Melanie," Joe said.

"Well, if all of you went together, I can't see any harm in that. I hope you kids had fun."

"Yes, ma'am. We had a real fine time," I said.

"If I were you boys, I'd take the food and get out while you still have hide on your backsides."

"Yes, ma'am," Joe said. We picked up the food and walked toward the door, then Joe stopped. "Sorry, Ms. Mollie. I can't do that. I need to speak with Ms. Gladys."

"Are you sure?"

"Yes, ma'am!"

Mollie walked into the kitchen, and I looked at Joe and smiled. "Now that's what you call being a man!"

"Why? I was just going to thank her for the food!"

"Tell her how you feel about Sharon!"

Gladys walked in and folded her arms as she glared at us. "Yes, Mista Joe?"

"Ms. Gladys, it's all my fault that Sharon accompanied us to the theater. We took Ms. Melanie along, and we really had a fine time. I just wanted you to know that."

Sharon was standing in the doorway behind Gladys. We smiled at each other.

"Ms. Gladys, I know you wanna protect Sharon and all," Joe said, "but the fact is, is that Sharon is a mighty fine woman, and I've had my eye on her for some time, and I love her. I would like to ask for your permission to marry her."

Oh my god! I couldn't believe he just said that. I thought Mollie was gonna fall off her chair. Sharon's eyes got real big; she looked like she was in shock. And as for Gladys, her face went blank. I don't know if she was also in shock or if she was thinking how she was gonna cook Joe for dinner.

"One show, one kiss, and you want to marry my baby?" Gladys said and then stormed into the kitchen, nearly plowing over Sharon.

"You kissed her last night, didn't you?" I asked.

"Yep. Twice!"

"No wonder you were smiling when you got back to the wagon."

"I'm surprised you remember."

"That's the last thing I remembered."

"That's a mighty steep proposal you've made there. You do realize she's from a different background?" Mollie said.

"Ms. Mollie, I know it seems out of place, but I can't help the way I feel! My stomach gets butterflies when I see her, and it's been like that for a spell now."

"You know, most people aren't gonna take a liking to the idea, but if that's how you feel, then don't let no man stop you," Mollie said.

"I appreciate it, Ms. Mollie," Joe said, and then we headed back to the firehouse.

"Damn, Joe. I can't believe you came right out and told Gladys!"

"Me neither."

We walked down the sidewalk, and Sharon was standing in the gangway between Quinn's and the building next door. We stopped, and she looked at Joe. "Did you mean what you said to my momma?"

I walked away to give them some privacy, headed to the firehouse, and went upstairs.

ACT 24

It was Saturday, September 30, 1871. I opened my eyes and thought about how today would differ from all the others. I got out of bed, walked into the front room, and opened a window. I stuck my head out. It would be a repeat of yesterday, sunny and hot.

"Hey, John. I'll give you a dollar if you jump!" Wayne said, and the rest of the crew laughed. I turned and smiled as I gave him the finger. After breakfast, we were downstairs preparing the equipment to go practice. Nicholas had said he had something new he wanted us to try, that he thought it would help us to ensure victory at the competitions.

"I got a joke for you," Wayne said.

"Let's hear it," Nicholas said.

"A cowboy was walking across the desert and sees a ranch and walks to it. On the sign, it said, 'Chief Red Bull's Horse Ranch.'

"The cowboy sees a bunch of corralled horses and walks over to the chief. After studying the horses for a few minutes, he asks, 'How much for the white horse?'

"Chief says, 'White horse not for sale. Horse not look so good!'

"'I don't care what the horse looks like. Here's twenty bucks. That should cover it!' he says and hands the money to the chief, and the cowboy rides off on his new horse.

"A while later, the trail turns to the left, and the horse goes straight into a tree, and the cowboy falls off. Gets back on the horse and rides a while longer until the trail turns right, and the horse goes straight into the river. By this time, the cowboy's mad and takes the horse back, 'Chief, I want my money back because this horse is as blind as a calf inside its momma's belly!'

"Chief looks at the cowboy and says, 'Chief try tell you, horse not look so good!'"

We laughed, then I heard a voice outside the barn say, "John!" I was standing near the horse stalls but saw no one. Who'd be looking for me? Everyone I knew was here in the barn, so I walked outside, and that's when I came face-to-face with Luther. It wasn't like before; this time, he had a pistol pointed at me. He aimed it and pulled the hammer back.

"Come on, Luther. You don't wanna do this," I said as I raised my palms toward him and stepped back. Was I scared? Hell yes! But then I thought, why would I travel to 1871 just to get shot?

"This will teach you to mess with another man's girl," Luther said, as he squeezed the trigger. Joe must've seen me back up with my hands out because he stepped out of the barn just as the shot rang out. Joe dropped like a sack of potatoes.

Luther tried to reload the gun but got wrestled to the ground by the crew. Nicholas and I rolled Joe to his side. He was unconscious and bleeding from the head just above the right eye. I ripped a strip off my shirt and applied it to the wound. It didn't look good, but at least he was still breathing.

"Dale, you and Billy get Jack hitched!" Nicholas yelled. "Daniel, get the police officers!"

After Wayne and Charlie wrestled the gun from Luther, Wayne stood and kicked Luther several times. "You sum-bitch, you're gonna hang for this!"

Within a minute, Dale and Billy had the wagon hitched and waiting. Joe was big, and it took four of us to load him. Nicholas and Dale hopped into the back with him, and Billy drove.

I walked over and looked at Luther. His nose was bleeding from Wayne kicking him. Charlie was towering over him with his fist cocked, daring him to move.

"I'll be back!" I said and ran to Quinn's. Mollie was standing near the counter, "Sharon! Where's Sharon?" I shouted.

"What's all the commotion?" Mollie asked.

"Joe! Joe's been shot!"

Sharon walked out from the back and put her hand over her mouth. I could see tears already in her eyes, then Gladys followed her out.

"It's Joe! He's been shot, and it doesn't look good," I said.

Sharon fell into Gladys's arms, sobbing. "Where is he?" Gladys asked.

"They took him to Mercy Hospital."

Gladys looked at Sharon. "Child, go to him!"

Mollie jerked her head back. "Huh?"

"Ms. Mollie, quit acting a fool. The children are in love."

Mollie looked at Sharon. "Take off your apron and get out of here!"

"Ms. Mollie, if you're firing her, then you might as well fire me too!" Gladys said.

"Who said anything about firing her? If her man needs her, then she should be by his side. John, my buggies on the side of the building. Take it and get Sharon to the hospital."

"Thank you, Ms. Mollie," Gladys said.

Sharon took off her apron and ran outside to the side of the building with me and stopped. I ran back inside the restaurant and shouted, "Ms. Mollie, there's five buggies outside. Which one is yours?"

"The black one with the sun cover!" she said.

I ran back out and helped Sharon up to the seat then untied the horse and climbed up. As I stared at the reins, that's when it hit me. I'd never driven one of these before. I can do this, I thought. I've been watching Billy drive.

Then I pulled the reins back, and then to the right. The horse moved to the street. It wasn't so bad I thought, then I shook the reins and the horse took off faster than I thought he would. Thank God, the buggy had a seat, or we probably would have fallen out the back.

"Whoa!" I yelled and jerked back on the reins, and the horse stopped. I felt like I was learning how to drive a stick shift.

Finally, after a little trial and error, I got the damn thing going. Then it dawned on me that I should've asked Sharon to drive. Sharon pointed the way to the hospital, and when we got there, we ran inside. The lady sitting at the reception desk looked up and then gave me a second look. She was the same lady who was working there during my stay.

"Where's Joe Weant?" I asked.

"Third floor!"

Sharon ran up the upstairs, and it took everything I had to catch her. We met Billy at the top of the stairs, and he pointed toward the rear of the room. The floor looked like the one I was on with beds lining both walls, but that level had curtains between each bed. Sharon briskly walked past Billy and down the aisle where a nurse stopped her. The nurse gave Sharon a once-over and said, "Sorry, sweetie, but we don't have any of your kind up here."

"Why don't you pretend to be a real nurse and act like you care about people," I shouted. The nurse jerked her head back and looked at me.

Sharon and I saw Nicholas standing partly behind a curtain a few beds from the end, and there were several nurses and a doctor next to him. We ran over there, and I expected to see Joe covered with a sheet, but when we got there and peeked behind the curtain, he was sitting there, laughing with Dale. When Sharon saw him, she smiled and then cried. She bent over and kissed Joe repeatedly.

"I love you, Joe. I love you!" she said between kisses. "I was so scared. I thought I lost you. Yes, I'll marry you!"

Nicholas and Dale looked at each other, baffled. "Did you know about this?" Nicholas asked. Dale shook his head.

Sharon sat next to Joe and held his hand, "Are you okay?"

"I'm doin' much better now. You say you'd marry me?"

"Yes, I'll marry you." Sharon looked at Nicholas. "Is he okay?"

"Doc says the bullet grazed him and knocked him out cold, but he's doing fine now. How long have you two been courting?" Nicholas asked.

"Since right now," Sharon said as she smiled at Joe.

Joe smiled back. "If I'd known you'd act this way, I'd got myself shot a long time ago."

"I can't believe you did that," I said. "You took a bullet for me. I don't know how I could ever repay you."

Joe glanced up at Sharon. "You already have."

"Yep. Looks like we might be having a hanging soon," Dale said.

"I don't think they should hang Luther. After all, it was an accident," Joe said.

"Accident? Joe, it's against the law to carry a gun in the city limits of Chicago. It's a crime to discharge such weapon within the city limits, and it's a serious offense to shoot someone, especially a police officer or fireman. Luther carried a gun, pointed it, and discharged it while aiming it and shot you in the head. How on God's green earth can you call that an accident?" Nicholas said.

"Because he was trying to shoot John, not me!"

Nicholas shook his head. "Now I have two men who've been hit in the head too hard. Let's get that doctor over here, so we can get you released. We still have training to do!"

ACT 25

After Joe was released from the hospital, we went to Molly's to take back the buggy and drop Sharon off. Nicholas, Billy, and Dale went directly to the firehouse. Charlie and the other guys watched as the wagon pull into the barn and were saddened when Joe didn't return with them. They thought the worst. "He didn't make it, did he?" Charlie said.

Nicholas jumped down from the wagon. "Yeah. He's over at Quinn's with his new wife-to-be."

"Huh?" Wayne asked. "You mean he gets shot, and instead of dying, he gets hitched?"

***

When we got back to the firehouse, everyone was happy to see Joe. "Man, we thought we'd lost you! The police officers took Luther away, and I don't think we'll be seeing him anytime soon," Daniel said.

"Now we have cause for a real celebration, one for God not wanting Joe yet, and for Joe's engagement to his fiancée, whoever she might be," Wayne said, and all the guys raised their fist and cheered.

"We'll stop by the Burlington after practice and get a few bottles of whiskey," Nicholas said. The guys raised their fist and cheered again.

"So, who's the unlucky woman?" Daniel asked. That's when the room went quiet, and everyone looked at each other. The ones who knew said nothing and looked at Joe.

"Ms. Sharon," Joe said. "And if any of you have anything to say, you'd better speak now, so we can settle it right here!"

"That's it!" I shouted. Everyone's attention focused on me. "The Burlington. The Burlington Warehouse?"

"Why? Have you heard of it?" Wayne asked. "Is your memory coming back?"

"I don't know."

"We'll stop there after practice. That way, you can get a good look at it. In the meantime, let's hitch up the steamer and head over to Twenty-Third Street."

After we left the firehouse, we parked about a half block from Twenty-Third Street. Nicholas and Charlie got down from the steamer and walked back to us. Nicholas pulled out a pencil from his shirt pocket and drew on a piece of paper. He drew a map of our location and the hydrant on the corner. "Listen up, men. I have a good friend from Cincinnati who told me about this new practice they're doing. We here in Chicago are accustomed to arriving at the fire and then running the hose to the fire hydrant. Not only is it hard work, but it takes both my hosemen and pipemen to drag hose down the street. Why not let Jack do all the work? Instead of calling it hand-jacking the hose, we'll just call it 'jacking the hose.'"

We laughed, but the guys were trying to figure out what he was talking about, but since it was standard practice in the future, I knew exactly where he was going.

"Now, my buddy says that they started doing what they call a forward hose lay, and it only takes one man to accomplish this feat. It's faster, and we can get water on the fire quicker."

"How does this forward hose lay work?" Dale asked.

"It's easy. Economy goes directly to the fire as usual, the wagon stops at the hydrant, Dale pulls off a length of hose, and then the wagon continues to the steamer as the hose falls off the back," Nicholas explained.

Everyone stood quietly while processing the plan. "Sounds good," I said. "Who knows, maybe one day, they'll use this as a standard practice everywhere!"

The guys looked at me, and then Wayne said, “Who cares about a standard practice. We care about winning the competition tomorrow!” Everyone laughed, and then we got to work. The first attempt was going smoothly until the hose snagged in the bed and dragged Dale down the street until he let go. Nicholas hopped down from Economy and scratched his head. He looked around and then walked over to the hydrant and kicked it, and then kicked it a little harder.

“What the hell is he doing?” Wayne asked.

Nicholas walked over to us and said, “The plug will make a good anchor. Let’s reload and try again.” He looked at Dale. “You okay?”

“Are you kidding? I get it worse wrestling my cows.”

“What do you mean an anchor?” Joe said.

“I think what he means is instead of holding the hose and being pulled through the streets, he should wrap the hose around the hydrant!” Billy said.

“That’s exactly what I meant.”

We reworked the hose and tried it again. This time, Dale wrapped the hydrant, and the hose came out flawlessly. Everyone was surprised at how fast it was. I knew that once all the other engine companies saw this evolution, it would spread throughout the department and become standard practice. I couldn’t believe it. I was witnessing history in the making.

After we finished, we sat around taking our break. Nicholas walked up and gave us the good news. He said we beat the company record by three minutes at laying 600-feet of hose. Everyone jumped up and hollered then threw their caps in the air. I raised my hand in the air, and Joe just stared at it, “What the hells that supposed to mean?”

“That’s how we celebrate in California. We give each other high fives.”

“Cool,” Joe said and high-fived me.

After we left from training, we went to the Burlington Warehouse, it was on the corner of Sixteenth and State Street. We got off the wagons and walked inside. An older man was sitting at a desk, and the other one was looking out the window. “Hey, Nicholas. How’s it going?” the man at the desk asked as he stood, and they shook hands.

“Well, Mr. Bellows, it’s only noon, and it’s been a long day already. Anyway, the boys and I have some celebrating to do and thought we’d stop by and purchase a couple of bottles of that fine Chapin and Gore whiskey.”

“Why certainly,” Bellows said and then glanced over at the man by the window. “Charles, go in the warehouse and get the city’s finest. Our finest.”

“Yes, sir, Mr. Bellows.”

“After that, I need you to move the rest of the empty barrels from the basement to the loading dock. We have a train leaving for Peoria in the morning. Let’s try to get out of here by five.”

“Yes, sir,” Charles said as he opened the door to the warehouse.

“By the way, this is our newest member of our crew, John Kirk.”

Bellows reached over and shook my hand. He had gray hair and looked to be in his fifties. “Nice to meet you, son. Nicholas is a real fine man, and he’ll teach you a lot.”

“Yes, sir,” I said. “Nice to meet you too.” Nicholas paid Bellows, and about that time, Charles returned with two bottles of whiskey in a paper bag.

We walked out to the wagons, and Nicholas handed the whiskey to Charlie. I turned around and asked, “So this is the Burlington Warehouse?”

“This is it,” Joe said.

I looked up at the massive three-story brick building. If I remember correctly, it extended 170-feet along Sixteenth and 130-feet up State Street and ended near the Chicago, Burlington & Quincy Railroad tracks.

I walked around the corner and out into the middle of State. I couldn’t take my eyes off the building. My insides were jerking around as I stared in awe. The crew followed me, and curiously watched me as I made my way to the rear, toward the railroad tracks. I walked up next to the building and dragged my fingers across the brick and looked up at the windows.

"Tell us what you see," Billy said.

When I got to the rear corner of the building, I walked back out into the street to get a look at the side and rear of the Burlington.

"What the hell's he looking at?" Nicholas asked the men.

"Beats me," Wayne said.

I was so fascinated as I studied the building. I probably could have told you how many bricks it took to build it. They continued following me, watching my every move. I turned and looked at the guys, and it made me laugh. It kinda reminded me of my kindergarten class when we'd take field trips and walk down the street, but my focus quickly returned to the building.

"Come on, John. Whaddya see?" Joe asked.

"Quiet. He may be on to something," Nicholas said.

I walked behind the building and a wooden platform extended out from the docks. It was a ramp for loading boxcars.

They followed me around the docks and across the railroad tracks to the other side of the building. I kept looking up at the windows on the second and third floors and couldn't believe that I was staring at a building that had burned 147 years ago but hasn't burned yet. This was getting confusing.

On the west side of the building was a large lot, and on the far side of it was a corral with two horses. Parked next to the corral were two buggies and two buckboards. I walked over and stood near the corral and looked back at the warehouse. From that vantage point, I could see the entire building. "Isn't there a Warehouse A and a Warehouse B?" I asked.

"Yeah. This side of the building is Warehouse A. The other side along State Street is Warehouse B. Both warehouses are in this building," Charlie said.

"Have you been here before?" Nicholas asked. I could tell he was eager for me to remember anything.

"No, not exactly," I said.

ACT 26

"You mind telling us why this building is so intriguing to you?"

"Wayne, remember the other day when I asked you if you knew something bad was going to happen, if you would warn people?"

"Yeah, something like that."

"You said, you would say something even though you knew they wouldn't believe you, right?"

"Yeah, yeah, I said that!"

"This is gonna sound crazy, but if today is really September 30, 1871, this building will catch fire sometime today!"

"I think his head's starting to swell," Dale said, and the other guys laughed.

Nicholas all but rolled his eyes.

"Are we having another spell?" Daniel asked.

"No, I'm not having another spell, but there's gonna be a fire in Warehouse A that starts in the broomcorn on the second floor. After it starts, it will spread to Warehouse B. The wind will blow embers onto the roofs across State Street, and by the time the fire's put out, three blocks will have burned."

I think they were more concerned about my mental state than what I was saying about the fire. Wayne smiled. "At least wait until you get some whiskey in ya before telling us these tales. Maybe that way, we'd feel more like laughing."

"You see, John, that's where your story becomes fiction. If you knew anything about this warehouse, you'd know that warehouses A and B are separated by an eight-inch firewall, making it impossible for a fire to spread from one side to the other. Your predictions could never become truth," Charlie said.

"Yeah, well, that's what they said about the Titanic."

"The Titanic?" Joe asked.

I closed my eyes. I couldn't believe I just said that. They had no idea what the Titanic is, because it hadn't happened yet, so I said, "Where I come from, the Titanic was a ship made of iron that they said was unsinkable. That God himself couldn't sink it. It sank on its first voyage."

Joe laughed. "Well, that's your problem. Everybody in their right mind knows that iron doesn't float!"

Dale stuck his finger in his mouth and then held it up. "The other problem with your imaginary story is that there's no wind out here!"

"Trust me, as sure as we're standing here, it will happen! And when we get here, the fire will be on the second and third floors of Warehouse A. Everyone will be so focused on putting water streams through the windows that you're gonna forget about the roof. The fire will vent through the top-floor ceiling, and then the winds will push the fire across the roof and over the firewall. By the time anyone realizes Warehouse B is burning, it'll be too late."

Nicholas looked at me and shook his head, then walked toward the steamer. "Let's get back to the firehouse."

As he and Charlie climbed on the steamer, Mr. Bellows walked out and handed Nicholas a third bottle of whiskey. "This is for you and your boys. Enjoy your celebration tonight."

"I speak for the boys. We sure do appreciate it. You need anything, just holler," Nicholas said. As Mr. Bellows started up the steps, Nicholas hollered at him, "Mr. Bellows, do you store broomcorn in the warehouse?"

"We sure do. We keep it up on the second floor of Warehouse A. Why do you ask?"

"Just curious. You have a fine day, Mr. Bellows." Nicholas said and then looked at me with an odd face.

"Billy, wait a minute," I said as I jumped off the wagon and ran up to the steamer. "Nicholas, I know none of this makes sense to you, and you probably think I'm a liar, but I have to tell you something else." Their faces were blank as they stared down at me. "Does the wonobago mean anything to you?"

"You mean the Winnebago? Yes, that's Engine 16, why?"

"Yeah, the Winnebago. Today, when the warehouse burns, the Winnebago will be fighting the fire from here on Sixteenth Street. This front wall will collapse on them and kill the crew and the horses. Even if you don't believe what I've told you, just remember that!"

Charlie laughed. "What are you, a prognosticator? That's some mighty strong accusations you're making there."

Nicholas sat there just staring at me. I believe at that moment if he would have had a gun, he would have shot me himself. "Get your ass on the wagon."

After I walked away, Nicholas told Charlie to have the boys keep a close eye on me; that if there was a fire at the warehouse, I'd probably be the one setting it. That kinda made me feel bad, but if I were in his, or the other guys, shoes, I'd probably be thinking the same thing.

When we got back to the firehouse, Lindsay was sitting on one of the chairs next to the front door. She had on a long white dress with ruffles around the shoulders. I jumped off the wagon, as they pulled around back.

"Hey, what are you doing here?" I asked.

"Waiting for you to get back. Word has it that Luther shot Joe, but I see he's on the wagon. Did he get shot?"

"Yeah, but it was just a flesh wound. Luther came gunning for me, but Joe stepped in the way and got shot instead."

"Oh my," Lindsay said. I held my hand out and helped her up.

"I must say, Ms. Lindsay, you sure do make a dress look beautiful."

"Why thank you, Mr. Kirk. You sure have a way of charming the ladies, don't you?"

"Only the ones who project such beauty as yourself," I said. "I need to go help with the horses. Will you stay until I finish?"

"Why most certainly, Mr. Kirk."

"Call me John. This mister business makes me feel old."

"Only if you call me Lindsay."

"Deal!" I said then went to help the guys unhitch the horses and clean up the wagons. Lindsay stood near the steamer and watched. Every time I looked at her, she smiled. I felt like Joe yesterday; I just wanted to give her a big ol' kiss.

Lindsay walked over to Jack's pen and asked, "Could I?"

"Of course, you can," I said.

Lindsay put her hand on his muzzle, and he just stood there. It was like an instant bond, like he too was drawn to her beauty. Lindsay's face was pure. She smiled, and Jack moved closer to her. My god, I was in love!

"What's his name?" she softly asked.

"Jack."

"Hello, Handsome Jack," she said as she put both hands on his face. If I didn't know better, I'd say Jack was mesmerized.

"If you aren't doing anything tonight, Melanie and I would love for you to come by for a game of cards. You can bring Joe and Sharon. I had so much fun last night, the most I've had in a long time. I really enjoyed your company."

"I would love to," I said. "I'll ask Joe." Then the Burlington popped into my head. "I forgot. We're gonna have a big fire at the Burlington Warehouse today, I'm not sure what time we'll be done with it."

"A fire at the Burlington? How could you know that?"

I wish I'd quit putting my foot in my mouth. I cleared my throat. "You've heard of the Burlington Warehouse?"

"Of course, I have. And how can you make such a preposterous prediction like that?"

"It's a long story. I'll have to explain it to you some time."

Lindsay looked puzzled but quickly brushed it off. 'Well, if you're wrong about this fire, please come by."

Joe walked up and tipped his hat. "Ms. Lindsay."

"Hi, Joe. Are you okay?"

"Yeah, I'm fine. It just grazed me. This bandage makes it look worse than it is."

"I'm so sorry."

"You got nothing to be sorry about. That Luther has been nothin' but trouble since the day he pained his momma. It was his actions, not yours. At least, now, he won't be bothering you anymore."

Lindsay walked up and gave Joe a hug. "Thank you."

"It was nice seeing you, Ms. Lindsay. I need to tend to the horses," Joe said and walked away.

"I should let you get back to work. Remember to come by after you get off work. I don't care what time," Lindsay said and raised her hands, and I lightly gripped them as we looked into each other's eyes.

I know what I wanted to do but didn't think it would be proper, so I didn't. "I'll see you tonight," I said.

After I held her hands for a few seconds, she let go and walked away. When she got near the door, she turned and smiled. If I didn't know better, I'd say she was a little disappointed. Damn! I should have kissed her.

A pile of hay slammed on the ground next to me. I looked up, and Joe was looking over the ledge, laughing.

"Oh, you're really funny," I yelled.

"You should have kissed her!"

"I see. Now you're the Romeo of romance! You shouldn't be spying on people!"

"Spread the hay behind the wagons. We're gonna let the horses out, so they can exercise," Joe said.

I grabbed a pitchfork while he pushed over another pile and then climbed down.

"You really think I should have kissed her?"

"That's why she stood there and held your hands for so long," Joe said.

"Nah." I laughed.

"Are you going over there tonight?"

"Yeah. She wanted me to ask if you and Sharon wanted to come. She said she'll be home about nine . . . That's if were done at the Burlington!"

"Don't worry. We're not going to have a fire—"

Just then, the deep tone of the watchman's bell echoed between the buildings, the sound almost frightening. We listened, and the bell rung eight times, then it paused for ten seconds and then rang five more times.

"Let the horses out," Joe shouted. I ran over and opened their stalls, and they ran out.

***

Nicholas and Charlie rushed over to the window. "Over there." Nicholas pointed to the northwest. Several blocks away, smoke rose above the rooftops and then spreading out horizontally. Nicholas looked at Charlie with curled brows. "The Burlington?" And then looked back at the smoke and noticed it wasn't rising.

"Is the wind blowing?" Charlie asked, and then the gong rang.

***

The horses ran right past the hay I had just laid out for them. They went directly to their wagons and stood there under their harnesses. As I helped Joe and Wayne harness Jack, the gong rang upstairs, and then Nicholas came running out. “Sixteenth and State!”

Everyone looked at me.

“That’s where the Burlington is!” Billy said.

ACT 27

Charlie and Nicholas climbed on the steamer. "Whaddya think?" Charlie asked.

"What do I think about what?"

"John?"

"We're not even sure it's the Burlington yet."

***

We left the station and headed east on Twenty-Second Street and then north on State toward the Burlington. It was only two blocks ahead. I turned around to see if I could see anything. Ahead, I saw a large blanket of smoke trapped on the road between the buildings. When we got to Sixteenth, Charlie and Nicholas stopped at the corner, and we pulled up next to them. The Burlington, on the northwest corner, had heavy smoke pouring over the roof and down onto State Street, where it was trapped between buildings by the wind.

Nicholas studied the flames ripping out of the upper windows of Warehouse A. "Joe, before we do this, was John with you all day?"

"Yes, sir," Joe said.

"All right then. We have a fire to put out," Nicholas said and directed us to the dirt lot on the west side of the warehouse.

***

"How's it possible?" Charlie asked.

"How's what possible?"

"This fire . . . that John knew this was gonna happen?"

"Coincidence!" Nicholas said, and then he jumped off the steamer. He walked over and told us to connect to the hydrant at Sixteenth and Clark, which was the next corner west of our location. I thought it was funny; he wanted them to hand-jack the hose instead of doing it like we practiced all day.

"Nicholas, I didn't see Bellows or Stein anywhere," Billy said. "They said they weren't leaving till five."

Nicholas looked over at the corrals where the same two horses we saw earlier were still standing, "Joe, you, Wayne, and John make sure they got out. The rest of you hook me some hoses, I want everything we've got aimed at the top floor," he shouted.

As we ran to the front, I asked Wayne, "What about a hose?"

"Hose? We ain't got time. If they're in there, we gotta get 'em out now."

***

Nicholas walked toward the rear of the building, staring up at the windows and the roof, looking for extension of the fire. He turned and walked back to the wagons. "Dale, grab a horse and get to the courthouse. Tell the watchman to dispatch me a 2-11 at Box 301. I don't see the chief anywhere, and if John's right, we need to get the roof covered."

"Got it!" Dale ran to the street where a man was holding the reins to a horse. He ran up to the man and said, "Fire business. I need your horse!" The man didn't hesitate. He handed the reins to Dale.

"Charlie, take full charge of the steamer. I'm gonna need Daniel on a hose." Nicholas said and headed toward the front of the building.

***

I followed Joe and Wayne to the front door and kept looking up at the flames leaping out of the windows. Wayne grabbed the knob, and as he opened the door, he said, "Wet your 'staches," and then walked through the door.

"What's that mean?" I asked.

"Don't you folks know nothin' in California other than Valley talk? It's an old saying to get ready to breathe some smoke. If you had a damn mustache, you could wet it, and it'd help filter the smoke!" Joe said.

I was nervous about following them into the building. My training has always taught me to never go in without proper gear, like a hose and breathing apparatus! We entered the front office, and the visibility was good with only a trace of smoke near the ceiling. There were no signs of Bellows or Charles. The door inside the office was containing the heat and smoke to the warehouse. "They must've gone inside," Wayne said.

Joe walked over and ran his hand across the top of the door. "It's a little warm, but not bad," he said.

"Open 'er up," Wayne said.

"You guys are nuts. We don't have any protection!"

Wayne and Joe wrinkled their noses. "You got your helmet and coat on, don't you?" Wayne said.

I would have laughed, but they were scaring the hell outta me. Joe turned around and grabbed the knob. I stooped down and took a deep breath, preparing for the worst. Joe opened the door, bowed his head below the smoke, and then walked through the door. Wayne followed him. I couldn't believe I was doing this, but I went in after them.

The warehouse was huge with rows of stacked crates that vanished into the smoke about seven feet up. The temperature was hot but tolerable.

"Mr. Bellows, Charles!" Joe yelled.

We stopped and listened for a few seconds, hoping to hear something, but we heard no replies. I was having a déjà vu moment of the other night when I was searching for Don.

"John, you go search the front. Joe, you take the middle, and I'll look in the back."

"You want us to split up?" I asked. "Are you fuckin' crazy?"

"It's a dangerous job. We'll cover more ground this way. If you're yellow"—Wayne laughed as he looked at my gear— "you can wait outside. Us men have a job to do!"

"I'll get the front," I said and headed that way.

***

Nicholas went to the front of the building, just as Engine 16 and their hose wagon pulled up and stopped. The men jumped off the wagons and ran a hose to the hydrant at State and Sixteenth Street. Engine 15 approached from the west. Nicholas signaled for them to go into the lot next to Engine 8.

He went over to James Enright, the captain of the Winnebago. "I sent three of my guys inside to search for two missing workers. Could you keep an eye open for them?"

"Sure thing."

Nicholas turned and walked toward the corner of State Street where he eyed the windows to Warehouse B, looking for signs of fire but didn't see any. When he reached the corner, he stopped, turned around, and stared at the flames coming through the windows of Warehouse A, and then at the Winnebago on Sixteenth Street with its horses still hitched, and then at the pipemen standing in front of the building with their hose streams trained on the upper windows.

"James!" Nicholas yelled.

"Yeah! What is it?"

"Unhook your hoses and get your men the hell off this street!"

"Something wrong?" Enright asked as he looked up at the building.

"I've got a bad feeling about this one. Something my new guy said, and I can't shake it!"

Enright stood for a few seconds, watching the flames rip through the windows and then at his crew. "You heard the man. Unhook your damn hoses and let's get the hell outta here!"

***

"Over here!" Wayne yelled.

I ran to the end of the aisle where I saw Joe standing a few rows down. He was looking back and forth. When he saw me, he hollered, "Did you see Wayne?"

"No!"

We hustled toward the back of the warehouse, and that's where we found him, kneeling at the bottom of a staircase. I looked at Wayne, and he pointed toward the top of the stairs. About halfway up, I saw legs protruding through the smoke.

"I'm going after 'im," Wayne said as he pulled his collar up over his neck. He rushed up the stairs on all fours, and when he reached the man, for reasons beyond me, Wayne stood up. His head disappeared into the smoke, and a few seconds later, he came tumbling down the stairs, yelling. He was beating his face, and his hair was smoking,

"It's too fuckin' hot!" Wayne said.

I looked up at the man and lowered my visor. "You're supposed to stay low, dumbass. I'll get 'im!"

I went up the same way as Wayne, low and on my hands and knees. When I got to the step below the man, I grabbed his ankle and dragged him down. That's when I noticed water was running down the steps. It was warm and black from soot.

When I got the man down to the floor, he was unconscious. We carried him to the office and laid him on the floor, so I could do a quick survey on him. Wayne closed the door behind us to buy more time.

After Joe and I laid the man on the floor, I surveyed the man's injuries.

"Charles must be upstairs," Joe said.

Wayne shook his head. "Well, if he is, there's no hope for 'im."

The man on the floor didn't look familiar. His face and hair were black from the soot. "You're saying this is Mr. Bellows?" I asked.

"Yeah. That's what we're saying," Wayne said.

I looked at the man's face. Other than it being dirty, it was red from the heat. He didn't appear to have any injuries, and his nares were not singed, meaning he didn't inhale anything too hot, so his lungs should be okay.

I took off my helmet and lowered my ear to Bellows' mouth and watched his chest, as I felt for a carotid pulse. His pulse was rapid but had no respirations, which meant his breathing had just seized.

I put my hand behind Bellow's neck and tilted his head back by placing my other hand on his forehead and pinching his nose and gave him several full breaths.

Joe and Wayne were horrified as they watched me. "What the hell are you doing?" Wayne asked.

"Trying to save this man's life," I said between breaths.

"Come on. The man's dead. Let's get the hell outta here!"

After I gave another breath, I felt for a pulse. He still had one. I looked at Joe and Wayne. "I'm not gonna let him die."

They didn't wanna leave me, so they got down on their knees and watched.

I gave another breath then stopped as my stomach tightened. I slowly looked up as the ceiling made the most unnerving groan. It passed overhead and stopped at the front wall, then the building shook.

"What the hell was that?" I asked. Joe and Wayne were staring at the ceiling, then I was hit in the face by a drop of water. That only meant one thing, and it wasn't good.

Wayne got off his knees and opened the door to the warehouse. All I could see was smoke rolling in under the door header and spreading across the office ceiling. The sound of dripping water came from inside the warehouse.

Wayne quickly shut the door. "We need to get the hell out of here!"

"What's happening?" Joe asked.

"Water's leaking all over the place. It's just a matter of time before the upper floors collapse!"

***

Outside, Nicholas had walked all the way around the building and back to the Economy and asked Charlie, "Where's the Winnebago? I told them to move off Sixteenth Street."

"I haven't seen them."

Nicholas looked up as the hose elevator reached the roof. The fireman on the platform looked across the roof toward the second elevator, hidden by smoke now. The fire had vented in the southwest corner, and the four-foot flames were making a run across the roof toward the firewall that separated the two warehouses. The firefighter on the platform turned and yelled, "Get me some water now!

***

The ceiling rumbled. I looked up, as it sounded like an earthquake. That time it was louder than the last. As it passed overhead, I could hear wood splitting. When the rumble hit the front wall, the whole building shook. There were a few seconds of silence, and then there was the sound of nails being ripped out of wood. Then there was a pop, and then the corner of the ceiling dropped about a foot and stopped.

Joe and Wayne's eyes got big as they watched. I'd be lying if I said I wasn't scared. I think they were too. I gave Bellows several more breaths, and that's when we heard a rumbling and loud crash outside the front door. It sounded like hundreds of blocks falling, and they kept falling.

ACT 28

As Nicholas walked away from the Economy to go check on the Winnebago, he and Charlie heard a thunderous crash resound between the buildings. They took off running toward the street, and as they got to the sidewalk, they saw a massive wall of dust and debris flying toward them. It looked as if a bomb had exploded. People across the street were screaming and scattering to the west. Nicholas and Charlie slowed down to a walk, figuring it was too late for the crew of the Winnebago.

"Dammit!" Nicholas said as he stopped.

Suddenly, the horses ran through the cloud, pulling the Winnebago and its entire crew.

***

"What the hell was that?" I said.

Wayne got up, walked over to the front door, and opened it, then quickly shut it. "The front of the building came down, and the doors completely blocked with smoldering bricks and wood."

"What happened?" Joe said.

"We're trapped. That's what happened! The whole fucking front of the building came down. If we'd have left when I said, we'd be outside right now."

"If we would have left when you said, we'd be buried under 500 tons of brick!" Joe said.

I was about ready to give up with trying to save Mr. Bellows. Maybe it was time to get out; no sense in us all dying. "Let me try one more time."

As I bent down and gave Bellows one last breath, I checked his pulse. Shit! His rapid pulse was almost impalpable; my first thought was a ventricular tachycardia.

"Don't die on me!" I said as I raised my fist in the air and hit him as hard as I could in the chest. Mr. Bellows lurched up and gasped for air, then he coughed.

"What the fuck?" Wayne asked as he looked at Joe.

Bellows looked confused as he tried to process where he was. Joe and Wayne stared at me in shock. Wayne got up and went over to the warehouse door and slowly opened it. The smoke poured through the opening. Wayne stooped down and went into the warehouse and shut the door behind him. When I saw how thick the smoke had gotten, my first thought was that we were all gonna die.

"Don't worry. We'll get out of here," Joe said. "We do this all the time. Wayne's good at his job. If there's a way out, he'll find it."

I don't know if he was just saying that to make me feel better, but from what I remember, I don't think it worked. Then the door opened, and Wayne rushed back in, a cloud of smoke following him.

"Mr. Bellows, can you walk?" Wayne asked.

"I think so."

"Good. I need you guys to help Mr. Bellows. We need to get him through the warehouse. Our only hope is the loading docks!"

We all looked up, as we heard another noise above us. That one sounded like wood bending, and then it snapped. That's when water poured into the office. Wayne looked at us. He was concerned and spoke slowly. "Listen. We need to keep our wits about us and hurry. The upstairs is ready to falter. Water is seeping everywhere!"

We helped Bellows to his feet and crutched him to the door. Wayne was standing there, waiting. He looked at us and said, "When I open the door, I'm gonna head to the docks and get them open. Stay low, and I'll come back to help you."

"Okay," Joe said. When Wayne opened the door, smoke rushed in, and we stooped below it and went into the warehouse. As we helped Bellows through the building, the upper floor was making unsettling noises. I had to block it out, so I could keep focus. Water was dripping all over, and it didn't take long for us to get drenched. It was coming down through the smoke like rain, and we were by then wading in about two inches.

When we got to the stairway, the one where we had found Mr. Bellows, water was rushing down it like a river and spreading over the floor, working its way to a ramp and then down into the basement. We stopped as a rumble went from the back of the warehouse to the front. Then to our right, there was a loud snap, and a section of the ceiling came crashing through the smoke and landed only a few feet away. The debris were on fire, and the ensuing deluge of water extinguished most of it. There was so much water, that the wave it created knocked both Bellows and me off our feet.

Wayne came back through the smoke, his face troubled. "Mr. Bellows, where are the docks?"

"Huh?"

"The docks. I went all the way back and along the back wall, and there's no fucking docks. Mr. Bellows, where are the docks?"

Bellows, a little incoherent said, "The basement."

"You mean down the ramp where all the water's going!" Joe said.

"Yes—"

Another sound crept across the ceiling, and that time, you could hear thick wood bend and then snap. Flaming debris fell all over the crates a few rows away, and they were catching on fire. The smoke was getting thicker and the heat more intense. The water was by then up to our ankles, as we waded through it, trying to get to the ramp.

When we got there, a torrent of water was rushing down. I stepped closer and lost my balance. Before I knew it, I was coming up for air in the basement. The water was up to my neck. Empty liquor barrels were floating and bobbing in it, and I tried to grab one to stay afloat, but I couldn't get my arms around it to hang on.

"Hurry, the water's getting deeper!" I yelled. I was terrified. I didn't want to drown. I fought to stay above the water as it continued to deepen.

Wayne, Joe, and Bellows slid down the ramp and splashed into the water just seconds before a loud cracking ripped across the ceiling followed by a boom that shook the warehouse. Right after that, flaming debris and smoke came flying into the basement through the ramp door. It sounded like most of the second floor had just collapsed.

Water rushed in from the warehouse, and it was rising fast. I was now bobbing to get a breath of air. Then I felt something grab my collar. It was Joe. He held Bellows and me above the water.

"You know this isn't right," I told Joe.

"What ain't right?"

"It isn't right that you're saving my life for the second time today!"

"I can let go," Joe said.

"No . . . Don't do that," I said between breaths. By that time, I had to tilt my head back so I could breathe through my nose. I tried to grab another barrel but couldn't hold on. I swore, if I got out of this, I'd never put water down a gopher hole again. I thought about the firefighters outside, and how they were pouring the water into the building that was gonna kill us. How ironic was that?

When we reached the docks, Wayne felt around under the water for the latch to the door. Finally, he found it and fought to unlatch it. He was now bobbing for air and then took a deep breath and went under to see why the latch wasn't opening. He resurfaced. "It's got a damn lock on it!"

Mr. Bellows hand came up out of the water. He held a large key ring with several keys on it. "It's the big one," he said.

Wayne swam over and got them and then dove under the water toward the doors. Just as Wayne got to the door, we heard another rumble and then an explosion. Not like dynamite, but the explosions you'd hear when something large and heavy hits the ground. That sound was nothing short of horrifying.

"Sounds . . . like . . . the second floor . . . just . . . came down," Bellows said as he bobbed his head in the water, gasping for breath.

"Oh shit!" I said. Out of the corner of my eye, I saw it rushing at us. It was a massive wave, and in it was all the empty barrels coming right at us. The wave must've been at least four feet high. If the barrels didn't kill us, the water would.

Wayne came up for air.

"Hurry! Hurry! hurry!" We yelled.

He looked at the water coming and then dove back down. He fumbled for the keyhole and then got the key in. Just as the wave hit us, he turned the key and slammed the latch up. The doors burst open with an incredible force and flushed us out onto the docks like we were guppies.

The water rushed out and drained on the railroad tracks. We sat there on the dock, quietly staring at each other in disbelief. Then all at once, we burst out laughing.

"Now that was fucking intense!" I said.

ACT 29

We got back to the firehouse around nine thirty that night. While the guys opened a bottle of whiskey and poured drinks, I got cleaned up.

"Gotta go," I said as I rushed out the door.

***

"And where is he going in such a hurry?" Nicholas said.

"He's got a hot date!" Joe said.

"A hot date? What the hell's that?"

"Beats me. That's just what he said. He's on his way to see Ms. Lindsay."

Nicholas shook his head. "That boy doesn't have a lick of sense, does he? After all that's happened, you'd think he'd stay away from that girl."

Wayne came out of the bathroom and sat down next to Joe. Billy laughed and reached over and ran his finger across Wayne's upper lip. "Don't we look purdy? Smooth as a baby's butt."

Wayne jerked away. "Get away from me, you jackass!"

"Isn't that about the third mustache in two months?" Charlie asked.

"Somethin' like that."

Nicholas leaned back. "So, how'd he do?"

"How'd who do?" Wayne said.

"John."

Wayne glanced at Joe and then back at Nicholas. "I'm not sure how to say this, but do you remember the other day when John said God had sent him here? I don't think he was joking!"

Billy reached over and took Wayne's glass of whiskey. "You've had enough!"

Joe smacked his hand on the table. "Y'all need to quit laughing and listen to what Wayne's saying! We saw John do things that were next to impossible."

"If it weren't for John, Mr. Bellows would be dead right now," Wayne said.

"Are you saying John's the one who rescued him?"

"Yeah, Charlie, that's exactly what I'm saying. I tried getting Bellows, but it was too damn hot, and my face caught on fire. Then John went up there and pulled him down. When we carried Bellows into the office, he was dead!"

"John did things we've never seen the likes of," Joe said. "Inside the office, he breathed the life right back into Mr. Bellows!"

"No, you got it wrong. Bellows didn't come back to life until John hit 'im."

Dale laughed. "You guys are full of shit."

"Then explain to me how he knew about the Burlington, and that it was gonna burn? Or how he knew it was gonna start in the broomcorn on the second floor? What about the Winnebago? How did he know they were gonna be fighting the fire on Sixteenth Street, and the front of the warehouse was gonna falter? If you ask me, the force of a higher power is with him. John saved a lot of lives today!" Wayne said.

"And horses too!" Joe said.

"This is absurd. These are nothin' more than coincidences!"

"Billy, if you don't stop using them big words, you're gonna make my head hurt," Wayne said. "Think what you want, but we witnessed it with our own eyes."

Joe crossed his arms and leaned back. "And if he hadn't stopped us from going outside when we wanted, Wayne and I'd be dead too, buried under all that rubble!"

Daniel got up and paced around the room, then he walked over and looked Wayne directly in the face for a few seconds. "We've known each other all our lives, and we've been through a lot of good times and some bad times. Hell, I remember, as kids, we used to sneak over to Mrs. Kowalski's house and steal pies off her window. I wouldn't hesitate for a second to give my life to save yours, and I know you'd do the same for me. With that said, the one thing I've learned over the years is whether or not you're lying by looking at your face," Daniel said and looked around the room then shook his head. "Think what you will, but I know one thing for certain, Wayne isn't lying!"

Nicholas leaned forward and crossed his arms. "To be honest, I'm at a loss for words. He did tell us about the Burlington, and when I saw those flames coming out those windows, I tried to dispel John's words, but I couldn't. Everything he says comes true! Inside my heart, I feel, if I hadn't acted upon John's words, we'd be attending services for the crew of the Winnebago."

"Don't forget about the horses," Joe said.

Everyone looked at Joe and laughed. "Yeah, okay, the horses too!" Billy said.

Charlie sat back in his chair and put a foot up on the table. When he saw Nicholas staring, he put it back on the floor. "Sorry . . . What if he is from the future like he says? I wasn't gonna say this, but when he walks into the room, it's like the air changes. Almost like the feeling when fall arrives."

"I've been thinking a lot about the night we found him," Daniel said. "We left that porch only for a few seconds. One minute he wasn't there, and the next he was. It was as if the house gave birth to him."

***

Thanks to a man who gave me a ride up Canal Street, it took only about twenty minutes to get to Lindsay's house. It was hard for me to get over how friendly the people were. Before stepping on the porch, I took my finger and brushed it across my teeth, and then cupped my hands over my mouth and blew. I smelled nothing, so I hoped my breath didn't stink. As soon as I stepped on the porch, the door opened. Lindsay stood there with a gorgeous smile on her face. "You came!"

"Of course, I did."

"I hope you're hungry."

"Starving," I said, and then I caught the smell of her cooking, and it made my mouth water.

"I made cowboy stew. It's my mother's recipe," she said as she stepped back to let me in the door. My stomach growled and she laughed.

"If it tastes anything like it smells. She must be an excellent cook!"

"Oh, she is."

I walked in, and the plates had been set. "Have a seat. You look tired."

"Thank you."

The table was square and had four chairs. I looked around the room, and Lindsay had her house fixed up rather nice. Off the main room were two doors. I imagined one went to the bedroom, and the other to the water closet or bathroom. "So, where're your parents?"

"Arizona Territory," she said as she set the pot of stew on the table. Next, she brought a skillet covered with a cloth. It was cornbread.

"What part of Arizona?"

"Tucson. My father's a soldier serving under Gen. George Crook at Camp Grant. I know, it's a tongue twister. They're at war with the Apache and Yavapai tribes."

"How'd you wind up here?"

"Melanie met her husband, Brian Flynn, while he was scouting near the Arizona border for renegades. They got married, and before they left for Chicago, Brian told me of the opportunities they had in theater. I came with them," Lindsay said as she set down a plate with what looked like a cube of butter on it, but it was white, and I prayed it wouldn't taste like lard.

I took a spoonful of stew and then a bite of cornbread and butter. "This is the best stew I have ever eaten. And the cornbread and butter, let's just say I've never tasted butter so creamy and rich in flavor. Can I come over every night for dinner?" I joked. She just smiled. "So tell me about your mother and father."

"Like I said, my father is in the army, and my mother is Papago."

"Your mom's Indian?"

"Yes," she said. "I shouldn't have said that."

"Why?"

"Because most people frown on it."

"On what?"

"You know, being half Indian or half-breed."

"Shoot, my great-grandfather was Comanche, so that makes me a quarter Comanche," I said.

Her face dropped. "You're Comanche?"

"Well, that's what I've been told. I've never met my great-grandfather. Why?"

"I've heard of the Comanche. They're as mean as the Apache. My father says the Comanche attacked a wagon and killed eight Texans. Now they're at war in Texas."

"Wow, maybe I shouldn't have said anything."

"That's okay. I don't think you're mean," Lindsay said.

I felt awkward. I had put myself in a spot and didn't know what to say, so I reached across the table and held her hands. "You know, the first day I laid eyes on you in Lincoln Park, I thought you were the most beautiful thing I'd ever seen."

"You mean that?"

"Absolutely! Without a doubt. And you still are," I said, and then that gorgeous smile returned to her face. "So how did your mother and father meet?"

"Well, my mother grew up in a small village in Southwestern Arizona, about a day's ride from a mining camp called Ajo. My mother's father was a strong leader of the Coyote clan. His name is Standing Eagle."

"Your grandfather's a chief?"

She smiled. "Yes, I guess you could call him that, but my father was living in Ajo and worked at a mine called the Old Bat Hole, which was in the Gunsight Mountains east of my mother's village. Once a week, my father and his miners, who worked for a guy named Childs, had to pass through our land to get to the mine. They would bring gifts, such as flour, furs, and guns in exchange for safe passage.

"One day, while the village warriors were on a hunt, a band of Mexican bandits raided the village. They shot the few braves that stayed behind and rustled the horses. They took the women and children and planned to sell them in Mexico as slaves. My mother was among those taken. A few of the Mexicans stayed behind and took what they could and set fire to the village.

"My father had been working in the mine and came out for a break. He saw smoke coming from the village and pulled out his spyglass. He saw the village burning and then spotted the dust trail the bandits made, as they rode to catch up with the others. My father rounded up the miners and told two of them to go fetch the braves while he and the rest of the miners rode to cut off the Mexicans before they reached the border."

"Wow! That's incredible," I said.

Lindsay got up and walked over to the cabinet next to the sink. I heard paper crinkling, and when she turned around, she was holding a paper bag in her hand. "Joe left this here last night. Thought you might like a drink." She reached into the bag and pulled out the bottle of whiskey, the one we didn't finish. The first thing that came to mind was, Oh shit! Not again! But I just smiled.

"Let's sit outside and I'll finish the story."

We went outside and sat on the edge of the porch. It was dark out, but the streetlamp at the corner provided a soft light, a light just bright enough that you could see. The wind from earlier had died down to a slight breeze; its cool air felt good across my face. Lindsay handed me the bottle, and I sipped it then gave it back to her.

"The two miners found my grandfather and explained what happened. The warriors returned to the village as fast as they could and saw it devastated. They painted their faces with red paint, and then they rode off to hunt down the Mexicans. My people, with their faces painted, had now become a war party.

"As night fell, the Mexicans had stopped to make camp in a dry river bottom. When my father and the other miners caught up to them, they snuck around the camp and across the river bed and waited near the trail to Mexico.

"Later, when the warriors got there, the half-moon provided enough light that my uncles, Silent Bear and Eyes Like Hawk, snuck up on the Mexicans that were guarding the camp and one by one killed them. Diego, the leader who wore a sombrero and had two guns with a bullet belt that crisscrossed his shoulders forced my mother into the bushes and used his knife to cut off her clothes. She said he looked crazy and had teeth like horses.

"My mother said she fought him the whole time, so he punched her in the face. Then the braves attacked, but before they could get to Diego, he grabbed my mother, threw her on his horse, and took off with two other bandits. My father and his miners heard the horses approaching, and when they came over the hill, my father stood up and with the butt of his shotgun, knocked Diego off the horse. My mother said my dad walloped Diego so hard that it knocked her off the horse too. The other two Mexicans tried to shoot it out, but the miners shot and killed them. Diego rolled over and tried going for his guns, but my father hit him in the face with the shotgun and knocked him out cold.

"After that, my father went to help my mother and took his shirt off to cover her nakedness. That was the first time my mother and father laid eyes on each other."

"What about Diego?" I asked, I was totally engrossed with the story. Lindsay took another swig and handed the bottle back. I took the last drink from the bottle; I was feeling buzzed.

"What happened to Diego?" she replied. "They took him and a couple of the surviving bandits back to the village and tortured them for days. My grandfather was so grateful to my dad for saving his daughter, Che'yah, that he accepted my father into the clan, and not long after that, he was permitted to marry my mother."

I took a deep breath. "And they say Romeo and Juliet was a good story!"

"It's funny. The same way my father rescued my mother from Diego, you rescued me from Luther."

"I hardly think that's a comparison," I said.

"Luther was a bad person and always treated me like he owned me, like I was nothing more than an animal. When Luther got mad at me, he'd pull my hair and drag me around and call me a no-good Injun. Other times, he would just punch or kick me or even throw things at me, and said if I ever tried to leave him, that he'd kill me," Lindsay said, crying.

It made me feel terrible, seeing her like that. I scooted closer and put my arm around her and wiped the tears from her face. She put her head against my chest for comfort. "I'm so sorry you had to go through that. He was blessed to have you."

She lifted her head and gently kissed me on the cheek. Her kiss put me in a trance, and I couldn't control myself. I turned and held her face and tenderly kissed her lips, then her forehead and cheeks. I was floating somewhere on cloud nine, like I had just drove into a dip in the road and my stomach fell out. After we kissed, I held her in my arms as we sat there, enjoying the peacefulness of the night.

Lindsay moved her head against my chest, and I put both arms around her and held her tight.

"Now that you know my story, let's hear yours."

"Whaddya wanna know?"

"Everything!"

I sat there for a moment and thought about what I should say. I was having a good time and was on top of the world and drunk! "Okay," I said. "I'll tell you everything because I don't ever wanna lie to you," I slurred.

"Okay," she said and leaned her head back against my chest.

"I'm not sure how to say this, but I'm not from around here."

"I know. You're from California, right?"

"Well, sort of."

"What do you mean, sort of?"

The alcohol was affecting my judgment, and instead of passing out, which I should have done, I continued being truthful. Whoever says alcohol isn't a truth serum only needs to drink whiskey from 1871. "Anyway, I'm not from the California you know. I'm from California in the future."

Lindsay jerked back. "What do you mean you're from California in the future?" That's the moment she went from speaking softly to a more direct tone. Apparently, she could hold her liquor better than me.

"I'm from the year 2018. I haven't been born yet."

Her face went blank, and she just stared at me for a few seconds, and then she scooted away from me. That's when I discovered that not only could she hold her liquor better than me, but she could hit as hard as a man. She slapped the shit outta me. She got up and went to the door and as she opened it, she said, "Just when I thought you were special, you turned out to be just like everyone else, a big liar! Do I look stupid?" And then she slammed the door.

"Fuck," I said. Now I'd done it. I sat there for a few minutes, trying to gather a little composure, and then got up and walked over to the door. "Come on, Lindsay. I'm telling you the truth . . . Please give me a chance to explain!" I said as I lightly knocked.

"You had your chance. Now get off my porch and leave me alone!"

I slowly turned and walked down the steps to the sidewalk. I turned around, hoping she'd open the door, but she never did. This is fucking great, I thought. I've been here for five days, and the only things I've accomplished was getting my nose and hand busted; my face fried; and become a miserable, brokenhearted, and homeless drunk staggering the streets. I felt like the dumbest jackass on the planet.

ACT 30

"John, get your lazy ass up!"

I opened my eyes. Wayne was standing right there, staring at me.

"Come on. We got a fire to put out!"

I jumped out of bed, got into my gear, and ran into the room where the crew was sitting at the table, laughing at me.

"You guys are a bunch of jackasses!" I said and walked over to the sink and ran water over my head. My head was pounding.

"Ahhh, come on, John. Tell us about your hot date. Joe said you were out late," Charlie said.

"It started off fantastic. We drank a little whiskey, and I got drunk, slapped, and thrown out on the street with no ride home."

Billy laughed. "Maybe you should keep your hands to yourself."

"It wasn't my hands. It was my mouth!"

"I don't think I've seen anyone hit as many times as you have been over the past few days," Nicholas said. "What happened?"

"I don't know. Maybe it had something to do with telling her that I was from the future, or that I hadn't been born yet."

***

I was in bed, crying, when I heard a knock at the door. Even though I was angry, I was hoping it was John. I opened the door, and it was Melanie.

"What's the matter?" she asked and gently wiped the tears from my face.

"Why am I so cursed?"

"What do ya mean?"

"With men. Why can't I find the right one?"

"Didn't John come by last night?"

"Yes," I said and cried again.

"What happened?" Melanie said as she hugged me.

"All the hopes I had for us, and he turned out to be no better than the rest. Things were going great until I told him the story of Mother and Father."

"What happened?"

"I don't think he believed me because he started telling me that he was from the future and hadn't been born yet—"

Melanie laughed. "I'm sorry, but he told you that?"

"And that was right after he said he'd never lie to me."

Melanie ran her hand through my hair and said, "I'm sorry, but don't worry. The right mister will come along. Sometimes it just takes a while."

***

"By the way, where's Joe?"

"He's over at Quinn's, waiting for breakfast to get done. Why don't we go help him?" Wayne said.

"Okay."

"You know, when you first told us you were from the future, we all laughed and thought you were crazy with amnesia. Even after witnessing you do the things, we've seen you do, I think most of us are still having a hard time coming to grips. So, don't get offended if at times I think you're full of shit!" Wayne said as we crossed the street. "Now, you take Ms.

Lindsay. She's never seen any of the things you've done, and then you go and lay this future shit on her. Did you really think she'd believe it?"

"I didn't want to lie about it."

"Look at it this way. It's like a cup of coffee. It starts off hotter than hell and it's hard to drink, but the longer it sits, the easier it gets to drink. You need to give some things time!"

I smiled. "You know, Wayne, that's probably the smartest thing I've ever heard you say!"

"Thank you!"

Gladys was standing at the counter taking money from a customer. She looked at us and smiled. "Mornin', Mista John . . . Mista Wayne."

"Good morning, Ms. Gladys," Wayne said as he took a seat next to Joe. Gladys kept eyeing me. I think she was getting used to me coming in with something wrong with my face.

"Morning, Ms. Gladys," I said.

"Nothing wrong with his face today," Wayne said. "Today he's got a broken heart."

"I'm sorry to hear that," she said, then she walked into the kitchen and returned with a pot of coffee and poured us a cup. Wayne took a sip of his coffee, and that's when I noticed his profile without his mustache. I almost fell off my chair, "Elkins . . . Wayne Elkins?"

"Yeah. Something wrong with that?"

"Can I ask you something?"

"I suppose since we got my name out of the way."

"Have you ever told me anything about your family?"

"What type of stupid-ass question is that? I don't talk about my family with no one except maybe Daniel."

"I have a story you need to hear," I said.

"Let's hear it," Wayne said.

"In 2018, I had a partner—"

"John," Wayne interrupted, "Remember, the coffee's still hot."

"I know, but you really need to hear this."

Joe moved forward, so he could see around Wayne and listen. Gladys looked up from behind the counter and stepped closer, trying not to appear as if she was eavesdropping.

"I started working for the Pine Valley Fire District in Northern California on September 24, 2018, and I was assigned a partner—"

Gladys moved closer and filled our cups. "Careful, Mista John. It's hot!"

I looked over at Wayne, and he smiled and shrugged. I took a sip. "Black coffee sure takes a little getting used to."

"Coffee isn't black in California?" Joe asked.

"Yeah, the coffee's black, but I like to drink mine with a little cream and sugar."

"That's how women drink tea."

I took another sip. "Anyway, my partner's name was Donald. My first night, we responded to a house fire, and after we made entry and were working our way to the fire, there was a bright flash, and the next thing I knew, I was waking up in the hospital here in Chicago, two thousand miles away and 147 years in the past."

Wayne rolled his eyes, but I think from what he said earlier, he wanted to believe me but was still on the fence. Common sense kept him from jumping.

"But here's the thing. Earlier that day, we were having lunch, and our captain said that Donald's third-generation grandfather helped fight the Great Chicago Fire!"

"The what?" Joe said.

"The Great Chicago Fire. It hasn't happened yet. I'll get to that later. But here's the kicker. Donald's last name was Elkins. That's why I pulled your mustache. You looked familiar. But now that you don't have one, the resemblance is undeniable!" I don't think they understood the point I was trying to make; they just stared at me. "Don't you see? Donald, my partner in the future, is your third great-grandson!"

Wayne stood up and tossed a coin on the counter. "That's enough. I've heard just about all I can handle."

"Wayne, sit the fuck down and hear me out!" I think my tone startled him because he stopped. Sharon walked out and sat our food on the counter then sat next to Joe. Wayne shook his head and then reluctantly sat back down.

Gladys inched over and wiped the counter top and looked into our cups, checking to see if we needed refills. It was so obvious that she was eavesdropping that I almost asked her to sit down too.

"After my captain told me about Donald's connection to the Great Fire, I decided to look up his genealogy on the internet. That's when I found his third great-grandfather and all the information about his wife and kids. His great-grandfather's name was Wayne Elkins. That's you!"

"Wait. I thought we were talking about his third great-grandfather?" Joe said.

"We are! It's just simpler to say grandfather, okay? Anyway, then I read about the Great Fire, and that's how I found out about the Burlington, and all the fires that are still going to happen this week."

"What's a genealogy and an internet?" Joe asked.

"Yes, what is it?" Gladys said as she stood there with her arms crossed.

"The internet is something like a telegraph, but not only does it send messages, it sends pictures. You can find all sorts of information on it that goes all the way back to the beginning of time." I paused as I heard a man behind me laugh. We turned, and he quickly looked down at his food. "Genealogy is where you can search a person's history, like I did with Donald's and found that you are his third great-grandfather. You can search for anything. It's like an electronic book with all the information about everything you could ever want to know."

"What's an electronic?" Joe asked.

I squeezed my eyes shut for a second while I thought. "The same thing that makes a telegraph work. I know this is all so confusing, but I don't have an easy way to explain it or the time. It's just something that hasn't been invented yet, so let's just skip that part."

"How do you keep coming up with all this future stuff? Your imagination is endless!" Wayne said.

"Yeah, okay," I said. "Now then, tell me if this is my imagination. Do you have any children?"

"Yes."

"How many?"

Wayne glanced over at Gladys, and they exchanged smiles. "One."

"How old is she?"

Wayne jerked his head back. "How'd you know she is a girl? She's one. Why?"

"Your wife's name is Sherry, and her maiden name is Setter. Your daughter's name is Rochelle, and the baby your wife is pregnant with will be born on January 25, 1872. At present, you're unsure whether it's gonna be a boy or girl, but if it's a boy, you plan on naming him Justin!"

Wayne looked frightened, and he attempted to stand but had to use the counter to stop from falling. The smirk was gone. "How did you know all of that?" Wayne asked and then looked at Gladys. "How could he have possibly known that? Nobody on God's green earth knew that if it was a boy, I was gonna name him Justin except me! Sherry and I agreed she would pick a girl name, and I would pick a boy's. We agreed not to tell each other until it was born. I picked Justin and haven't told a soul because I didn't want to ruin the surprise for her."

I bent over and whispered in Wayne's ear. "I hate to spoil the surprise, but it's gonna be a boy!"

Wayne stood straight up and held his arms up like he was trying to hug the world. "Oh, thank you! Thank you," he said while looking up at the ceiling. "I'm gonna have a boy!" Then he stopped and looked around. "This mustn't leave this room. Sherry can't find out!"

Gladys put her hand over her mouth. "Oh, my Lord, I know there was somethin' special about you. I knows it since the first time I saw you."

I whispered in his ear again, "Here's another spoiler. Save some of that excitement because you're gonna have three more boys after Justin. I already know their names, but I'm not gonna tell you. I don't want to be the one who names them, if you get my meaning."

Just as I took the last gulp of coffee, Wayne asked, "By the way, where's Ms. Mollie?"

"Good golly, Ms. Mollie went to Six Corners to fetch up some supplies from Brenner's." When Gladys said that, I couldn't help it. I busted up laughing and sprayed the counter with the coffee in my mouth. Gladys grabbed a rag. "Are you okay, Mista John?"

"I'm sorry, that reminded me of a song I once heard. Ms. Gladys, I can clean up my mess."

"You just get that food over to the men before it gets cold."

"Yes, ma'am."

As we walked out the door, Wayne looked at Joe. "Remember what John said about the first man walking on the moon?"

"Yeah, why?"

"Believe him. I don't think he was lying!"

ACT 31

I remember that morning after we got back to the firehouse; breakfast seemed a little odd because no one said much. It seemed like when Nicholas said nothing, no one else did either. Finally, Charlie laid his fork on the table, then Billy laid his down, and then the rest of the guys did too. When it was my turn, I didn't wanna put mine down because I was hungry, but after I saw the guys glaring at me, I decided it might be in my best interest to get my mind off my stomach.

"Speak up, Nicholas!" Charlie said. "Tell us what's on your mind?"

"Word has it that while we were out practicing, so was the crew of the Long John. Seems Tige Jenson and Jeremy Wallace shattered our record by nineteen seconds on the 600-foot hydrant pull." We looked around at each other for a few seconds and then busted out laughing. Then we continued eating. "After we finish with breakfast, Billy, you and Dale recheck the hose and make sure it's bedded properly."

"You got it," Billy answered.

"John, are you quick at coupling?" Nicholas asked.

"Yeah . . . pretty quick."

"How quick?" Charlie asked.

"Speedy Gonzales quick."

"Good. Let's see if you're quick enough to rid my nose of these boogers before anyone sees you!"

Everyone thought that was funny because they all laughed.

"Kiss my ass," I said and threw my cap at him. He jerked his head to the side, and the chair fell out from under him. I laughed. "Now that was funny."

"What the hell's a Speedy Gonzales?" Joe asked.

"Give me two couplings, and I'll show you!"

After breakfast, Joe and I fed and watered the horses then went outside to the corral and fed the crew's horses. I couldn't get Lindsay off my mind and what happened last night and didn't want it to end like this. I was so much in love with her. "Hey, Joe, can I ask you something?"

"Sure. Go right ahead, little brother."

"What would you do if you were in my shoes?"

Joe looked down at my feet and said, "Get me a bigger pair!"

I laughed. He was always so literal. "You know that's not what I meant. What would you do about Lindsay?"

"Well, that's kinda funny because just the other day you were giving me advice. Now you're asking me?"

"Yeah, I suppose."

"Well, a smart lady once said that when it comes to the heart, you shouldn't listen to other people's advice because it's cheap. They don't have to live with the consequences. You do."

I shook my head. "You're a jackass."

"You gotta follow your heart. If you love Lindsay, then you must fight for her. You have to convince her that your love is real!"

"But how?"

"You're a pretty smart guy. That's something you'll have to figure out."

I patted Joe on the shoulder and said, "You know, you're the best brother I ever had!"

Around one o'clock, we arrived downtown. We parked on Clark Street, about a half a block north of Adams. It was exciting to see so many fire engines and hose wagons in one place. On Clark, south of Adams Street, I saw two hook and ladders and hose elevators. We all got down and stood next to our wagons and waited for Nicholas to check in.

"You see those guys up the street next to that hose wagon?" Joe said.

I looked and saw two firemen standing there, sneering at us. "What's their problem?" I asked.

"That's Tige and Jeremy. They're pipemen for the Long John."

"Oh. They're the ones who shattered our record."

"That's them. Hold your nose when we walk by 'em," Wayne said.

"Hold my nose?"

"Yeah. They go around acting like their shit don't stink. That'll let them know it does!"

"See the man who just walked up to them? That's Schimmels, their captain," Billy said.

Schimmels walked to the rear of the hose wagon and lifted the top layers of hose. Under it, the hose was bedded in such a way, it formed loops, just like our hose on Engine 342.

"You guys see where the hose is folded under? Those are loops to help them pull the hose off the wagon. It makes it faster and easier. I counted six loops, so that means each man will grab two and run. That's how they beat your record!" I explained.

"That's mighty clever," Charlie said.

We walked toward the corner of Adams, and as we passed Tige and Jeremy, they made a few comments about how we ought to get ready for a real humiliation. They laughed and tried rubbing in their breaking of our record. We ignored them, and I did what they said to do. As we walked by, I held my nose. That's when I noticed that none of them were holding their noses, and they were laughing at me. I couldn't believe it. They just punked me.

When we got to the corner, I looked west on Adams Street toward the river. It surprised me there were so many people lining the streets, probably over a thousand. They were noisy and having a good time, and the smell of hickory filled the air as they readied the firepits for the afternoon celebration.

The next street to the west was Wells. On the north corner of Wells and Adams was a makeshift wooden stage with a podium on it. I would have never thought that the monthly competitions were so popular.

A stumpy, red-faced, balding man walked up on the stage and over to the podium. He looked to the sky and rubbed the top of his head. He reached down and picked up the megaphone next to the podium and waited for the crowd to silence.

"I should have worn my hat today, because if it gets any hotter, my family's gonna look at my head as dinner for tonight." The crowd laughed as the man looked up and down the street. He seemed pleased with the large turnout and smiled. Again, he raised the megaphone. "Without further ado, let me introduce to you, Mayor Roswell Mason!"

The crowd cheered.

The mayor took the podium and smiled. "Ladies and gentlemen, boys and girls of all ages. First, I would like to give my humblest gratitude to the men who display outstanding bravery and dedication to protecting the citizens of this great city of Chicago. Let's hear a well-deserved round of applause." The crowd cheered wildly.

This was so cool, I thought. Why couldn't they have events like this in my time?

The mayor took out a handkerchief and wiped the sweat off his forehead. "Bob's right, if it gets any hotter, I might just be joining his family for supper!" The crowd busted out laughing. "Today, we have our top six companies by time. They include Company 3, the Atlantic, led by Captain George McCagg. Company 5, the Chicago, led by Captain Jefferson. Company 6, the Little Giant, led by Captain Fred Bragg. Company 7, the Liberty, led by Captain John O'Neil. Company 1, the Long John, led by Captain Christian Schimmels. And then we have our returning champions, Company 8, Old Economy, led by Captain Nicholas DuBach."

The crowd cheered. I almost felt like I was at a football game while the players were being introduced. Roswell lowered the megaphone and stepped back and waited for the cheers to die down. He wiped the sweat from his forehead and cheeks, then he stepped back to the podium.

"These are the rules," Roswell said and cleared his throat. "All companies will line up on Adams Street, east of Clark. The race will begin when Marshal Brandon Theis fires his shotgun in the air. The first two companies to lay hose and connect to this fireplug will continue the race," Roswell said, as he pointed at the corner hydrant. "Companies unable to make their connections to the hydrant will be disqualified from the competition and sent to man the firepits. The first company that has their engine parked at the corner of Adams and Market and has water spraying into the Chicago River will be deemed the victors!"

The crowd cheered. This time they were chanting for their favorite companies. They filled the air with excitement; it was so unbelievable.

Schimmels and his men walked over to us, and Jeremy and Tige were smiling as Schimmels said, "Well, boys. We hope you've enjoyed your place at the top because today it's coming to an end!"

"Whateverrrr!" Joe said.

Roswell took a drink of water and then walked back to the podium and waited for the crowd to quiet down. "Furthermore, thanks to your generous donations and the money given by the insurance companies, the company who wins today's competition will get the usual one month's paid meals from the eatery of their choosing. And because Christmas is nearing, this month and next, we will be adding a ten-dollar cash bonus for each member of the winning company."

The firemen that lined the street threw their hats into the air and yelled, Jeremy and Tige shouting the loudest, and the crowd applauded.

We all headed back to our wagons and then moved them around the block, so we'd be facing west on Adams Street at the starting line. The steamers were in front, and the hose carts a few feet behind. I glanced at the hydrant on the next corner and then at Tige and Jeremy to our right. I smiled at them. In front of all the hose wagons, the smoke from the steamers created a cloud that drifted over our heads. The steamers were ready to pump.

Nicholas looked over his shoulder and winked at us. We were all ready and set to go. Schimmels looked over at Nicholas. "You wanna put a little wager on the race?" he yelled.

"Nah. We don't need your money. We'll be satisfied with the ten dollars!" Charlie hollered back

"Well, that's where you boys are completely misinformed. Unless you're yellow, let's wager. The losers cook at the next shindig."

Nicholas smiled at Charlie and said, "That's fair. You're on!"

"Yeeha," Schimmels shouted.

Tige and Jeremy kept eyeing me. "I was gonna ask," Tige said. "Your yellow coat and trousers, is that so everyone knows you're yellow without asking?" They laughed.

What a couple of asses, I thought. The horses stood and stomped their hooves. They were just as anxious and excited as we were. They wanted to run.

ACT 32

We focused up the road as Marshal Theis walked out into the street and pointed his shotgun in the air. He stood there for a minute, making sure that we all saw him, and then he braced the butt against his shoulder.

Nicholas turned around and shouted, "Don't disappoint me, boys!" And then there was a loud blast as the marshal fired both barrels. The steamers took off, and the crowd cheered. Marshal Theis laid the smoking gun on his shoulder and calmly walked out of the street. We took off a few seconds later and drove into the black smoke cloud the engines left behind. We were racing side by side with Hose Company 1 on our right and Hose Wagon 5 on our left. I waved at firefighter David Kenyon, and he waved back and smiled. Engine 3, the Atlantic, was pulling out in front of the others, and then the Long John inched ahead, but for only a few seconds. Fast and Faster turned it on and then edged out the Long John. That was exciting and scary at the same time, the speed these horses were pulling the steamers. As the steamers raced up Adams, Billy slowed Jack, and Hose Company 1 pulled ahead. Tige and Jeremy looked back at us and were laughing.

"What the hell are you doin'? Turning yellow?" Jeremy yelled.

As soon as they got ahead of us, Billy pulled to the sidewalk and stopped in front of the hydrant. The cheers from the crowd went quiet as they watched us, trying to figure out what we were doing. Dale jumped down and pulled an armful of hose from the wagon and wrapped it around the fireplug, then we took off. As we drove toward the steamer, people pointed and cheered as they saw the hose flying off the back of the wagon. After we had laid about a hundred feet, Dale quickly unwrapped the hose and made his connection.

About a hundred feet before reaching the Economy, we passed the other crews running their hoses to the hydrant. They had 500 feet to go. I laughed at Jeremy and Tige as we passed them. Now they had to get to the hydrant before Dale opened it up, or they'd lose their opportunity to make a connection.

When we got to the Economy, I jumped down and pulled off another section of hose, uncoupled it, and then ran the end to Charlie. Then Daniel and I uncoupled the hoses Wayne and Joe were pulling, and we ran our ends to the steamer and connected them. We had to hurry because Charlie had made his connection and called for water.

Dale cranked the valve open and water shot into the hose. We had just pulled off a shutout; once the hydrant was opened, no one else could make their connections. Tige and Jeremy saw the water rush by them in our hose, and they stopped. They threw their hose on the ground and kicked it. All we had to do was get water into the river.

As soon as Daniel and I made our connections, Daniel yelled, "Pull!"

Charlie pulled open the discharge valves, and within a few seconds, Wayne and Joe had water flowing into the river.

Mayor Roswell raised a flag and waved it to signal a victor. He raised his megaphone and his first word was "astonishing!" He wiped his face. "The men of Old Economy and Nicholas DuBach have won the competition with an unbelievable time of two minutes and thirty-five seconds!"

The cheer of the crowd could be heard for blocks. Joe and Wayne made their way back to the steamer, and we high-fived each other. Then over our shoulders, we heard someone say, "Cheaters!" It was the loudmouths of the Long John. Joe and Wayne looked at each other and smiled, then they opened their nozzles and shot two streams at Tige and Jeremy. The streams were so powerful, they knocked them on their asses. Joe and Wayne kept the water trained on them until they scrambled to their feet and ran down the street. We all laughed.

Schimmels walked over and shook his head. "Nicholas, I don't know how you figure shit out, but I must say, you're one smart sum-bitch."

Nicholas grinned and shook hands.

The crowd walked off the sidewalks and into the streets. The festivities were now in full swing. Plumes of white smoke shot up as slabs of meat hit the grills, and across the street, dueling banjos took to the stage. We gathered around the steamer and celebrated. As we laughed and joked, I glanced over at the crowd, and a woman's hat caught my attention. It was large and colorful. I squinted to get a better look. It was Lindsay. We made eye contact for a few seconds, then she turned away and disappeared into the crowd.

I rushed over to the sidewalk, but by the time I fought my way through the crowd, she was gone. I scanned the crowd and ran down the walkway, searching for her, but she was nowhere to be found.

We got back to the firehouse around three o'clock, and shortly after that, the city bell rang. We responded to a duplex fire on Prairie that a witness said was started by two boys playing. As we finished up with that fire, the bells rang again and again. It seemed like, for the next couple of hours, fires were breaking out all over the city. We responded with the Long John to a fire at the Northwestern Railway freight office which turned out to be a roof fire. Fortunately, we put it out quickly, and it caused little damage. Three more fires were received throughout the city into the evening, then it died down. I remember thinking that those fires were a prelude to the Great Fire. The fuse to one of the country's worst disasters had just been lit.

It was around sunset when we got back to the firehouse. Joe and I fed the horses and allowed them to run loose inside the barn, so they could get some exercise. They'd been hitched and standing in place almost all day.

"John," Dale yelled from the stairs.

"Yeah? What's up?"

"You have any plans for tonight?"

"No, not really. Why?"

"Dawn wants to go to the theater. You wanna go with us?"

"Who?"

"Dawn . . . my wife."

"Sure," I said.

"Get cleaned up. She'll be here in a bit," Dale said.

I looked at Joe. "You wanna go?"

"Nah. Go get cleaned up. I'll finish down here."

"Okay, thanks," I said and then ran upstairs.

After I got cleaned up, Dale and I waited outside, and a short spell later, two horses pulling a buckboard stopped in the street. The driver was a woman, around twenty-three and had blonde hair past her shoulders. "You two handsome strangers in need of a ride?"

"No thanks. We're waiting for Dale's wife!"

Dale slapped me on the back of the head. "Dumbass! She is my wife!"

"Oh, sorry!" I'd been hanging around Joe too much, I thought.

We climbed on the wagon, and Dale took the reins. "Giddyap!"

"I'd been here sooner, but the chickens were dead set against going to bed early," she said and then turned to me. "I'm Dawn."

"Nice to meet you."

"I hear you and Lindsay have an eye for each other."

I smiled. "I thought we did too until I said something stupid. Now she doesn't want anything to do with me."

"Like what, if you don't mind my asking?"

"John told her he was from the future."

Dawn put her hand over her mouth to keep from laughing. "I'm sorry, but why would you tell her that?"

"That was my first reaction too. I laughed and thought he was crazy. But somehow, he's convinced Wayne and Joe that he's telling the truth," Dale said. As we passed the Burlington, Dawn stared at the charred ruins of Warehouse A and the workers that were cleaning up the rubble off Sixteenth Street. The smell of burned wood was pungent.

"You wanna hear something funny?" Dale said.

"Sure."

"John told us yesterday that that fire was gonna happen hours before it did."

"Nah . . ."

"He did, and believe it or not, it happened exactly the way he said it would."

Dawn looked at me and said, "He's joshing me, right?"

I raised my eyebrows. "I wish he were."

"That's absurd." Dawn sat there for a few seconds until the smile left her face. "Why do Joe and Wayne believe him?"

"Let's just say he did a few things inside the warehouse that amazed them," Dale said as we pulled into a lot behind the theater. Dale jumped down and tied the horses then helped Dawn off the wagon.

"If you really like her, fight for her," Dawn said as we walked into the theater. Our seats were in the front row of the second balcony. She sat between Dale and me and held his hand. As we waited for the show to start, Dawn leaned over and whispered, "So, what part of the future are you from?"

"You're kidding, right?" I said.

"Are you or aren't you from the future?"

"Two thousand eighteen," I said as I stared at the stage.

"Two thousand eighty?"

"No, 2018."

The lights dimmed, and the spotlights came on and brightly lit the stage. As the curtains opened, I sat back. Lindsay walked onto the stage and began singing her opening song. Instantly, I was transported into another world. I leaned forward and laid my arms on the railing and rested my chin on my hands. I enjoyed every minute, and the show seemed to fly by. After her final song, I stood and whistled and yelled. Lindsay looked up at the balcony and saw me.

"Blow her a kiss!" Dawn said.

As soon as I did, she rushed off the stage. Dawn looked at me. "Don't be fooled. That girl's in love with you!"

That was all the encouragement I needed. "I'll meet you at the wagon."

I rushed into the aisle and fought my way downstairs to the lobby then ran across the auditorium to the stage doors. They were closed.

I ran up to the usher. "Please, can I get in? I need to see Lindsay!"

"Is she expecting you?" The six-foot, two-hundred-fifty-pound usher asked. He looked more like a bouncer.

"No, not exactly."

"Then I'm sorry. I can't let you in."

I threw my arms up and walked away. I met Dale and Dawn at the wagon.

"Why the long face?" Dawn asked.

"Because I seem to have the worst luck in the world. When I got there, the doors were already locked."

ACT 33

"Wake up!"

I opened my eyes as a boot hit the wall behind my head. "What the hell, dude?"

"You need to get up. We have a 2-11!" Joe said and ran out of the room.

I thought for a second and was skeptical after what happened yesterday, but I grabbed my boot wedged between the bed and wall and ran into the living room. Everyone was gone. I barely made it down to the wagon and jumped on as Billy pulled out of the barn.

"We're gonna have to take some of that straw outta your mattress. You sleep too damn good," Wayne said.

"Give 'im a break. The boy had a rough night," Dale said over his shoulder.

"Didn't you all go see Lindsay last night?" Wayne said.

"Yeah, but she wouldn't see him," Dale said.

"It's not that she wouldn't see me. They locked the doors before I got there."

Wayne shook his head. "Face it. She didn't wanna see you!"

"Don't worry, little brother. She'll come around."

"Thanks, Joe, but I'm starting to have my doubts."

"Yeah. Dawn says you're a pretty nice guy, and she's a pretty good judge of character."

"I don't know about all that," Wayne said. "She married you!"

"Kiss my ass!" Dale said.

I laid back and looked up. It was another blistering day with no clouds, and the wind hadn't even started blowing yet. We went to an alarm on Twenty-First Street that turned out to be a carpenter shop on fire. The shop, two outbuildings, and about an acre of grass burned. We spent about two hours there. Minutes after returning to the firehouse, we got another 2-11 at Rice and Jackson. The fire was in a row of brick buildings and spread to several outbuildings and a nearby house.

"Man, these fires are killing me," Dale said as we headed back to the firehouse finally.

"Better get used to 'em."

Wayne raised up on his elbow and looked at me. "What's the hell's that supposed to mean?"

"Exactly what I said. You'd better get used to it because between now and Friday night, there's gonna be twenty more."

"You're full of shit," Dale said as he laughed.

Wayne rolled over and said, "I wouldn't laugh if I were you. Everything he says happens!"

When we arrived at the firehouse, the fire chief's buggy was out front, tied to the hitching rail. While we put the equipment up, Nicholas headed upstairs to meet with them.

***

"Nicholas," one of the two men standing in the room said.

"Fire Marshal Williams. Marshal Benner," Nicholas said and shook their hands. "What can we do for you?"

"We're here to discuss that hose pull your men performed yesterday. We were impressed by the speed you had water flowing out of your pipes," Williams said. "Furthermore, we have been throwing around the possibility of making your hose lay as standard practice within the department. Imagine the time this practice could save and the property that would be spared."

"Mr. DuBach," Benner said. "We would like to know if you and your men would consider demonstrating your hose lay to the companies who weren't afforded the privilege of witnessing it."

"Sirs, I'm sure I speak for my men in saying that it would be our privilege to demonstrate it although I must confess, it isn't mine to stake claim to. It was passed on to me from a close friend who works for the Cincinnati Fire Department. He said they're already using it as a practice. It's called a forward hose lay."

"Very well," Williams said. "I'm sure your demonstration at the competition would have made them proud. We'll be in touch."

"Good day, Mr. DuBach, and congratulations on proving once again the fine leadership skills you have. You represent the department proudly!" Benner said.

"Thank you, sir," Nicholas said as the two men walked out to the barn stairs.

***

"Those are our chiefs, Williams and Benner," Joe said as they came down the stairs, Nicholas following closely behind. I was nervous because Williams and Benner walked directly up to me.

"Excuse me, son," Williams said.

"Sir, I'm John Kirk," I said and saluted them like we did at the academy.

"A military man, I see," Benner said.

"I saw you at the competition yesterday, and at the Burlington Warehouse fire day before yester, and noticed you wearing that yellow coat and pants. I don't rightly believe they are approved clothing for our department!" Williams said.

I didn't know what to say, and thank God Nicholas was there. "Chief Williams, John is my new hire from California. This is what they're wearing out West, so I gave him permission to use it, and to be quite honest, I think we should have the department study it. It seems to enable him to get closer to the fire."

Benner stepped forward and picked up my helmet off the hose wagon. He lifted it up and down, feeling its weight and then flicked the top with his finger. "Ouch, this thing is as light as a feather but hard as a rock. What's it made of?" He lowered and lifted the visor and then turned it over. "Bullard PX, thermoplastic shell, NFPA certified." Benner wrinkled his nose. "What the hell does all that mean?"

Williams shrugged. "Your guess is as good as mine."

Benner handed the helmet to Williams, and he knuckled the top and then handed it back. "It's hard as hell, but I think it's too light to be of any value. Half the time, I don't know what the folks in California are thinking. Nicholas, see about getting him a proper helmet. Until then, wear it, but be careful," Williams said.

"Yes, sir."

"We'll get back with you when we set up a time for your demonstration," Williams said. He and Benner walked out to their buggy and drove away. The crew went upstairs to play cards. Joe asked if I wanted to sit in on a hand, and I told him I'd stay down and spend time with the horses. I put my helmet back on the hose bed and wanted to laugh at what Benner said. If he only knew.

My coat had soot on the upper arm and shoulder. I picked it up, and as I was brushing it off, a glove fell out of the pocket. I picked it up and stuffed it back in, and being curious, I checked my pockets. I found nothing in the outer ones, so I checked on the inside. In the first pocket I found nothing again, so I reached into the other. As soon as I did, I felt something small and square. I pulled it out and said, "Fuck!"

I couldn't believe what I was holding in my hand. It was a twenty-dollar bill tightly folded around a five. I had put them there if I needed money while on a call.

As I unfolded the five, I smiled when I saw Abraham Lincoln's face. I threw my coat down and ran upstairs. When I walked in, everyone looked at me. "If you run up those stairs any harder, you're liable to break them!" Nicholas said.

I walked over to the table and smiled then laid the five- and twenty-dollar bills down. "There. Check that out!"

Joe leaned forward. "Hey, that's Abe on a greenback. How'd you do that?"

Dale picked up the bills and gave them a closer look then handed them to Nicholas. He studied them for a minute and handed them to Wayne. While Wayne looked at the five, the others passed around the twenty.

"Who's Dallas?" Wayne asked.

"Dallas?" I said.

"Yeah, he has his name in this circle. Who's Dallas?"

Joe looked at the bill, then took his cap off and hit Wayne upside his head. "Don't you know anything about the country you live in? Dallas is a new city in Texas!"

"Yeah, dumbass. It says Bank of Dallas," Dale said.

Wayne's face dropped as he stared at the bill.

"What's wrong?" Nicholas said.

Wayne took a deep breath and slowly released it. "I told you jackasses that he was telling us the truth!" He handed the bill to Nicholas. "Look at the date posted next to Abe's picture."

Everyone moved in for a closer look. It was almost comical. They all looked at the bills as if the bills were possessed. Nicholas blinked and took another look, then picked up the five with Abrahams Lincolns face on it. "Nineteen sixty-nine."

"Hey, 1969. That's when Neil Armstrong landed on the moon!" Joe shouted out.

I looked at the clock. It was two minutes before six. "I need to be somewhere," I said and picked up the bills. I left the firehouse and ran most of the way to Lindsay's house. Where are all the nice people when you need them? When I got to her porch, I had to stop and catch my breath and then went up the steps. I knocked on the door and waited then knocked again. I stood there with my ear as close to the wood as I could get it, hoping to hear movement inside.

"Lindsay, it's me, John. If you're home, please answer the door. I need to talk to you. All I'm asking for is just a minute, then if you want me to leave, I promise I'll leave and never bother you again."

I slowly walked away from the door and sat down on the steps and buried my face in my palms. I was so confused and in love at the same time. I couldn't believe this is how it was gonna end. The first love of my life and a bottle of whiskey destroyed it. I sat there for a few more minutes, trying to relax before trekking back to the firehouse. Then as I got up, I heard the door creak behind me. I quickly turned, and Lindsay was standing behind the crack of the door.

"You want a minute, I guess I owe you that much," she said and then walked over and sat down next to me on the stairs.

I sat back down. "Lindsay, I just want you to know how sorry I am and that I love you more than anything in this world."

"People who claim to love someone don't lie and make up fantasy stories about being from the future!"

"But it's not a lie!"

Lindsay shook her head and got up. "I'm sorry, but I can't."

"No, please don't go. You said you'd give me a minute, and I promised I'd leave if you want me to. I saw you at the competition, so I know you at least feel something!"

She stopped, and I stood up and said, "I'll prove it!" I reached into my pocket and felt around for the bills, but they weren't there. I checked my other pockets, and I was going into a serious panic. Then I checked my back pockets; nothing. Just as I was about to give up, Lindsay looked around me and squinted. I turned, and on the walkway leading to the porch were both the five- and twenty-dollar bills. They must've fallen out of my pocket as I ran up. I picked them up and gave them to her. "This is what I wanted to show you. This is money from the future!"

She stared at the five and then the twenty, fixated. “This can’t be right,” she said. “This is utterly impossible!” She sat back down on the porch and kept staring at the bills. “I don’t know what to say!”

ACT 34

Lindsay held up the five-dollar bill and stared at it. "I'm so sorry I didn't believe you," she said. "So what year are you from?"

"Two thousand eighteen, but I was born in 1994."

She smiled. "This greenback says 1969."

"I know. It's an old one."

She raised her brows and looked at me.

I laughed. "I know it sounds strange, but its older than I am."

"If this greenback were printed in 1969, that would mean it hasn't been made yet, and if it hasn't been made yet, then how is it possible that I have it in my hand?"

"Puzzling, isn't it? I had the same thought as I walked around the Burlington before the fire."

"So, if you're from the future, how is it even possible that you're here?"

"I don't know. That's the mystery I haven't figured out yet."

We sat there for a while, talking, and then she got up and said she'd be back. Lindsay went inside and, a few minutes later, returned. She had changed from a day dress to a pair of pants.

"Come on," she said as she grabbed my hand and led me next door. We snuck into Mr. Johnston's barn and saddled his mare.

"Are we gonna get in trouble for this?"

Lindsay leaned over and kissed me. "Only if we get caught."

I laughed. Right then I was seeing her wild side, and I loved it. We led the horse to the alleyway behind the barn, and she got on. I climbed up behind her. No sooner had I got on did she kick the horse, and it took off. I had to grab Lindsay's waist just to keep from falling. Apparently, she was no stranger to horses.

We went down the alley to Clinton Street and then up to Harrison before she slowed the horse. From there, we headed east to Lake Michigan, which was only a couple of miles away. We rode the horse out onto the beach and tied it to a hitching post near the tree line. Then we took our shoes off and walked arm in arm along the beach, laughing and kicking the sand between our toes. We walked out on a wooden pier and sat on the end. We dangled our feet over the water and held each other as we watched the moon rise and cast its reflection across the lake.

We spent most of that night talking, holding hands, and kissing on the end of that pier. That, by far, was the best night of my life, and to think that God had given us the ability for us to experience such passion. It was truly a gift. We stayed there until daybreak, and then Lindsay took me back to the firehouse.

After I got down, she bent over and kissed me. "Come by tonight. I'll fix you dinner."

"I'll be there," I said and then watched her ride off. I was tired, and instead of going upstairs and waking Joe, I went into the barn and lay down in the back of the hose wagon.

I was in a deep sleep when something crawled on my nose woke me. I opened my eyes and saw Joe and Wayne sitting there laughing at me, holding a string over my face. I swatted it away and said, "What the hell?"

"He's alive!" Wayne said.

I felt a few bumps and sat up. We were hauling ass down the street with the steamer in front of us. It had white-and-black smoke pouring out of the stack. "Where are we going?"

"Two-eleven downtown," Joe said.

I glanced over my shoulder to see where we were. We were on North Michigan, just passing Harrison. I recognized the area because that was where Lindsay and I spent most of the night. "Hey, Joe, do I have a silly smile on my face?"

"More tired than silly. Why?"

"Because I was wondering if love made me look as silly as it does you."

"Cool. You made up with her," he said and slapped me on the shoulder.

"Yeah. We spent most of the night at the lake."

We looked to our left as Billy slowed the wagon and turned. The buildings on both sides of the street were tall, and about two blocks down, heavy smoke was billowing from the upper floors of a five-story building on the right. I saw the Long John and two hook and ladders rescuing people from the fifth-floor windows.

Nicholas stood up and yelled back to us, "Connect to the corner hydrant!"

We stopped so Dale could jump down and grab the hose while we continued to the fire. When we got there, Nicholas jumped off the steamer and ran over to Schimmels. "What do you need?"

"Looks like the fires on the fourth floor near the west end. All my men are helping with the rescue, so I need your men to get inside and stop it."

"You got it," Nicholas said. "Wayne, take Joe and John and get me some pipes inside!"

"Yes, sir!" Wayne shouted.

We pulled a shitload of hose and two pipes off the wagon and dragged them into the building. The grand stairway was directly in front of us; it was wide so we didn't have much problem climbing it with our hose. When we approached the fourth floor, we could tell that was indeed the fire floor. Smoke filled the hall at about chest high and was going up the stairway to the fifth floor. We peeked over the top of the stairs, and to our left, we saw flames at the end of the hall.

"I count fire in two flats," Wayne said.

Our hoses stiffened and we had water. Wayne got on his knees and scooted toward the fire and then lay down on his belly. He blasted the flames, moving across the ceiling, then lifted his arm in the air for a few seconds. Then he got up on his knees.

"Why'd he put his arm in the air like that?" I asked.

"He's was checking to see if it's too hot to get up!" Joe said as he stood and moved toward Wayne. I followed and pulled the hose from behind. We stopped about halfway down the hall and got back down to keep under the smoke, which was quickly filling the hallway.

Joe looked at Wayne. "We need a plan to get rid of this smoke and get the fire burning the other way. Otherwise, we're not going to get close enough to put it out."

The flames rolled back out into the hallway, and Joe and Wayne opened their nozzles, putting them out.

Wayne crawled to the next apartment and felt the door. He opened it, and then crawled in. A few seconds later I heard him yell, "Charlie, have those ladder monkeys throw a boot through the last window west of me!" Then he came back to the hall, and for a third time, the fire in the last apartment ahead of us spread out into the hallway and across the ceiling. Then I heard glass breaking, and the flames sucked back into the apartment. That was awesome, ventilation working at its best.

"Okay. Let's get it!" Wayne said, and then they crawled at a fast pace toward the fire. Wayne turned his head. "Come on, John!"

I laughed. "You guys are crazy," I said. As I watched them crawl away, I thought, What the hell. I couldn't believe I was doing it again without a mask, but at least, at the moment, we had hoses. We crawled down the hall to the first burning apartment. Flames were trying to come out, but they were being drawn to the oxygen outside the broken window. Wayne opened the nozzle and shot his stream into the room, and Joe shot his across the ceiling. It seemed like a matter of seconds and they had that room put out. Wayne lay there for a few seconds then said, "We're good. Let's get the next one!"

Joe looked at me and said, "Stay here and keep an eye on the flat. We don't want it coming back to life and trapping us."

I stopped and looked into the apartment from the hallway; the fire was still smoldering, but nothing threatening. Then I heard Joe yell, "Yeeha!" then they opened their pipes into the second apartment and knocked down that fire. Then they shut their nozzles to a trickle and sprayed each other. When they got back, Wayne said, "Go up and open the bulkhead."

"Bulkhead?"

"Yeah. The door at the top of the stairs that leads to the roof."

"You want me to go up there through all that smoke and open a door at the top of the stairs. Are you fucking kidding me?"

Wayne and Joe laughed. "How else are we gonna clear the smoke out? How do you guys do in the future, stand outside in the streets and let it air out on its own?" Wayne said.

I turned and looked at the stairs. I didn't want to do it, but I refused to be called yellow. I rolled my eyes and headed toward the stairs.

"John!" Wayne yelled. I stopped and turned. I expected them to laugh and say they were kidding, but instead, I was knocked down by a stream of water. "Breathe through your wet shirt. It'll help filter out the smoke."

About halfway up the stairs, the smoke was static. It had filled the fifth floor and had nowhere to go. I grabbed the banister and lowered my head below the smoke and took two deep breaths. The third one I held, and I headed up into the smoke. I followed the railing up as fast as I could. It reminded me of a blackout drill where they'd put tape over our mask to simulate this type of situation, but this was different. Not only could I not see, I couldn't breathe.

I held on to the rail and counted twenty steps then stepped on a flat area. This must be the fifth floor, I thought. I was curious and opened my eyes to see what I could, but that was a mistake. Not only could I not see, but my eyes were burning badly. I was running out of air, and I needed to hurry. I continued following the rail around and then started up another flight of stairs.

I wanted to breathe, but my body wouldn't let me. As I hurried as fast as I could, I lost count of the stairs and had no had no clue how many I had left to climb before reaching the top, and bam, I ran face first into the door and almost fell back down the stairs. I frantically felt around, trying to find the way to get the door open. Suffocating and in near panic, that's when my hand hit a lever and the door sprung open. I fell out onto the roof, gasping for air

I looked up at the sky as smoke poured out of the building and over my head. I laughed. "Oh my god, this is unbelievable," I yelled. I had never experienced an adrenaline rush like that.

***

Joe and Wayne sat on the top of the fourth-floor stairs, cooling down after the smoke lifted. Joe smiled. "Looks like he made it."

Nicholas rushed up the stairs and looked around. "Where's John?"

"On the roof," Joe said.

"You sent him to the roof?"

"Yep. We didn't wanna do it!" Wayne said then laughed. "By the way, why are we the only crew up here?"

"The crew of the Long John is helping pull people off the fifth floor. All the other engines are on different fires throughout the city. We're all there is."

***

I was standing near the parapet, looking down at all the people, when Joe walked out on the roof. "You okay?"

I turned with the biggest smile on my face. "Joe, I love this."

"Love what?"

"Fighting fires in the 1800s. I've never felt so scared, horrified, and thrilled at the same time."

ACT 35

That evening after we got cleaned up and it neared six, Joe and I sat in the bunk room, talking. He said he was going to Sharon's after work, and he'd be happy to give me a ride to Lindsay's house. Joe was sure spending a lot of time at Sharon's, and Gladys seemed to be taking a real liking to him.

Dale hollered down the hall, "John, somebody out front wants to see you!"

My first thought was that the last time someone wanted to see me, I almost got killed. I walked out to the front windows and looked down. There was a horse and buggy below, but no people. Cautiously, I went down the stairs and opened the front door. Lindsay was standing there with a big smile.

I smiled back. "Is that Mr. Johnston's horse?"

"It could be!"

"I don't know about you," I said and gave her a kiss.

"Come on. I've got plans."

"Oh yeah? What type of plans?" I asked as I climbed on the wagon.

"Plans!"

"Aren't you working tonight?"

"Nope. They closed the theater for a week, so they could do some repairs. You got me for the whole week!"

After I told Joe that I had a ride, Lindsay and I went directly to her house. I was sure hungry and was looking forward to a home-cooked meal. Instead, she went to her room and brought out a stack of clothes and handed them to me. There were three pairs of pants and several socks and flannel shirts. She told me to try them on.

I don't think I've ever been so happy to get new clothes than I was at that moment. I went into the water closet and tried them on and was surprised that they fit perfectly. When I came out, Lindsay was standing there in a beautiful evening dress. I swear, she made everything she wore look good. She was nothing short of being stunning.

"How'd you know my size?"

"I wear dresses for a living. I know sizes," she said and grabbed my hand. I followed her out to the buggy. We were like high school kids in love.

"Whose buggy?"

She laughed. "Mr. Johnston's."

"You took his buggy too?"

"He said he didn't like two people riding his horse, so he told me if I was gonna steal his horse again, that I should steal the buggy too."

I laughed. "He knew we took his horse?"

"That busybody sees everything!"

She took me to the north side of town and showed me some sights. Then we went to Chicago Avenue and Pine Street to see the new water tower they built just two years earlier. It was designed like a castle, and the tower stood nearly 140 feet high. Looking at it made me feel like I had when I went to Disneyland as a child. We got down and ran around the building, checking it out, and then she handed me a nail and told me we should scratch our names in the limestone. She kept watch while I etched a heart and wrote John loves Lindsay in its center. She looked at it and smiled then wrapped her arms around my neck and kissed me. Just then, the church bells rang seven times. I felt like I was in a dream.

"Come on," she said and grabbed my hand. "You hungry?"

"I'm starving!" With all the fun I was having, I had forgotten about eating.

"Good. We have a seven-thirty reservation at Wright's dining room at the Crosby Opera House."

"Wright's dining room?"

She smiled and then shook the reins. Her smile made me wonder what type of surprises she had in store for me. When we got to Wrights, I was stunned. I couldn't stop staring at the woodwork and how it was crafted. The chandeliers were sparkling, and the tables were covered with white cloths and had burning candles on them. I was standing in the lobby of a high-class restaurant full of high-class people, probably millionaires.

A woman standing behind a podium smiled at us. "Good evening. My name is Jenny, and I'll be your hostess," she said. "May I have the name on your reservation?"

"Kirk . . . John Kirk!" Lindsay said.

"Yes, of course, Mr. and Mrs. John Kirk," she said as she looked down her list. I jerked my head and looked at Lindsay. She just smiled.

"I have your reservation right here," she said and signaled to a girl standing nearby. "This is Jamie. She'll show you to your table."

As we followed, I whispered to Lindsay, "Are you serious?" I was in awe. I'd never been in a place so fancy.

"Am I serious about what? The Mr. and Mrs. Kirk?" she whispered back.

"That too."

She smiled and put her finger over her lips, kissed it, and then put it over mine. She just had a way about her that just melted me. I didn't want that moment to end.

We sat down at a table next to a window overlooking the city lights. Then a man, dressed in all black and a bow tie walked up to our table. His dark hair was slicked back, and he had a serviette draped over his arm. "Madam, sir, my name is Fredrick, and I'll be your server," he said as he sat two menus in front of us. "Can I start you off with a bottle of fine wine? Perhaps a Verdelho Solera or Cama de Lobos?"

"Yes, Verdelho Solera would be fine," Lindsay said.

I looked at Lindsay because I had no clue what he'd just said, but she seemed to have understood every word.

I picked up the menu, and they were serving boned turkey or quail. Fredrick returned with two glasses and a bottle of wine. He opened it and filled the glasses then set the bottle on the table. Lindsay suggested the quail, so that's what I ordered. First, they brought us soup, then vegetables, bread and butter, appetizers, and then our main course. It was so cool being pampered like I had money. Finally, we finished our six-course meal with cake. I was so stuffed that I didn't think I'd be able to walk out on my own.

On our way out, I saw a poster for the Crosby Opera House announcing their reopening on Monday, October 9 with a show starring Conductor Theodore Thomas.

We left Wright's, and she said she had to show me something. We ended up on the beach in Lincoln Park, the first place we saw each other. We kicked off our shoes and danced around in the moonlight, laughing, then stared into each other's eyes and kissed. Then she jerked away.

"Come on," she said and pulled me by my hand. We ran up the beach to the other side of the park and into a grove of trees where there were thick bushes and a fence.

"What's this?" I asked.

She looked at me and smiled. Oh shit, there's that smile, I thought. I followed her down the fence line to a small opening, and we squeezed through it to the other side. I squinted to see in the darkness and saw shadows of what looked like cages. "Where are we?"

"We're at the zoo."

"The zoo? I know I'm going to regret asking, but are we allowed to be here?"

"Only if we don't get caught!"

"That's what I thought!" I said and then laughed. Suddenly. a whistle blew and a lantern came on in the zookeeper's house behind the cages. Lindsay and I ran into the bushes and hid behind a tree. That was exciting. As the light came closer, I held Lindsay's face and kissed it all over. I looked into her eyes and saw her soul staring back at me. I had no other way to explain it. I was in love.

After a few minutes, we walked out from behind the tree and came face-to-face with the guard. He scared the shit out of us.

"Who goes there?" he said as he lit a stick match. "Is that you, Ms. Lindsay?"

"Yes, sir."

The old man looked over at me and held the match to my face. "And who might you be?"

"This is John Kirk. He's a fireman."

"Nice to meet you, son," he said and shook the match out. "Now you two know it's a violation of city law for you to be here while the zoo is closed?"

"Yes, sir, but John has never seen a zoo before. He's from California!"

"California? Well then, I guess there's an exception to every rule. You do know we just got two elk? Now we have in our zoo two swans, a puma, three wolves, four eagles, and eight peacocks. Oh, and the two elk I just mentioned," he said as he lit his lantern. "By the way, I'm Mr. Anderson, the zookeeper. Let me show you kids around."

ACT 36

The next morning was October 4, 1871, four days before the great fire, when I woke to the voices of the crew in the living room. I looked up and focused on something crawling across the ceiling. It was a freaking spider. I moved away from the bed, so it wouldn't fall on me.

That morning, we practiced for two hours, and when we got back, the guys talked me into playing cards. I had watched them play all week, so it didn't take long to catch on. I think I pissed them off because I won the second hand. After Billy dealt the next, we were quietly sorting our cards when someone let loose the longest, squeakiest fart I think I had ever heard. It broke the silence, and everyone looked at Wayne. He sat there and smiled. "What? It's not bad manners, just good food!"

Daniel and Charlie got up and went to the windows and opened them. Soon, we were all at the windows, getting fresh air while Wayne sat at the table laughing.

That day we had three fires: two small houses they called cottages and a roof fire at a local business. After work, Joe dropped me off at Lindsay's on his way to Sharon's.

When we finished dinner, Lindsay cleared the table and then wrapped her arms around me from behind and whispered in my ear, "I hope you enjoyed your dinner." Her warm breath on my neck sent chills down my spine.

I reached up and gripped her arms. "It was delicious. Thank you," I said.

She bent down and kissed my neck; her kisses paralyzed me. She slowly released me and walked over to the sink.

While we cleaned the kitchen, Lindsay asked, "So, what part of California are you from?"

"Northern California. A small city called Pine Valley."

"That sounds like a quaint place. What year did you say you were born?"

"Nineteen ninety-four."

She thought for a moment and said, "That means you were born 123 years from now?"

"Yeah, something like that."

"How is that possible?" she asked.

"Since I've been here, I've been asking myself the same question."

"Tell me about 2018."

"It's a complicated place. The cities are so much larger, and Chicago has as many people as most countries, and the buildings are a lot taller. They are so tall that they'd make the water tower look like a toy."

"How tall are they?"

"Well, for the longest time, Chicago had the tallest building in the world. It stood 1,450 feet and had 110 stories."

Lindsay's mouth dropped open. "That's as high as the heavens!"

I smiled. "It's pretty tall. In 2018, people don't ride horses unless they do it for fun or live on ranches. We have cars and trucks instead, with motors that burn gasoline instead of coal."

"What is gasoline?" she asked.

"It's a liquid fuel that comes out of the ground. As a matter of fact, your generation will discover it. Then we have what we call airplanes that fly in the air—"

"You mean like a bird? What do you do with them?"

“They carry people. Let’s say you needed to be in Los Angeles tomorrow. You could catch a plane today and be there tonight.”

Lindsay sat there with a blank stare. I could tell she was having a hard time comprehending what I was telling her. It was as if she were a grasshopper trying to figure out how a TV works. Finally, she asked “Is that fast?”

“Yeah, that’s fast,” I said.

Lindsay thought for a moment and then sat up. “That’s impossible!”

“I’m serious. We have military planes that can fly at 1,500 miles an hour. They could make the trip in a little over an hour. In 1969, we sent the first men to the moon. It took only four days to get them there.”

“That’s a bit to take in,” Lindsay said.

“Yeah, I can only imagine,” I said as I swirled my glass and watched the tornado form from the sediment inside the water. The funny thing about it? I wasn’t going to think twice before drinking it.

“Is something wrong?” Lindsay asked as she saw me looking at my glass.

“Not at all,” I said.

Lindsay and I spent hours talking, then we lay down on her bed and cuddled. I held her and thought about how I had traveled 147 years to find my soul mate and wondered how all this was gonna end.

About ten thirty, there was a knock at the front door. I must have dozed off because it took a few seconds to figure out where I was. I was still lying on the bed with Lindsay in my arms. I didn’t wanna get up, but the knock persisted. Joe had stopped to see if I needed a ride back to the station, being as far and as late as it was, I took him up on the offer.

On the way, Joe said he needed to check up on his mother, so we did. She lived near Polk and Ellsworth streets. We helped her out with a few chores and had coffee and talked. She was a nice lady. I believe her name was Isabelle.

After we arrived at the firehouse, we went up to the roof and lay there on the cots and talked. He told me all about him and Sharon and how he felt when they were together. I could tell he loved her every bit as much as I loved Lindsay.

"So, when are you gonna marry her?" I asked.

"I haven't given it much thought," Joe said.

"What about Gladys?"

"I think she loves me too."

"I'm really happy for you." I told him about the last few nights I'd had with Lindsay and the crazy things we did and the places we went. When I felt something crawling on my arm, I screamed and jumped up. Joe busted up laughing. I brushed my arm and saw a damn spider fall on the roof. "I hate spiders," I yelled and stepped on it. Joe was still laughing and said I sounded like a girl screaming.

I looked the cot over before lying back down.

"Do you think we'll have any fires tomorrow?" Joe asked.

"I'm not sure. All I know is that between Sunday and Friday there's gonna be twenty-five. I've wanted to tell everyone about Saturday and Sunday, but I'm tired of being called crazy and looked at as a liar."

"I don't think you're a liar. I don't think Wayne does either."

"I know, and that's why I tell you the things I do. It's like I told Wayne, the night before I came here, I did a lot of reading about Chicago. It said Saturday, there's gonna be a big fire at a planing mill, and it's gonna be called the Saturday Night Fire, the biggest fire in Chicago history. But Sunday night, a barn will catch fire, and it'll be known in history as the Great Chicago Fire. The funny thing about that fire, they'll try to blame a cow for starting it."

"Is that the one you were talking about the other day?"

"Yeah. It'll be the biggest fire ever and kill a lot of people."

Joe sat up. "Then we gotta tell Nicholas!"

"I want to, but I don't want to be a disappointment to him."

"Whaddya mean?"

"Look how many chances he's given me. I don't want to ruin it." I said.

Joe lay back down and just stared at the moon. I think we both yawned at the same time.

"Let's get some sleep," Joe said. I don't think it was but a minute and I was out.

The next thing I knew, something was climbing on my bed. I was afraid to open my eyes, thinking it would be a giant spider. Then I felt tender lips gently kissing me. I opened my eyes and was eye to eye with Lindsay. She kept kissing me, my forehead, my nose, and my neck. My eyes rolled back in my head as chills tingled my bones. She slowly climbed under the covers and whispered, "I want you."

"Is that proper?" I said. "Shouldn't we be married first?"

She put her finger over my mouth. "Shhh," she said and put her head under the blankets and kissed my chest. Oh my, I felt like I was on a roller coaster and falling off the back. Then I heard Joe cough and opened my eyes. It was quiet, and the only thing I saw was Joe rolling over in bed. Lindsay wasn't there. Damn, I was dreaming. I jumped up and got dressed.

"Joe, pick me up on your way back from Sharon's in the morning. I gotta go see Lindsay!"

"Okay," he said. "By the way, what's not proper?"

"Just forget you heard that and go back to sleep. See you in the morning."

I ran most of the way to Lindsay's, and when I got there, I took a minute to catch my breath, and then I knocked. I waited a minute and knocked again.

"Who's there?"

"John. It's me, John!"

The door opened and Lindsay stood there half asleep in her nightgown. I couldn't believe how much I was in love with her. I walked in and held her face between my hands and gently kissed her, and she kissed me back.

"Why are you here?" she said between kisses.

"Because I love you, and I need to be with you!" I said as I pushed the door closed with my foot.

"But that wouldn't be proper. Shouldn't we be married first?"

"I promise I'll marry you tomorrow!" I said as I kept kissing her.

ACT 37

The next morning, I woke to a ray of light shining directly in my face. I glanced down, and Lindsay was sleeping with her head on my chest and arm wrapped around me. I looked back at the light shining through the curtains and watched the tiny dust particles as they floated in the air.

"Oh shit!" I yelled. "I gotta get to work!"

Lindsay lifted her head, and I gave her a quick kiss and got up. I grabbed my clothes and headed for the front door while trying to dress at the same time. She followed me, and I told her I'd get the afternoon off, so we could get married. She wrapped her arms around me and smiled.

"I gotta go," I said as I pulled away from her and ran to the street while putting on my boot.

A farmer was generous enough to go out of his way and get me to the firehouse on time. When I walked in, Nicholas looked up at me. "It's about time you got here. A few more minutes, and we would've had the posse out looking for you. Grab some grub before it gets cold."

"Sorry I couldn't pick you up," Joe said. "Horse threw a shoe."

"That's okay," I said and laughed. A horse with a flat tire, now that's funny. I sat down and dug in.

"What's with the goofy smile?" Dale asked.

I took a bite and noticed that everyone else was staring at me too. "Nicholas, I was wondering if I could get the afternoon off?"

"Let's see," Nicholas said and looked up at the ceiling in deep thought. "Since Monday, I count sixteen fires. Now I have no claim on arithmetic, but the closest I can figure, take sixteen away from twenty-five, and that leaves nine fires between today and tomorrow. No, I can't spare you!"

It surprised me when he said that. When I looked at Joe, he smiled. "You believe me?"

"I'd be a fool not to," Nicholas said.

"Whaddya need the day off for?" Billy asked.

"I told Lindsay I'd marry her."

"A wedding?" Nicholas said.

"Yes."

"Well, why didn't you say so?"

"So I can have the afternoon off?"

"No," Nicholas said, "but if you're wanting to get married, we'll throw you a company wedding!"

I got excited. I asked if it would be possible to get married in Lincoln Park, the place where I met her.

"You should get married in the zoo," Wayne joked. The rest of the men laughed.

"Now that might not be a bad idea," Nicholas said. "I mean, they have a stage there, a building connected to it, and there's plenty of seats for an audience."

"Good idea!" Billy slapped Wayne on the shoulder. "How cool is that, a wedding at the Lincoln Zoo." Wayne just stood there with a blank face.

I looked at Joe, and then I thought about Sharon. "Joe, since you and Sharon are engaged to be married and we are brothers, why don't we both get married?"

Joe's eyes got big. "That's a great idea," he said. "But what about Sharon and Lindsay?" I jerked my head back and he laughed. "Gotcha!"

"Then we'll plan a double wedding for Sunday," Nicholas said.

"Sunday?"

"Yeah. That's normally the day folks get hitched around here," Charlie said.

"Yeah. You get hitched Sunday morning and then go to church afterward and pray that it works out!" Wayne said. That made everyone laugh.

"We can't do it Sunday," I said.

"Why not?"

"Trust me, Nicholas. I'll explain it later, but I've gotta do it today!"

Nicholas looked at me for a minute then said, "Boys, we have a wedding to set up."

"Yeeha!" Joe yelled and ran out the door, then ran back in. "I need to let Sharon know she's getting married today!"

"Hold on, Joe. We need to find out what time first or even if the pastor can do it today. Dale, saddle your horse and go tell Pastor Starcevic that we need him to perform two ceremonies this afternoon. Billy, go ask Mr. Anderson if we can use his stage for a wedding today," Nicholas said.

Dale and Billy took off. About fifteen minutes later, Dale came running back up the stairs, half out of breath. "I told him John and Joe wanted to get married today at the zoo. He said to be there at two o'clock, and he'd perform both ceremonies at the same time!"

"Good deal. Joe, hitch up my horse, and you and John go let your girls know," Nicholas said. "But if the bell rings, get back here as fast as you can."

As we headed to the stairs, Billy showed up. "Mr. Anderson said he'll have the place waiting."

Everything was falling into place and fast. Our first stop was Quinn's. We ran inside, and Joe went directly into the kitchen where Gladys and Sharon were. A few minutes later, he came out all excited, jumping up and down. He grabbed me and gave me a big hug.

"Put me down before you squeeze the life outta me," I said.

"She said yes!" Joe shouted.

"What's all the racket? Can't you see I have paying customers in here?" Mollie said.

"We're gettin' married today," Joe said. "And you're invited!"

"I'll be darned," Mollie said, and then she walked over to the dining area. "You people need to hurry up and eat. I'm closing early!" She walked over to the front door and turned the Open sign around as a man tried to walk in. "I'm closed," Mollie said. "Can't you read?"

"It's not even noon. You can't be closed."

"Listen, this is my restaurant, and I'll close it any damn time I damn well choose. Now git!"

The man tucked his head and walked away. We left Quinn's and went to Lindsay's, and she was ecstatic. Then we went to Joe's mother's house to let her know. And then, would you believe it, , shortly before noon, the damn fire bell rang. We had an alarm on Twentieth Street, which turned out to be two sheds and some land. It was started by grease in a smokehouse. Well, I guess the meat really did get smoked. A few minutes after that, we got a house fire on State Street, started by a kerosene lamp. Now why in the hell would anyone be using a kerosene lamp during the day when they could open the damn curtains!

I was getting anxious. It was close to two o'clock. We got the fire knocked down, and as Wayne was going over hot spots, I yelled at him, "Come on. It's out!"

He looked at me and said, "It's still smoking. There are embers still burning."

"A little smoke never hurt anyone!" I said. He smiled and shook his head and shut off his pipe.

"Come on, Joe. Let's go get you guys married," Wayne said.

***

Sharon and I got ready in the room behind the stage. Melanie and Gladys French-braided our hair and made sure our dresses were perfect. There was a knock at the door, and we got excited. At first, we thought the firemen had arrived, but it was the pastor's wife, Pamela. She said it was a few minutes after two, and the firemen hadn't come yet. The pastor had another engagement at three, and the latest he could stay would be two twenty. If they didn't show up by then, we would have no choice but to postpone the wedding till Sunday. Then she left.

I was stressed, and Gladys walked over and rubbed my shoulders. I guess she could tell I was a nervous wreck by looking at me. "Don't worry, child. If the Lord wants this to happen today, they'll be here!"

We heard something out front. "I'll go check," Melanie said.

She opened the door and peeked out into the crowd of about forty. She looked around but saw none of the firemen. The guests, mostly family, friends, and a few spectators were gathered to enjoy a zoo wedding. After all, who had ever heard of a zoo wedding that didn't involve animals? I saw Nicholas's wife, Susan, with their newborn son, Frankie, sitting with Joe's mother. But still, there was no sign of the men.

A few minutes later, there was a soft knock on the door. Melanie rushed over and answered it. It was Pastor Starcevic. "Ms. Melanie, ladies," he said, talking with his face turned so he couldn't see inside. "I'm sorry, ladies, but it's two twenty-five, and I must be—" He paused when he heard bells ringing. And they were getting closer.

We ran to the door and looked out and saw the steamer and hose wagon coming, and there was a whole parade of fire engines and wagons following them.

"Like I was saying, ladies, we're having a wedding," Starcevic said.

Sharon hugged me and said, "I'm nervous!"

We laughed and I said, "Me too!" But under it all, we were the happiest girls on earth.

We anxiously awaited inside as we heard the men stepping onto the stage. Then the door opened, and Pamela told us to come on out to the stage. When I saw John and the men, I almost laughed. Their faces were black with soot and their clothes dirty. But none of that mattered. I was getting married.

***

When Lindsay first saw me, I could tell she wanted to laugh, but hey, we made it. I leaned over to Joe and whispered, "You know we look like shit, right?"

He smiled, and I'll always remember him saying, "No, we look like real firemen!"

The preacher moved us around, and then Wayne and Daniel stepped up on the stage, "We'll be their best men." Daniel said.

Then Nicholas stepped up and so did Billy, Dale, and Charlie. Nicholas said, "Pastor, we'll all be their best men. After all, we're family!" That brought a tear to my eye, and I swear, if he were ten years older, I'd consider him a dad.

The pastor smiled and said, "A little uncommon but very well."

Lindsay looked at me and smiled and, out of the corner of her mouth, said, "You stink."

"I know. I was hoping you wouldn't notice."

"I'm just glad you got here when you did."

Joe stood next to Sharon, and they smiled at each other and held hands. They were a cute couple, and Sharon had on a Victorian dress. She was a sight, an absolute beauty.

Starcevic smiled and seemed antsy, as if he was pressed for time. "Folks, we're here gathered at the Lincoln Park Zoo." He looked at the wolves staring back from their cages. Then he looked around at the bushes and then up at the trees. "Although we have vicious animals lurking in our presence, we must remember that they are all God's creatures. And then, the setting of the zoo could resemble that of the Garden of Eden, a real paradise. I stand here before you today, to serve as an instrument of our Almighty God to join two couples in holy matrimony, John Kirk to Ms. Lindsay, and Joseph Weant to Ms. Sharon."

Starcevic turned to Lindsay and me. "John, do you promise to love, honor, and protect Lindsay in health and in sickness as long as you both shall live?"

I made eye contact with Lindsay, and she had the most beautiful smile on her face. "I do!"

"Ms. Lindsay, do you in return promise to love, honor, and obey John in health and in sickness as long as you both shall live?"

"I do!"

"Joe Weant, do you promise to love, honor, and protect Ms. Sharon in health and in sickness as long as you both shall live?"

"I do!" Joe said.

"And do you, Ms. Sharon, promise to love, honor, and obey Joe in health and in sickness as long as you both shall live?"

"I do," Sharon said in a soft voice. She had tears rolling down her cheeks.

"You may place the rings on your bride's fingers," the pastor said. Joe and I looked at each other. That's the part I had forgotten about. We looked at Starcevic, and that's when Nicholas stepped forward and handed Joe and me a ring each.

"The boys and I figured you might need these until you can get some of your own."

"I don't know what to say," I told him.

"Just put the damn ring on her finger," Wayne said.

Lindsay held her hand out, and I slowly put the ring on her. It was a copper O ring and fit loosely, but that didn't matter. I smiled at Nicholas and said thank you. He smiled and winked at me.

The preacher held his Bible in the air and said, "With the power invested in me by Almighty God, and the City of Chicago, I now pronounce you Mr. and Mrs. John Kirk and Mr. and Mrs. Joe Weant. You may now kiss your brides."

ACT 38

The next morning, Friday, October 6, 1871, I woke up with tears in my eyes. I had been dreaming about my mother. It saddened me; she couldn't be there at my wedding. I looked at the curtains, and the light hadn't shone through yet, so I knew it was still early. I looked down at Lindsay, and she was snuggled against me. I reached up and ran my fingers through her hair and then stared at the ceiling. Then it hit me. I thought I knew how I could message my mother. It would be a long shot, but in theory, it could work.

"Yes!" I shouted.

Lindsay opened her eyes and smiled at me. "Did you say something?"

"Do they make jars in the 1870s?"

"Huh?"

"Jars. Do they make them?"

"You mean like canning jars?"

"Yes!"

"Of course, they do. Why?"

"Where can I buy one?"

"You don't need to. I have a whole cabinet full of them. Why?"

"Cool. Is there anywhere to get a wooden box about the size of the jar?"

"I'm sure we could find one somewhere. Maybe we could get Luke at the woodshop to make us one," Lindsay said as she sat up. "What do you need a jar and a box for?"

"I was thinking about my mother, and then remembered a movie I saw where someone was sending another person messages in the future. I figured if I were to put a note in a glass jar, and bury it for a hundred years, I just might be able to get a message to her."

"But what about the box?"

"I would put the jar in the box for protection," I said.

"But if someone were to find it, how could you be certain it would get to her?"

"Faith in humanity," I said. "I could put the note in an envelope and ask if they could deliver it to my address on September 25, 2018. That would be the day I got here. I could tell her everything."

Lindsay smiled. "You can send her a picture too!"

"What?"

"Didn't you see the photographer in the back, taking pictures of our wedding?"

"Are you serious?"

"Yes. He was from the Tribune and said the story would be a good piece for the paper. He said he's never heard of anyone getting married at the zoo before and said this could bring attention to the zoo. And who knows, this could become a popular tourist event and possibly help us get more animals!"

"Sweet!" I said and jumped out of bed. "Where can I get a newspaper?"

"They sell them at newsstands and in most shops . . . What's a movie?"

"Do you have a pencil and paper?" I asked as I grabbed my clothes off the chair and got dressed.

Lindsay got up and walked into the kitchen. She opened a cabinet and got a pencil and some paper. "How many pieces would you like?"

"Give me about five sheets." She brought me the paper and pencil and observed as I fold each page into fours. I licked the creases on each sheet and made twenty smaller pieces. I took the pencil and drew a little circle on each piece, each offset a little from the last, then put the pages together and made a small book.

"In the future, they make a camera that takes about thirty pictures a second. Then they put the pictures on what they call film and then play it through a machine called a projector. It's like this paper when I turn the pages; it looks like the circle is moving," I explained as I showed her by flipping through the pages. She was fascinated as she watched the circle bounce up and down.

"That's magic!" she said.

"No. That's what we call a movie in the future."

"Can I try?"

"Sure," I said.

Lindsay smiled as she flipped through the pages again and again. I looked out the window, and Joe had just pulled up. I gave Lindsay a quick hug and then left.

It was another clear day but not as hot. A cool breeze was blowing from the southwest and bringing with it—yes, wouldn't you know it—that overwhelming stench of the Union Stockyards located off Halsted Street. The Union Stockyards covered nearly four hundred acres and processed over two million cattle, hogs, and sheep yearly. See, I hadn't just been chasing girls while I'd been here. I've been learning a little about the city.

"Morning," Nicholas said as Joe and I walked into the firehouse.

"Good morning," I said as I sat at the table. "Man, it sure does stink out there this morning."

"I noticed that on my way in," Nicholas said. "It's kinda odd for the wind to be blowing this early in the morning."

Daniel pushed a cup to me and then the coffee pot. I poured me a cup and sipped it then asked, "If you wanted to bury something and didn't want it found for a hundred or more years, where would you bury it?"

Dale laughed. "Under all that cow shit at Halsted and Thirty-Fifth Street."

Nicholas laughed and then leaned back. "The lake."

"Huh?" Wayne said. "Why the lake?"

"Because it's been here forever and doesn't seem to move much in either direction. I don't see anyone building on it, and I'm sure, in a hundred years, it'll still be where it is today. I'd say, near a tree along the edge of the lake."

"That's why if you need to know anything, you ask Nicholas. He knows everything," Joe said.

A short while later, Mollie put the red flag out front, and Wayne, Joe, and I set out to get breakfast. That morning we had eggs, fried potatoes, and bacon. I could say one thing for sure, the bacon on my plate smelled a lot better than the pigs down the street!

"What're ya wantin' to bury?" Billy asked.

"I was thinking of burying a letter in a glass jar. It's called a time capsule."

"Why bury it? Why not just throw it in the lake? Everyone else does," Wayne said.

"Because I want it to reach my mother, not some old man fishing in Canada!"

"Canada's on the other side of the lake? I thought it was Michigan." Joe said.

Nicholas laughed and shook his head.

"You said you couldn't get married on Sunday, and you'd explain later. Well, we threw you a wedding, and now I believe it's come time for you to explain. Also, I'm curious about this Saturday Night Fire you've been telling Joe about," Nicholas said.

I looked down at my food and twirled my fork in my eggs and thought for a minute. "The Saturday Night Fire, that's gonna happen tomorrow—"

"Well, that would only stand to reason since tomorrow's Saturday!" Billy said, and the rest of the guys laughed.

"This fire's gonna start at a lumber company, and it's going to burn nine blocks before we get it out. It'll be the biggest fire the city's ever seen."

"Nine blocks, I should certainly say so," Charlie said.

"What lumber company?" Nicholas asked.

"I don't remember. All I remember is that it's a planing mill," I said and took another sip of coffee.

Charlie looked around at the guys and laughed. "This is Chicago. We don't get fires that size."

"Charlie, think about it. I read about this stuff the night before I got here. It's part of my history. How do you think I knew about the Burlington? That's how I know there's gonna be five fires today. You need to believe me because a lot of lives are going to depend on it. I'll tell you what, if we don't get five fires today, I'll go to the lake and drown myself out of humiliation!"

Charlie stood and reached across the table. "Fair enough. And if we get the five alarms today, then that'll be all the convincing I need," he said and firmly shook my hand.

Finally, I felt I was winning their trust, or at least they were open-minded right then.

"One thing," Daniel said. "If you drown yourself, can I watch?" Wayne took his hat off and threw it across the room and hit Daniel in the face. "What's that for?"

"For being an ass and making fun of John!"

"Nine blocks? I've never seen a fire that huge," Billy said.

"You haven't, but you will," I said. "But still, it's gonna be nothing compared to the fire on Sunday."

"I suppose it'll burn sixteen blocks," Dale said.

"Sixteen blocks would be a good thing," I said. "History will call this the Great Chicago Fire, and like the Saturday Night Fire, which will be the largest the city has ever seen, the Great Fire on Sunday will be the biggest the country has ever seen."

"How would we fight this fire?" Charlie said.

"We need to think about tomorrow's fire first. While in California, I mostly fought wildland fires, and there's a tactic we used that I think will help stop the fire tomorrow."

"What's that?" Nicholas asked.

"The biggest problem we'll be facing tomorrow night will be the wind. The fire will be moving at a fast pace and burning everything in its path. When we fought wildfires, we would cut fire breaks and remove the fuel in front of the fire. I know this isn't fighting a wildland fire, but we could use the same tactic and remove its fuel to slow it down enough, so we could stop it."

"How do you propose us removing its fuel?" Dale asked.

"We knock the buildings down. With the buildings lying on the ground, it will take a lot longer for them to catch on fire. That's how we stop it!" I looked over at Nicholas and saw he was in deep thought, but he said nothing.

Billy laughed. "So, you're saying we need to destroy perfectly good buildings to stop a fire? How does that make us any better than the fire?"

"That's exactly what I'm saying. And how does that make us any better? It's called triage! We sacrifice a few to save a lot . . . Look, if we can stop this fire with only a couple blocks burned and save six or seven, then that's how we're better than the fire," I said. "But it's not my decision. It's just something for Nicholas to think about."

ACT 39

After breakfast, we trained until lunch. I was getting used to the hard workouts because I was performing as well as the other guys, if not better. That morning, we didn't have any alarms. I could tell the guys were on edge, expecting something to happen, but it didn't. After we finished, we went back to the firehouse. For lunch, we had sandwiches and soup. Don't ask me what type of soup it was. I had no idea, but I know it was good.

After lunch, Joe and I took the dishes back to Quinn's, and he spent a few minutes with Sharon before we headed back across the street. As we reached the sidewalk near the station, the fire bells sounded. It was our first alarm of the day. When we arrived at the scene, it turned out to be a chimney fire. Flames were shooting out from the flue. I volunteered to get on the roof with a hose and put it out, but Nicholas laughed. He said to watch and learn how we do it in Chicago. I followed him into the house, and he rolled up a towel and soaked it in water. Then he threw the towel into the stove, which instantly turned the moisture to steam, which went up the chimney and put out the fire. The old lady gave Nicholas a hug and thanked him for saving her house. I stood there, dumbfounded. In a million years I would have never thought of doing that.

After that, we had a 2-11 downtown at the European Hotel. It was also a chimney throwing sparks, but by the time we got there, it was out. Then we got a boxcar fire, and then two more chimney-related fires. We finally finished up around seven-thirty and got back to the firehouse. No one said anything, but they had that stare about them. I sensed they were in disbelief about the five fires and were thinking about what tomorrow and Sunday would bring. For once, I think they were taking me seriously.

“John, help me hitch my wagon, and I’ll give you a ride home,” Nicholas said in a somber tone. I figured Joe wanted to get straight home to Sharon, so I accepted Nicholas’s offer. On the way, Nicholas sat, just staring ahead and jiggling the reins. I could tell he had a lot on his mind, and then he finally asked me, “What time’s this fire gonna happen tomorrow?”

“I’m not sure, but I imagine sometime after dark.”

“Well, it being called the Saturday Night Fire. That would only stand to reason. Can I count on you to be there?”

“Absolutely!” I said.

“I think maybe you should stay home and spend some time with your girl tomorrow. Why don’t you come in around five?”

“Tomorrow night?”

“Yeah. I think gettin’ some rest tomorrow would be a good idea. Maybe that’ll give you some time to go bury your note.”

I looked at Nicholas and smiled as we pulled up to the house. I reached over and shook his hand. “Thanks. I appreciate the ride.”

I met Lindsay on the porch and gave her a kiss, and then we went inside. I glanced at the table and smiled. There was a glass jar, a wooden box, and a pencil and paper sitting there. But the thing that made me laugh was that Lindsay had sat around, creating flip books. She even got creative and made one with a stick man running and jumping.

“I got the items you wanted. I told Luke at the woodshop that I needed a box that we could bury for a hundred years, one our great-grandchildren could open. He put something called creosote on it and said he didn’t know if it would last that long without rotting.”

I picked up the box, and it was heavy and smelled like railroad ties. The jar fit in it perfectly.

“You did well. Nicholas told me to come in at five tomorrow and said I should bury the box near the lake. You wanna help me find a good spot?”

“Yes,” she said. “But how can you be sure someone will find it?”

"I thought about it over and over, and I can't be sure, but I figure if I put a piece of iron in the box—"

"Iron?"

"Yes. In the future, they'll invent a machine that detects metals, and they'll become a popular hobby in the late 1960s. People will take them to the beaches and parks, looking for money and jewelry lost in the sand. I'm sure it will only be a matter of time before someone finds our box." Lindsay had the sweetest expression on her face. I could tell she was trying to understand what I had just told her. I kissed her on her forehead. "Trust me. It's gonna work. Now all we need is a hammer and nails."

"Mr. Johnston, next door. Let's go ask!" Lindsay said.

"You want me to go like this? I'm all dirty and smelly."

"It makes you look and smell like a working man. He'll like that."

"All right, if you say so." I grabbed the box, and we went next door. We didn't even make it to the front door before Mr. Johnston opened it and stood there with a lantern. I guess he heard us come up the steps, and then I thought about what Lindsay had said; the old coot heard and saw everything.

"Hello, Ms. Lindsay," Johnston said and then looked at me.

"Mr. Johnston, this is John. He's my husband. We got married yesterday."

"Married? Nice to meet you, son," he said as he gave me a once-over. "A working man, I see. Good for you!" Johnston shook my hand and told me to call him Clint. I looked at Lindsay, and she smiled at me. Clint turned and shouted through the door, "Betty, heat up some coffee. We have company. You would like some coffee, wouldn't you?"

"Yes, sir."

"Well, come on in," Clint said. "We're about to have supper, liver and onions. Would you kids like to join us?"

That did not sound appetizing. As a matter of fact, it sounded gross.

"Thank you so much," Lindsay said. "John's been working hard all day, and I'm sure he's starving."

I gave her a smile, you know that smile you give someone when they volunteer you to do something you didn't want to do, like eating liver.

We sat and talked for a while and then ate. Mr. and Mrs. Johnston were nice people, and to my surprise, the liver and onions were damn good. I ate seconds. It turns out Clint was retired from the military, and he had some wild stories about being out West. Betty was a school teacher and taught arithmetic. Before we left, the Johnston's gave us permission to use their mare and buggy in the morning to go out to the lake.

ACT 40

The next morning, we were up before daylight. While Lindsay made breakfast, I wrote my mother a letter. I glanced up and watched Lindsay put cream and sugar in her tea. "Can I have some of that in my coffee?"

"Cream and sugar?"

"Yes, it tastes good in coffee too."

She shook her head and smiled. "I've never heard of anyone putting cream and sugar in coffee."

After breakfast, we went next door and hitched the horse. I was sure glad Lindsay knew what she was doing because I had no clue. It made me laugh.

"What's so funny?"

"I feel stupid, following you around like a child, not knowing what to do."

She smiled as she tightened the bridle around the horse's face. "And I'd feel silly trying to put out fires like you do."

We led the horse to the street and climbed in the buggy. It was still dark out, but the roosters had begun crowing. It was funny, as soon as one crowed, another down the street would crow followed by another. It was as if they were competing.

As we rode away, I couldn't believe how trusting everyone was. I mean, like Mr. Johnston had no problem with letting us use the buggy. It was like handing your neighbor the keys to your car.

We drove south on Clinton for a few blocks, and then I asked her to stop. The sky was turning light, light enough I could make out things, such as the street sign I was staring at. "This is DeKoven Street?"

"It has been ever since I've lived here. Why?"

"Is there a family that lives around here called the O'Learys?"

"You're silly. You mean Patrick and Catherine? They live at the other end of the block," Lindsay said and pointed west. "Why? Do you know them?"

"Let's just say I've heard of them." I sat there for a minute, thinking, then turned around and looked toward our house. The fire is gonna burn in a northeast direction, which put our house directly in its path. "Can we go by there?"

"Sure." We turned right on DeKoven and went toward the end of the block. On the north side of the street was a wooden house that looked like it had been built in two parts, a front and a back. Each section had a chimney, and the yard was enclosed by a fence. In the rear of the house was a small barn. As we passed, I saw a sign above the front door that read, "The O'Learys," and below it, the numbers "137."

I felt like I was in a dream and having déjà vu simultaneously, if that makes any sense. I had seen that house on the internet only a few days ago, and it is where the fire will start Sunday. It was a trip, looking at a home that will have so much to do with the future and will affect people forever.

"You all right?"

"Yeah," I said. As we drove by, a cow mooed. Talk about eerie.

We turned on Jefferson and went south to Twelfth Street and then east to the lake. The whole way I thought about the O'Learys and got a sickening feeling in my stomach, thinking that our house wouldn't exist in just a few days.

"You're sure quiet," Lindsay said. "Are you sure there's nothing wrong?"

"No, I'm okay. Do you think you can invite Melanie and Brian over before I go to work? I need to tell you all something."

"I'll see what I can do."

A few minutes later, we crossed over the tracks of the Chicago and Michigan Central railroads. A dirt trail led through a grove of trees and out onto the beach. I still couldn't get over how big that lake was. The sun was rising and cast a reflection on the water. It was stunning.

A little way up the beach, there was a cove, and on the north side of it were two medium-sized trees. "That looks like a good place," I said, and we drove over there. We jumped down from the buggy, and I carefully studied the area. "This is the spot!"

We carried the box with the jar and letter to the trees. Lindsay handed me the shovel and I dug about three feet down before stopping. We carefully placed the box into the hole and put four horseshoes on it and then buried it. It was emotional for me as I packed the dirt down under my feet, knowing that was the only chance I had to get a message to my mother, and it wouldn't reach her until after I was dead.

Lindsay put her arms around my neck and kissed me. "It'll get to her. I feel it in my heart."

"I hope so. She needs to know what happened to me and how happy I am."

"I know what would make you happier."

"Oh yeah?"

"Yeah, but you'll have to catch me to find out!" She took off running across the beach. I kicked off my boots and chased after her. She was fast, but I was a little faster, and as I got closer, she screamed and hollered. I grabbed her and pulled her down on top of me. Her hair hung down around my face, and then she kissed me. "John Kirk, I love you!"

ACT 41

That morning after we got home, I took a nap. Lindsay left and did errands and invited Melanie and Brian for an early dinner. They came over around three, and that was the first time I'd met Brian. He was tall and intimidating, especially when I thought about what he did for a living: hunting down criminals and sometimes killing them.

I wasn't sure how-to bring things up. I just pulled out the five-dollar bill and laid it on the table. Brian looked at it, somewhat interested in the design, then he flipped it over. Being observant by nature, he noticed the date. "Is this some sort of joke?"

"No, it's real!" I said.

"How could it be. It's stamped 1969?"

Melanie turned her head away from Lindsay and looked at Brian and me then walked over and looked at the bill. She said nothing, just gazed at me. Lindsay set the food on the table.

"Fried chicken, my favorite!" Brian said. I couldn't believe all the fried food everyone ate. It's surprising that people weren't dropping dead from heart disease at thirty.

"Now, back to the greenback. You gonna enlighten us?" Brian asked before taking a bite of his drumstick.

"Do you have plans for tomorrow?" I asked.

"Bright and early, me and the boys are heading out on a three-week expedition north." Brian paused as he took another bite. "Got word of smugglers crossing the northern border, and they were spotted traveling down the Red River near a place called Grand Forks. Why? What's on your mind?"

"Grand Forks?"

"A town bordering North Dakota and Minnesota. Why?"

"You need to cancel it!"

Brian laughed. "And why's that?"

"Because this morning I realized where DeKoven Street was, and tomorrow night, the O'Learys barn is gonna catch on fire—"

"How does that have anything to do with me going to North Dakota? Isn't DeKoven a few blocks from here, and how do you know it's gonna catch fire?"

Lindsay looked up at me and said, "Is that why you were so interested in their house this morning?"

"Yes," I said, and then explained how I knew about the fire and how big it would be. Brian picked up the five-dollar bill and looked at it while he ate. Every so often, he would eye me, but didn't say anything. I told them how the fire will spread throughout the city and that our houses will be in its path. Lindsay looked worried, but I don't think Brian and Melanie believed me. I told him he should warn the other guys in his posse, and then he should pack up their things and head West. I read that people took refuge in the prairies.

"So, let me get this straight. You want me to warn my boys of a fire that hasn't happened yet, pack up all my belongings, and move my wife to the open prairie because you say I should. Is there anything else I should do?"

"Yes . . . Could you take Lindsay?" Lindsay jerked her head back and looked at me.

Brian smiled. "Listen here, John. You have two things going for you right now. One, you're married to Lindsay, and the second is that I don't have my gun with me!"

Melanie said, "You're not kidding, are you?"

“I wish I were, but no. Listen, the only thing I have to offer you as proof is this five-dollar bill, and that there’s gonna be a big fire tonight on Canal Street.”

Brian shook his head. “What do the guys at the firehouse say about all this?”

“They’re getting some rest for tonight. Nicholas told us all to come in at five!”

ACT 42

After dinner, Brian gave me a ride to the firehouse. He didn't say much, but on the way, he asked if I liked to hunt. I wasn't sure how to answer because I didn't know whether he meant if I liked to hunt, or if he was talking about taking me out and using me as the game. Too many movies, I guess.

Most of the guys were already at the firehouse, and those who weren't wandered in one by one over the next few minutes. Joe and I went downstairs to feed and water the horses. While they ate, Joe handed me a shovel and bucket and told me to go clean Jack's stall. After I did that, we took the muck out back and dumped it near the corral. Joe said that once a week, a farmer came by to pick up the pile. He used it to fertilize his crops. It seems everything got recycled. I guess it's true: one man's shit is another man's treasure. The funny thing about it, three weeks ago, I would've looked at this type of work as disgusting and would have never done it. But ever since I was doing it, I kind of enjoyed it and could see myself working on a farm.

Nicholas walked out and yelled for us to come upstairs. He was handing out our pay, and I was paid seven dollars. I was happy. Between that and what I had left over from the competition, I felt I was getting rich. Charlie received the most, eleven dollars and fifty cents.

Wayne looked at me. "Whaddya gonna do with all that money?"

"I'm giving it to Lindsay. She's gonna need it!" I said and thought about how nice it would be to have Charlie's salary.

"I think that's a wise move," Nicholas said.

We sat around the table and played cards as darkness fell. The darker it got, the more anxious everyone seemed to get, and as more time passed, doubt set in. Nicholas got up and walked over to the window and stood there for a few minutes and looked around, and then went to the windows in the back of the hall.

"Well, it's been dark for a while now, and it's getting late." He pulled out his pocket watch. "It's ten. Let's say we play one more hand, and if nothing happens, we'll call it a night."

It took about twenty minutes to play the next hand, and Billy won. I think that was the first hand he'd won since I'd been here. Everyone threw their cards on the table and got up. Nicholas walked over to the front window and looked out. "Well, it's late and doesn't look like anything's going to happen. Let's say we shut down these lights and get out of here." He looked at me, his expression a little disappointed. It made me feel bad because I had gotten them to believe in me, and at the moment, their trust in me was getting ready to walk down the stairs. I know this is gonna sound terrible, but for the first time ever, I wanted a fire to happen. Joe said he'd stay the night, and everyone else headed to the stairs, and then that familiar bell rang.

They stopped. Charlie counted the tones with his fingers as he and the crew rushed over to the windows. The bell rang eight times, and then it rang another ten times. "Ward 10!" Charlie said. And then everyone ran to the back windows. We couldn't see anything because the ward was a couple of miles away. We needed a more elevated position. We followed Nicholas up to the roof.

"Over there!" Wayne said, pointing to the northwest. A few miles away, there was an orange glow. It wasn't as high as it was wide. It reminded me of a wind-driven wildfire spreading fast. The dark smoke blew ahead of the glow and quickly vanished into the night.

Charlie came out on the roof, and the wind almost blew him off his feet. "Canal and Van Buren!" he yelled as he held his cap on his head.

Staring at the glow, Nicholas asked me, "What did you say was going to burn?"

"I remember it started in the boiler room at a planing mill."

"With a glow that size, it's more than just a boiler room. Boys, the long-dreaded day of a fire in the Red Flash District has come upon us."

"Whaddya thinking? Lull and Homes?"

"That's exactly what I'm thinking." Nicholas said.

"What's a Red Flash District?" I asked.

"It's a name the insurance companies gave that area because of its high risk for fires," Joe said.

"Charlie, take the men down and hitch the wagons and get the steamer fired up," Nicholas said.

"You sure? We haven't been requested yet."

"Yeah, I'm sure. The way of the wind, and the size of the glow, they'll be calling us shortly."

Charlie looked at us and said, "Whaddya waiting for? You heard the man!"

We ran down the stairs, and by the time we got the horses harnessed, Daniel had the fire going. Then Charlie pulled the steamer out to the street so the barn wouldn't fill with smoke. We jumped on the hose wagon and waited for Nicholas to climb on the steamer, then we took off. As we turned up Wentworth toward Sixteenth Street, we heard the fire bells ring again. They were now requesting a 2-11.

Wayne looked at me and asked, "You ready for this?"

He reminded me so much of Don. I smiled and said, "I was born ready."

Then the bells rang again. "Sounds like it's bad," Joe said.

"Why's that?" I said.

"They're calling out a 3-11, which means they're requesting Wards 1 and 2 from downtown.

I nodded and then looked over my shoulder to see if I could see anything. It was hard because of the light from the streetlamps. It was kinda like trying to look at the stars with a full moon out. The wind was blowing so hard that it was blowing the smoke ahead of the steamer. A strange feeling came over me as we rode up the street. The city bells were ringing nonstop and echoing between the buildings, the winds howling at our backs, and the horse's hooves clacking in the darkness. It was like I was in Sleepy Hollow, and the only thing missing was the Headless Horseman.

We arrived at the fire a few minutes later and stopped at the corner of Canal and Van Buren. I looked up Canal, north of Van Buren, and both sides of the street were on fire. Flames swept across Canal to the northeast. West of us, on Van Buren, several fire engines were set up with hoses stretched between a row of homes on the north side. They were trying to prevent the fire from working its way south to the houses. The Lull and Holmes Planing Mill, a two-story brick building straight ahead on the left side of Canal was fully engulfed by fire. A two-story house north of the mill also was burning and so was the building north of that. On the right side of Canal Street, just north of Van Buren, was the Union Wagon Works Company, and behind it were large stacks of lumber. There were several hose lines there protecting them. Several buildings north of the lumber piles were on fire along with everything north of that.

Engine 15 pulled up behind us and then from the left came the chief's buggy. It was Chief Benner. He yelled to Nicholas, "I need you to take your men to the north side of the fire. It's jumped Jackson Street. I'm trying to pull everything I can over to Adams Street. I wanna stop the fire there. I have six engines making a stand between Clinton and the river. I need you and Engine 15 to head up there and give 'em a hand!"

"Yes, sir," Nicholas said.

"Follow Nicholas!" the chief yelled at Engine 15. "You'll have t' take Clinton up to Adams. Canal is impassable!"

We followed the Economy, and Engine 15 and their hose wagon followed us to Clinton Street. As we drove up Clinton, we passed the John Foster Paper Box Factory. It was totally engulfed. The rest of the block was full of large stacks of burning lumber and outbuildings. The erratic flames and sparks that were flying in the air reminded me of videos I watched of the Oakland Hills Fire that burned in 1991.

We crossed Jackson Street, and there was another box company on fire. A row of houses facing south along Jackson Street was also on fire. We continued north to Adams Street and then turned right. We were now a block ahead of the fire. There were steamers lined up all the way to the river, which was two blocks east of Clinton. We stopped at the corner of Adams and Canal.

Nicholas jumped down and met with two captains from other engines, then he hustled back to us. "Joe, I want you guys to pull everything off the hose wagon and run a supply line to the hydrant at Clinton. Dale, I need you to unhitch Fast and Faster and take them with Jack and the hose wagon to safety. A farmer is taking in equipment and horses three blocks west on Adams. We're either gonna stop the fire, or we're going to lose everything trying. We don't need the horses to be part of it."

We dumped all the hose, nozzles, and hand tools, and Joe and Wayne lifted the fuel box down to Billy and Daniel. They carried it to the steamer and set it down near the furnace. I kept looking over my shoulder at the fire. It was still a block away but was coming fast. Sparks and heavy smoke were coming right at us and flying overhead. I looked over my other shoulder toward the northwest of Canal and Adams. The owner of the corner saloon had opened his doors and was handing out whiskey and cigars to the crowd watching. He was convinced his place was gonna burn and didn't want the alcohol to go to waste.

A man walked up to me and tapped me on the shoulder. He had concern on his face. "I've been trying to get to my house, but I can't. I'm looking for my wife. Have you seen her?" he asked, and then he described her and said she had an injured ankle and may have a hard time walking.

"Sir, we just got here," I said as I connected the hose coupling. "I haven't seen anyone wandering around, but I'll keep my eyes open. Right now, you need to go find a safe place."

ACT 43

As soon as I turned back to the hose, someone grabbed my shoulder. "Sir, I said you need to get to safe—" I turned, and Nicholas was standing there. "Thought you were some man looking for his wife."

Nicholas was in deep thought, and then he looked at the people standing across the street on the corner. They were unaware of the danger heading toward us, but that clearly wasn't what Nicholas was thinking about. "What you were saying about the fire tomorrow night and about clearing its fuel, do you think it'll work here?" he said.

"It should as long as we watch for hotspots!"

"I hope you're right. Come on."

I followed him across the street to the crowd outside the bar. An older man handed Nicholas a bottle of whiskey and told him to have a drink. Nicholas took the bottle and looked at the men. They raised their bottles in the air, and then Nicholas took a swig and handed it to me. "Take a drink." I did, and the men cheered and drank from their bottles.

"Listen up, men!" Nicholas yelled over the crowd. "If we're going to stop this fire, I'm gonna need all of you to help!"

The old man took another swig from his bottle and said, "Ya name it, laddie. Ya be one of us now!" he said with a robust Irish accent. The men behind him cheered.

"The fire's coming at us like a raging bull, and I believe there's only one way we're going to stop it from reaching the depot. We're gonna need to remove its fuel."

"How do you propose we do that?" a man shouted from the back.

Nicholas looked at me then back at the crowd of about fifty. "All those sheds and small buildings around the old woman's house, we need to knock them down!"

"Tear dem down?"

"Yes, we need to knock down all those buildings. It'll slow the fire, so my men can put it out. Can I count on you?"

The old man in front yelled, "Yes! Let's have some fun, mates!"

The men grabbed the sledgehammers and axes we had dumped on the sidewalk and headed toward the buildings on the north side of Adams. It was only a matter of a few minutes, and the buildings were coming down. Nicholas patted me on the shoulder. "You want the Irish to help, you gotta win 'em over with a drink. I hope you're right about this because I'm gonna feel like a real ass if it doesn't work."

I smiled. "That's how we do it in the future. It works well."

I headed back to the other side of the street and had to hopscotch to keep from stepping on the hoses. There were so many, it looked like spaghetti.

In the distance, the roar of the fire was getting louder and the smoke thicker. The sparks blowing in the air were landing on the houses in front of us. I've been in some hairy situations before, but that was getting scary.

I picked up my pipe and stood there waiting. Joe stood about fifteen feet to my right and Wayne to my left. Beyond them, I counted fifteen pipemen stretched along Adams Street from Clinton to the river. Daniel tapped me on the shoulder from behind and handed me a large, straight-bore nozzle tip. "Change your pipe. You'll need a heavier stream. That small tip you have on there now will be like pissing in the wind!"

"Thanks," I said and changed tips.

Another strong gust blew a wave of sparks through the air, but by that time, sparks were also being blown between the houses and onto the ground in front of us. The smoke was burning my eyes, and snot was running from my nose like a faucet. I put my visor down to protect my eyes. Then flames leaped in the air behind the houses in front of us, and the roaring sounded like a freight train. The buildings behind the houses were catching fire.

"Charge all fire hoses," someone behind us yelled through a megaphone. My hose filled and then kicked. Wayne tapped me on my left side and handed me a handkerchief.

"What do you want me to do with this?"

"Get it wet and then put it in your mouth. It'll filter the smoke."

"Are you kidding, it's used!"

"Rinse it out. Smoke will kill you. Snot won't!" I cracked the valve to my nozzle and did like he said. It seemed disgusting to me, but he was right. I stuffed the rag in my mouth and then heard shouting behind me. I looked, and it was coming from the little house on the northeast corner of Adams and Canal. Some of the Irishmen were trying to get the old lady out of her home, but she was refusing to leave.

Word came down the line that it was time to move toward the fire and stop it. I looked at Joe and then Wayne. They both smiled at me. These guys are nuts, I thought.

The rear of the houses in front of us was right then catching fire. I opened my nozzle and shot the stream over the roof. That's when I was glad I switched nozzles, because the last one would have never had the distance. I felt bad for the other guys because they had nothing to protect their eyes from the flying embers and water blowback.

We advanced toward the fire and were trying like hell to stop it. East of Canal, piles of lumber and several buildings were burning. Farther down, along the river, firefighters were trying to save the National Grain Elevator. I sprayed as long as I could take it; my eyes were burning to the point that I couldn't see, and it was hard to breathe. I could hardly see Wayne or Joe through the smoke. Wayne motioned for me to move back and shut down my hose, and we both retreated to the sidewalk.

"You okay?" Wayne said.

I pulled the handkerchief out of my mouth. "Other than being hotter than hell and unable to see or breathe, yeah, I'm okay!" I rinsed the handkerchief and put it back in my mouth.

"How does my snot taste?" Wayne said and laughed.

I smiled, gave him the finger, and headed back into the fire. We had to hold it and keep it from crossing Adams, or it was gonna be unstoppable. To the east, the winds had pushed the flames under the Adams Street viaduct that spanned the Fort Wayne and Chicago Railroad. The dry trusses caught fire, and the flames, driven by the winds, quickly spread to the north side of Adams Street and to the old woman's house. It took only a matter of minutes, and her house was on fire. Luckily, the Irishmen pulled her out minutes before the fire reached her.

Wayne, Joe, and I broke away with a couple of other pipemen and ran across the street to fight that fire. We confined it to the house and put out several spot fires started by flying sparks. We ran our asses off.

After we knocked down the fires, I pulled out the rag and rinsed it. It was black and full of soot. After I cleaned it and took a drink from my hose, I put the handkerchief back in my mouth and headed back to the main fire. We would fight the fire for a while and then pull back for a break then go at it again and again. The wind and sparks were relentless, but we held our ground. We fought until the sun came up, and I was proud to stand alongside those men. They were the bravest men I have ever known.

As the sun rose and daylight was finally there, the fire was deemed under control. I looked toward Van Buren and then Clinton. Everything was destroyed. It seemed as if a bomb had gone off and reduced buildings to burning piles of rubble. To my amazement, the National Grain Elevator to the east was still standing high. It was untouched and was a testament to the firemen who worked so hard to protect it.

Nicholas came over and told us to break down our hoses. We had been released. There were still piles of lumber and downed buildings burning, but it wasn't going to spread anywhere. The chief decided to release engines, so they could be freed up to respond to other alarms. It made me laugh when I looked across the street, and the man's bar was still standing. He gave away all that alcohol and cigars for nothing.

I took off my helmet and coat. The cool breeze felt good on my face and gave me a chill as it blew across my sweat-drenched clothes. As I broke down the hose and drained the water, Nicholas told Wayne and Joe that several engines had been destroyed on Jefferson, and others were damaged and out of service. He said ten in total. Charlie walked up and said that some men had found the bones of a missing woman, and her husband was collecting them and waiting for the undertaker to come for them. I felt terrible. It was the same man from last night.

ACT 44

It was about eleven thirty Sunday morning when we finished loading the equipment back on the hose wagon and had the horses hitched. I had been up for some thirty hours, well minus the two-hour nap, but I was drop-dead tired, and I could tell everyone else was too!

On the way back, we stopped by my house, so I could check on Lindsay. She said Brian had seen the fire last night and came by that morning to say he was sending two wagons over to pick her and her things up. He was also sending men over to get Sharon, Gladys, and Joe's mother.

I glanced over at the Johnston's house, and Clint was loading his buckboard.

"Did you say something to them?" I asked Lindsay.

"Of course, I did."

"What did he say?"

Lindsay laughed. "Something you need to know about Mr. Johnston. He's a firm believer in the apocalypse and said a fire would be a good enough reason to cause it. He then told Mrs. Johnston to start packing. To him, it's a dream come true. He has been waiting for this day for years."

"Really?" I didn't know if the old man was crazy, believing in the apocalypse, or crazier, believing me about the fire. "Come by the firehouse and let me know where Brian's taking you, so I can find you after the fire."

"Okay," she said.

I got back on the wagon and told Joe that Brian was sending some of his men to get Sharon and Gladys. Around noon, we were back at the firehouse and got all the equipment back in order. Nicholas told us that if we needed to check on loved ones, we should do it now and be back in two hours so we can get some rest for tonight.

Joe asked if I wanted to ride with him, so I took him up on the offer. We left the station and saw Nicholas walking down the street. Joe stopped and asked if he needed a ride. Nicholas laughed and said he lived only two blocks away.

On the way to Joe's house, I watched the people walking around, and buggies filled the streets going about their merry way as if the day was just another ordinary day, unaware of the conflagration to happen in only a few hours. I wanted so much to tell them, but I knew they'd mock me the way they mocked Noah before the flood.

We got to Joe's house, which surprised me because it was right next door to Gladys. We stayed there for about an hour and helped pack, and before we finished, four wagons pulled up out front. It was Brian's men. The wagons were loaded, but each had enough room to carry a little extra.

"You John?" one man asked.

"Yeah, John Kirk," I said.

The man threw me a box of matches. "Brian told me to tell you that if this fire doesn't happen tonight, you better make sure one does because he said he'd kill you!"

I laughed. We loaded as much as we could on their wagons, and they said they were heading to a post in Hammond, Indiana. We took Sharon and Gladys back to the firehouse with us because they would travel with Brian, Melanie, and Lindsay. It was a thirty-mile trip, which doesn't sound far by automobile, but by wagon, it was an all-day journey.

Around three thirty, I held Lindsay tight in my arms and kissed her. "I'll see you at the end of the week," I said. "Joe and I'll come to Hammond and find you."

"Do be careful, and remember that I love you and want to come home to you."

"I'll see you Friday," I said and gave her a kiss goodbye. My eyes watered as I watched her climb up on the wagon. It was hard seeing her go, but I knew it was only for a few days. I looked over at Joe standing next to his wagon with Sharon. They were lip-locked. Sharon didn't want to let loose of Joe but eventually did when Brian said it was time to go. Sharon climbed up next to Gladys, and they all rode away.

Joe walked over and put his arm around me. "Don't worry, little brother. It'll just be till Friday. Let's get some sleep!"

***

After we left John and Joe at the firehouse, we knew it would be a long journey to Indiana. A few minutes later, we met up with four more wagons: Joe's mother Isabelle, Dawn, Wayne's wife Sherry; and Daniel's wife, Renee. For the next hour, there would be six wagons in our group until we met up with Brian's men and their families. Seven more wagons joined our party, which by then made it thirteen in our group.

We stopped a few times to feed and water the horses, and it felt good to get down from the hard seat and stretch our legs. Brian looked around and saw many people staring at us and commented, "They must think we're Mormons returning back to the East!" His men laughed.

Around six thirty, after traveling about seven miles, Brian decided it was time to stop and make camp while we still had enough light to see. I helped the women cook dinner while the men pitched the tents and moved the wagons in a circle around the camp. That was a practice Brian and his men did to protect against Indians, although in that part of the country, I don't think there was much risk of being attacked.

After dinner, some of us were escorted by a couple of men to a watering hole near the camp, so we could wash dishes. As we cleaned the plates, coyotes howled in the night. It reminded me of growing up in the Arizona desert, but I think it scared some of the other women.

After the tents were up, the men collected wood and built a fire. I sure wished John could have been there. Although we told stories and laughed, I think everyone was worried about the fire, wondering if it would even happen, and if so, was it going to be as bad as John said?

ACT 45

I woke up around eight o'clock that evening and walked into the main room. Nicholas, Wayne, Joe, and Charlie were sitting at the table. On the stove was a pot of boiling coffee with the pressure so great that the steam rose all the way to the ceiling.

"Have some coffee. It's fresh," Nicholas said.

"That's if there's anything left in the pot," I replied. "Did you guys get any sleep?"

"Yeah. We just got up a pot ago," Charlie said.

"So anyway, after I left Susan and Frankie, I went to see Chief Benner," Nicholas said, continuing his conversation with the other guys. "I told him everything, even how John was predicting all these fires and especially the one last night. When I tried telling them about tonight's fire, he and his driver laughed me out the door. He told me it's been a long night and that I should go home, have some whiskey, and get some sleep."

I sat down directly across from Nicholas at the table and smiled. He stared at me for a few seconds then said, "I sure hope you're right about this, because if you're not, I'm going to look like a real ass and probably lose my job."

Billy walked into the room, rubbing his eyes and looked around. In a raspy voice he asked, "'Sup?"

"What the hell did you just say?" Wayne asked.

"'Sup. It's short for saying, 'what's up?'. John says that's what they say in the future."

Everyone glanced over at me. "You folks must be getting lazy in the twentieth century, making up a shorter word for what's up!" Charlie said and laughed.

"It's no different from all you hicks saying 'y'all.' And by the way, it's the twenty-first century!"

"Pardon me," Charlie said and rolled his eyes.

Soon the rest of the guys were up and pouring coffee. Nicholas kept looking over his shoulder at the clock on the wall. It was twenty minutes after eight. Dale offered to throw down cards, but Nicholas said no and walked over to the rear windows. He stood there for a few minutes, sipping his coffee. "Well, one thing for certain, that wind is sure stirring up out there."

"So, when's this great fire supposed to happen?" Dale said.

Daniel laughed. "Probably like last time, when we're ready to go home."

"That's one thing I don't remember seeing."

Nicholas came back to the table and sat down. "Then fill us in on what you do know."

"Well, I read a lot about the fire, and the one thing that fascinated me was the way it was gonna burn. They said it had the same characteristics as a wind-driven forest fire."

"Whaddya mean by that?" Joe asked.

"When the fire starts, the wind will push it to the northeast and it will jump the river—"

Everyone laughed. "That there should tell you the story's fiction. If the fire jumps over the river, I'll eat horse shit!" Daniel said.

I looked at Daniel. "Then if I were you, I'd be getting the salt and pepper ready! In the rear, the fire will flank the main burn both on the west and east sides. After these flanks widen out, they'll make runs alongside the first burn, and this will happen over and over. Then at one point, the wind will shift and spread the flames to the west. After this happens, the fire's course will change and head north again sending a five-mile-wide and two-hundred-foot high tidal wave of flames across the city. By the time the fire's out on Thursday, only 10 percent of Chicago will be untouched, and 3,350 people will be dead. But I think we can change that!"

"I should say so. If you read all that, then you must know where the fire's gonna start," Billy said. "We could be there and put it out before it spreads!"

"Yeah," the rest of the crew agreed.

"You know, I thought about that too, but the more I thought about it, the more I realized we can't do—"

"Why the hell not?" Charlie said.

"Because if we did, think of the impact that would have on the outcome of history."

"Isn't that what we want?" Wayne said.

"If it were only that easy," I said. "Just think about what would happen if we changed history. Because of this fire, they've learned valuable lessons on how to prevent fires like this from ever happening again. They'll implement fire codes, improve building standards, firefighting equipment, and the way we fight fires. The list goes on and on, and because of this fire, thousands and thousands of lives will be saved throughout time. The exact number will never be known. It will make the next century and my century safer!"

"Yeah, but they'll learn that over time anyway!" Dale said.

"Oh yeah, at what cost? And why haven't they figured it out yet? When I got here, I couldn't believe how close the houses were built and what they were constructed of. In my time, you would never see that, and it's a direct result of tonight's fire. We even have a National Fire Prevention Week every October to commemorate this fire."

"Okay. I get where you're coming from, but how do we fight it?" Nicholas asked.

"Once the fire gets going, you gotta remember, it'll be unstoppable. I remember reading one man's words: 'You can't put out the wind with water.'"

"Oh yeah? What idiot said that?" Wayne said.

"Some idiot that watched tonight's fire 147 years ago!"

"So we need to get to the north side and set up?" Charlie asked.

Nicholas threw down a city map on the table. "Show us where the fire's going to burn."

I glanced at the map and remembered it was the same one I had seen on the internet. "There, that's where it's not gonna burn," I said as I put my palm on the far southwest corner of the map. Everyone looked at me simultaneously with that oh-shit expression on their faces. Now mind you, the map was table-size and my hand only covered a small portion. I pointed at the area west of the river. "Since the fire hasn't started yet, all I can say is that it will begin in the southwest division, and to answer your question, Charlie, no. We can't get in front of the fire and stop it. We'd be like a handful of ants trying to stop a train!"

"I see where you're going with this," Nicholas said as he rubbed his chin. "You're thinking if we stay on the south- and west-side of the fire, we could prevent it from flanking, which in turn will prevent the second and third waves?"

"That's exactly what I'm saying. We can stop it from becoming the fire it did and still give history its fire. Maybe then, instead of history saying the Great Chicago Fire, it'll be the Great Peshtigo Fire, and National Fire Prevention Week will be named in their honor."

"Peshtigo Fire?" Billy asked.

"You wouldn't know about that yet, but today, Peshtigo, Wisconsin, is having the worst forest fire in American history. It's going to kill 2,500 people, and there's another large fire in Michigan."

"What the hell's going on, the Second Coming of Christ?" Daniel said.

"No. It's just a bad day in history," I said.

ACT 46

Around eight forty-five, Dennis Sullivan, who lived on the south side of DeKoven Street, was sitting on the sidewalk in front of his house when he noticed a light flickering behind the O'Learys' house. Dennis watched it for a couple of minutes, and when he noticed it was growing, he went to investigate. He peered over the O'Learys' fence and saw the barn on fire.

"Fire! Fire!" he yelled.

Rogan, a neighbor who lived directly across from the O'Learys, heard Dennis's cry and ran to help. When they got to the barn, the entire second floor was ablaze, and they tried to save the animals. They were only able to rescue a calf that had been burned. The fire was too intense, and they were forced to retreat.

***

William Brown, the night operator of the fire department's telegraph alarm system, was chatting with his sister in the courthouse tower. He noticed a light flickering through his window in a southerly direction. Brown got up and walked over to get a better look. "Do you see that?"

Mary got up and stood next to her brother. "What do you think it is?"

William stared for a minute and said, "It's probably a rekindle from last night."

A few minutes later, William noticed the glow had increased in size and went back to get another look. Mary asked, "What do you think, a new fire?"

"Yes, it appears to be. It's getting larger." William turned to his sister with a puzzled face. "Now why hasn't there been any alarms called? Why hasn't Mathias sounded one?"

Uneasy, they continued watching the fire.

Mathias Schaffer, the watchman on duty in the courthouse cupola, above the Browns, had a bird's-eye view of the city. Around the dome was an outside walk where Schaffer could move around the tower and view the entire city in all directions. On his walk around, the wind was fierce, and he had to hold the railing to keep his balance. As Mathias made his way to the south side, he noticed the fire and quickly ran inside for his spyglass. After looking at the fire for a few seconds, he determined the location to be at Halstead and Canal Port. Mathias rushed back inside and got his chart, located a nearby alarm box then rang down to Brown to send an alarm for Box 342. Seconds later, at nine thirty-two, Mathias rang the tower's bell for Ward 7.

***

It was a strange feeling as we all sat in the room with no one speaking. It was ominous, and the tension increased with each passing minute. Just as my mind wandered and started thinking about Lindsay, the bell rang. I almost jumped out of my skin. It rang eight times and then seven more. Then the gong went off, and the ticker tape punched. Charlie rushed over and pulled his chart from the shelf. He glanced at the tape and said, "Alarm Box 342," then ran his finger down the chart. "Halstead Street and Canal Port Avenue!"

I stood up and said, "That's not right."

"What isn't right?" Nicholas said.

"The location. The fire's on DeKoven Street. That's where we need to go!"

Nicholas stared at me and then rushed to the window. "Are you saying the fire's in Ward 9 and not 7?"

"If that's where De Koven is, then yes!"

Nicholas walked away from those windows and went to the ones in the back. He stood there for a few seconds, looking around, then he turned. "Hitch the wagons. We're going to DeKoven Street!"

"Are you sure, Nicholas? DeKoven is more than a mile from Canal Port. Why would anyone pull an alarm that far away?"

"I don't know, Charlie, but we're going to DeKoven Street!" Nicholas said, and then he looked at me. "I sure hope you're right about this!"

"I am!"

After we left the firehouse, we went north on Wentworth to Sixteenth Street and then turned west. As we crossed the river, we got our first glimpse of the fire. There was an orange haze in the air, blowing northeast. We turned up Clinton and went past DeKoven to Forquer. That's where the fire was, and it was rapidly moving northeast. Only four structures were burning: the O'Learys' barn, two barns behind it and a house on the northwest corner of Forquer and Clinton. The fire was burning in an east-northeast direction. I saw one other engine and a hose cart on the scene. It turns out, the hose company saw the fire before it was dispatched, and the watchman at Firehouse 6 spotted the fire and placed its location at Jefferson and DeKoven, and they self-dispatched.

As soon as we stopped, a man ran across the street and told Nicholas that if he'd put out the fire in his coal pile, he would give Nicholas shares of the profit. Nicholas looked at the coal company on the east side of Clinton and then gave the man a stern stare. "I get paid by the city. I don't work for bribes!"

We connected hoses, and Joe, Wayne, and I ran to the fire and tried to stop it, but the wind was too strong and was blowing the fire from rooftop to rooftop, and those houses were on the ground in a matter of minutes. By the time we got the fire in one house, it had knocked down, two more would be on fire. The fire swept down a row of homes on the north side of Forquer and then jumped the street to the south and was spreading in the block north of Taylor.

Nicholas told us to disconnect and move to Taylor. He wanted to stop the fire from flanking farther south. While we were connecting hoses, three other engines showed up. It was unbelievable how fast it was spreading, and what made it worse, the wind was blowing embers ahead of the fire and starting new ones.

Nicholas ran to the corner and pulled the alarm box, and within a minute, the fire bell was ringing for Ward 9. A short time later, it rang again, and they kept ringing. The winds were increasing in speed. and in just a matter of minutes, we watched the fire burn past Canal, Beach, and Ellsworth streets, and it was licking at the banks of the Chicago River. It left a path of burning destruction behind it, but we kept it from crossing to the south side of Taylor.

Nicholas commandeered a horse from a man and yelled, "Charlie, get the hoses loaded and head to Jefferson and Ewing. I just got word the fire is flanking back on itself and moving west against the wind. I'm going to the armory. I'll meet you there in a few!"

When I heard Nicholas say that, I yelled at Joe and Wayne, "We're moving. Load the hose!" As soon as Charlie shut down the engine, we drained the hose and threw it in the back of the wagon. When we got to Jefferson and Ewing, we hooked our hoses and waited. Through the smoke, we saw a steamer coming west on Ewing. It was Engine 16, retreating from Canal Street. They had been overrun by the fire on its northward push, and Engine 14, the Fred Gund, went north. I couldn't believe it; their whiskers were singed and their faces red and blistered, and they still wanted to be in the fight. I saw one of the horse's tail smoldering and took my nozzle and sprayed it down. I remember saying to myself that that shit was getting serious.

The captain of Engine 4, half out of breath, said, "The fire's burning against the wind and heading this way. It's crossed back to the west side of Canal. Damndest thing I've ever seen. We sent out a message. Did you get it?"

"Yeah. That's why we're here," Charlie said. "We stopped it on the north side of Taylor. Nicholas will be back here in a few!"

I looked east and saw the fire about two blocks away, and it was coming our way, slowly but surely. It was just like I had read: the fire was coming back for the buildings it missed in the first wave. It wasn't leaving any survivors.

ACT 47

"C'mere, c'mere!" a young boy yelled from outside the tent. I was in the tent with Melanie, Sharon, Gladys, and Isabelle, Joe's mother. We had been talking and when we heard the child, we looked at each other, puzzled.

"Now why isn't that child in bed?" Gladys asked.

We got up and walked outside to see what all the commotion was about. The campfire was burning, but we didn't see anyone. As I focused beyond the fire, I saw the men standing on the outer edge of the wagons, all facing the northwest. As we walked up to them, one boy said, "Look!" and pointed toward Chicago.

My first thought was shock. I couldn't fathom what I was witnessing and fell to my knees and cried. The sky over Chicago was bright, bright orange from the fire. It had happened. The city was on fire. Sharon collapsed next to me, and we hugged each other and cried. We were terrified for our husbands. We didn't know if they were okay or not.

Gladys kneeled behind us and put her arms around us for comfort and said, "Don't worry, children. I'm sure they'll be fine."

"Thank you, Ms. Gladys. I sure hope you're right," I said.

Melanie walked over to Brian and put her arm around his waist.

Brian looked at the men. "I'm gonna need three of you to get the women to Hammond. The rest of you are coming with me to Chicago. With a fire that size, they're gonna need help in some capacity. Get some sleep. We're leaving at first light!"

***

A few minutes later, Nicholas returned with four covered wagons with U.S. Army written on the sides. He had been to the army and asked for help. The wagons were full of dynamite and kegs of black powder, enough to blow up everything west of the Chicago River. Nicholas glanced at me and grinned. "Last night we did it your way. Tonight, we're doing it my way!" I think that was the first time Nicholas made me laugh.

The man standing next to him stepped forward. "I'm Major Bradley, and these are my men. Our specialty is making things disappear, and by the looks of it, we have a lot of work ahead of us. I have a few things to say before we get started. The dynamite without the blasting cap is relatively safe, but the black powder is a different story. You strike one spark near these kegs, and I damn well guarantee you that they'll do more than pop your ears."

The major paused as we heard a wagon approaching from the north. It was Hose Company 5. The men jumped down, and David Kenyon walked over to us and said they were fighting the fire up on Canal and Mather. "Engine 5 quit running, and our captain went to help with repairs and put me in charge," Kenyon said.

The fire was moving to the northwest, and the church on Mather and Clinton was burning. Kenyon said it had caught fire before the main fire even reached it.

"What about the rest of the houses east of the church?" I asked.

"I'm sorry, Mista John, that whole block is on fire!"

My stomach sickened. That meant our house was gone.

"We'd be obliged if you and your men could give us a hand," the major said.

"Yes, sir," David replied.

"Listen up. This is what we need to accomplish," Nicholas said. "We need to keep the fire on the east side of Jefferson. If we can do that, we can corral it into last night's burn and run it out of fuel."

"For us to put Nicholas's plan into action, we need to place explosives in the houses facing Jefferson Street on the east side. My men will instruct you on how to handle it, how many to place, and where to place them. When the fire gets near, we'll set off the powder, removing these structures from existence. If all goes well and we wait for the right moment, we should be able to create enough force from the blast to blow most of the fire out. Just remember one thing: once the chain has been lit, there's no turning back!" Major Bradley said.

"Why's that?" I asked.

"That's because once the fuses separate, you might be able to defuse one, but you won't be able to get the rest. And if one blows, you'll be feeding fish in Lake Michigan!" The soldier standing next to Bradley said.

"Oh!" I said.

It was about twelve thirty when we got busy. The fire had crossed Clinton and was heading right for us. The winds shifted to the east, which slowed the wall of flames, giving us more time, at least right then. Counting the soldiers and David's crew, there were twenty-one of us.

The major assigned a crew of five to each wagon. It was Joe, David, two soldiers, and me in my group. We had four wagons of explosives and had four blocks to level, so each wagon was assigned a separate area. We were given the most northern block, the one between Harrison and Van Buren. Ours was the critical one. If the fire got past us, it would continue spreading across Jefferson and then flank north around last night's burn, and history would repeat itself. If that happened, then there would be two fires, the west and the east fires, each being separated by the Chicago River. The west fire would prove to be the deadliest and most destructive of the two.

We stopped in front of our houses, and the two soldiers got down. They studied the homes, which looked like mansions.

"Listen up," the one soldier said. "That first and second house, I want two barrels in each, and the third, I want four!"

It took about a half hour to get the barrels and dynamite placed in all houses. The last home, near the corner of Jefferson and Van Buren, was beautiful inside. There was no doubt that money lived there, and I hated destroying it. But then again, I'd never seen an explosion that big, so I was excited.

Joe and I stayed in the big house while David and the soldiers went to the others. Before the soldiers left, they said that when the fire got to us, to light the chain and run like hell. We stood in the kitchen and watched out of the back windows. We could see the sky lit on the other side of the houses behind us but could see no flames.

I got a strange thought. "Joe, has anyone bothered checking upstairs?"

"Huh?"

"Upstairs, did anyone check upstairs. We're getting ready to blow this house to smithereens. What if someone's up there sleeping?"

We both looked at each other for a second and then took off upstairs. We ran through the halls checking the rooms, and luckily, we found no one. We went back downstairs and looked out the windows. We couldn't believe what we saw. The house behind us was engulfed in fire.

A few minutes later, we heard a loud explosion that came from the south. Joe and I looked at each other and figured it was one of the other crews blowing up the house assigned to them. I could feel the heat radiating through the window from the fire behind us, and then I remembered one of the soldiers said that the black powder could be set off by heat. I was getting nervous and glanced at Joe. "Let's do this!"

He looked at me and grinned. "Okay!" Then we heard another blast and then another. Joe pulled out a match and tried striking it on the floor, but the head broke off. He tried another but couldn't get it to strike.

"Come on, Joe. The wall outside is on fire!" I hollered and looked back out. The flames were on the outside wall and burning up to the roof. Finally, Joe got the match lit. I grabbed the end of the chain and held it, then he put the match to it. When it lit, white sparks shot out the end. It reminded me of a Fourth of July sparkler. I dropped it, and we ran like hell out the door and across the street. We got behind a wagon, and the house blew. I couldn't believe how powerful the explosion was. Wood flew over our heads and then dropped out of the sky and all around us. A couple pieces even hit me in the head. Thank goodness I had my helmet on.

After everything finished falling, I stood up. "Damn, Joe. Check that out!" The major was right; their specialty was making things disappear, and that's precisely what they did. Everything across the street was gone.

ACT 48

The blasting worked. It had stopped the fire. Nicholas said we needed to head into the city because they would need us. We got on our wagons and headed east on Van Buren with Hose Company 5 and Engine 16. A block east of Canal Street, we saw the burned remains of the Fred Gund. Out of respect, we saluted the steamer in silence as we passed by. It was a real somber moment, as we wondered what happened to the crew.

When we got to the Van Buren bridge, it was impassable. It had burned and the parts of it not smoldering were missing. We jumped off the wagons and climbed up the charred banks of the Chicago River and looked across. The fire had jumped and was taking a strong foothold in the business district. We watched in disbelief as the wind pushed the fire from building to building at the speed of a grass fire. I saw a block of houses burn in less than a minute. Joe said that was a place called Conley's Patch. Then we saw a section of flames swirl and form a tornado. It must have been five-hundred feet tall and was throwing burning debris everywhere. In its own way, it had a beauty to it as the flames danced in the wind and the shower of sparks filled the sky. It was mesmerizing.

We headed north to the Madison Street Bridge and found it was still intact, but the people fleeing the city nearly made it impossible to cross. As we pushed our way east, countless wagons were filled with belongings. I even saw pianos in a couple. It was chaotic. As we neared the other side, I saw coffins bouncing upright, as if they were walking among the crowd. That was eerie, and with the undertaker dressed in all black, I thought of the Grim Reaper.

Once we made it to the other side, the fire was burning to the southeast. Although most buildings were tall and blocked our view of the fire, we knew it was about a half mile away. At the corner of Wells and Madison, we met up with four more engines and hose companies. They had been on State Street and Adams, attempting to level a few buildings with black powder, but it didn't stop the fire, so they headed west out of its path.

The fire was so immense that it lit the night as if it was daytime. East, down Madison, the light became blinding, and then we saw it. Flames swept across Madison and onto the buildings on the north side of the street. As I focused, my heart sank. It was McVicker's Theatre catching fire. Within a minute or two, the Green Room was on the ground, and McVicker's engulfed. At that same time, the bell at the courthouse rang, and unlike the ringing it had done all night, it rang nonstop, almost as if it were a distress call. Then it stopped. A few minutes later, the bell rung two more times, but those had more of a hollow tone and then we heard a thud. We looked at each other and knew that would be the last time we'd ever hear it ring.

After the main fire front swept across Madison, the street was burning, and the residual flames were spreading in our direction but at a much slower rate. The engineer from Engine 16 tapped open a hydrant to flush it. The water pressure was gone, and the water just leaked out. They reasoned that the waterworks had been destroyed.

Nicholas looked up into the air. "Listen up. It's not the fire coming from the east that we need to be concerned with. You see those embers overhead? They're coming from a second wave of flames heading our way. If we don't leave this area, we're going to be trapped in a sea of fire!"

"Where do we go?" one captain asked.

"We need to cross the river to the north division and make our stand there."

"Yes. We need to cross the river!" another captain said.

We got on our wagons and headed north on Wells. Most people were just standing around, transfixed by the fire, just watching it as if they were hopelessly doomed. Others looted, drank, and danced in the streets. They didn't seem to grasp the danger they were in.

Each block we passed, I saw buildings burning to the east. The speed at which the fire was spreading was incredible. As we neared Randolph, several wagons passed through the intersection, traveling west at full speed. The backs of them were on fire. I had to blink a few times just to make sure I'd actually seen what I thought I did. I looked east down Randolph, but the fire hadn't made it that far north yet.

We were slow at getting across the bridge because of the fleeing refugees, but the pace allowed us to see the fire. I could see McVicker's, the Crosby Opera House, and the Chicago Tribune office burning with the other tall buildings. Flames were reaching three-hundred feet in the air, and the flames went on for miles across the city. Watching it gave me the same feeling I had when I went to Mount St. Helens. I had read about it and seen pictures of the eruption, but not until I saw the devastation in person did I appreciate the magnitude of its power. I remember sitting on the observation deck in awe, thinking how small and insignificant I was.

After we got to the north side of the river, we regrouped at the passenger depot at Wells and Kinzie. Nicholas talked with the other captains and decided that the best plan of action was to spread out along Michigan and keep any spot fires in check. Nicholas said that in a worst-case scenario, if the fire was to take hold, then we could retreat to the north branch of the river. It's wider there, and the wind would be working in our favor. We would also have the river to draw from if we needed to.

We split up into groups of two engines, and ours went to Michigan Street and Clark. Nicholas told us to get a little shut-eye because if the fire jumped the river, we'd have one hell of a fight on our hands. The rest sounded good because I was having a hard time keeping my eyes open.

I lay in the wagon with Joe, Billy, and Wayne. The rest of the guys lay on the grass across the street. Joe must have been tired because, as soon as his head hit the hose, he was snoring.

"I hope it stops at the river," Wayne said.

"If not, we'll be getting help tomorrow."

"From where? I heard earlier that we only have twelve engines left."

"Don't you ever watch the weather?" I said.

"It looks the same as it did yesterday, hot and dry."

***

Sharon and I sat outside of the tent and watched the light over Chicago as it got brighter and brighter. We did our share of crying, and even though we were exhausted, we were too worried to sleep. Dawn and Gladys walked up from behind and handed us a cup of hot coffee. Usually, I'm a tea drinker, but for that moment, I didn't care as long as it was hot.

"I figured you'd be asleep by now," I told Dawn.

"I tried, but my man's out there too!"

"Oh my," Melanie said as she walked up and saw the size of the glow. She sat next to me and wrapped her arm around me and held me tight. "He'll be fine. Why don't you come to bed and get some sleep? We're going to have another long day tomorrow."

I looked at her and smiled. "You're right," I said as I got up.

"Sharon, you need to get your rest too," Melanie said.

After giving the fire one more glance, I went to bed. At first, I just lay there thinking of John, but my eyes grew heavy, and eventually, I fell asleep

***

I lay there thinking of Lindsay and wondered where she was, and if they had made it to Hammond. Even though I knew she was in good hands, I was still worried about her.

"John, you still awake?" Wayne asked.

I opened my eyes and saw the sky full of sparks. It was like the Fourth of July. "Yeah. I'm still here."

"I just wanted to say you're one hell of a fireman, and I wouldn't hesitate to trust my life in your hands."

That made me smile and brought a tear to my eye. "Thanks, Wayne. That really means a lot."

"I also wanted to say I'm sorry for calling you a liar all those times and thinking you were a cow short of being a full herd."

I raised up on my elbows and looked at him. "I don't remember you ever calling me a liar."

"Oh, well then, I apologize for all the times I thought you were."

"Just when I thought you were being nice. You remind me so much of Don that it's not funny."

"Who?"

"Don . . . your great-great-great-grandson!"

"Oh yeah? Tell me about 'im."

"Well, for one, he looks a lot like you. As a matter of fact, if you were standing side by side, you'd almost look like twins. But he's better looking."

"Shit!" Wayne said and smiled.

"I only worked with him for a day but got to know him pretty well. He was always making everyone laugh and saying crazy things, kinda like you," I said and lay back on the hose. "He definitely has your personality and the same love for fighting fires. He's an excellent firefighter, and I do know one thing for sure, he was really proud of you."

Wayne smiled. "Thanks. I appreciate that. So... what type of help are we getting tomorrow?"

I thought I'd have a little fun, so I put my finger in my mouth and then held it in the air. "Rain. It's gonna rain tomorrow."

"Sheeeit," Wayne said as he pulled his cap down over his eyes. "I take back all my apologies."

I stared back at the sky. The embers were getting closer but were still a good mile away. It was kinda pretty, like a million fireflies in the air. I watched them for a few minutes and fell asleep.

ACT 49

It only seemed like a few minutes later, and Charlie was yelling at the top of his lungs, "Git up! Git up! The fire jumped the river!"

I opened my eyes, and it was daytime. The thick smoke was blowing overhead and blocking out the sun. Being pushed by gale-force winds, the fire was moving northeast of Rush Street. We weren't concerned about the east flank of the fire because it would burn itself out when it reached the lake, but north, it was headed straight to the waterworks and the Chicago Water Tower. We had to stop it.

We went to Rush and Huron while the Titsworth, Little Giant, and the U. P. Harris went to Chicago and Pine. The other two engines stayed along the riverfront to watch for spot fires. A good plan in theory, but we just didn't have the equipment or manpower to pull it off. We would've had better luck throwing a handful of rocks in the air and them coming down as gold nuggets.

We hooked the hydrant at Huron and Rush Streets, and Joe took two sections of hose down the street and hooked them to a hydrant there. He was using the hydrant pressure to fight the fire. We fought it back for about an hour until we suddenly lost water pressure. Charlie yelled at us, "I just lost my water supply!"

Nicholas's worst-case scenario had happened. Losing the water pressure meant one thing: the three engines sent to stop the fire from reaching the waterworks near the tower had failed.

"Disconnect. We're retreating to the north branch!" Nicholas yelled.

As we threw the hose in the back of the wagon, the three engines came down Rush Street at full speed. Captain Musham of the Little Giant told

Nicholas the fire came at them like a hurricane, and they had to leave their hoses behind in order to survive. The Little Giant still had a hose connected to it and was being dragged down the street. That wasn't good. Not only did the city not have water, but we had three engines without a stitch of hose.

As we piled our hose into the wagon, Joe stopped and looked up at the sky. "Did you feel that?"

"What?" Wayne said.

Joe looked up for a few seconds and then finished throwing the hose in the back. We jumped on the wagon, and Charlie said, "Son of a bitch!"

I looked over my shoulder and saw a wall of flames to our southwest. A few blocks past that was another fire. Nicholas stood up in the steamer, shouting, "Let's go! Let's go!"

We had to get around the flames before they joined and cut us off. If we got trapped between fires without water, we'd be doomed. We all took off, heading west on Huron and met up with the other two engines, the Frank Sherman and the J.B. Rice, a couple of blocks down the road at Huron and Wolcott. I could not believe it, but the six engines, hose wagons, and carts in our group were half of what remained of the Chicago Fire Department. We had no idea where the other six engines were or even if they made it through the night.

Joe looked up at the sky again and said, "That!"

Wayne and I looked up, and water hit me in the face; it was sprinkling. Wayne glanced at me and smiled. "Son of a bitch." He looked up and closed his eyes as the cool droplets wafted across his face. It only lasted a couple of minutes, and then it stopped. The smoke had been so thick that none of us had noticed the clouds above it.

Every couple of blocks we rode west on Huron, the fire moved north a block. We were literally in a race for our lives. Joe eyeballed it to be at Illinois and Clark Street. You could literally see the flames sweeping north unimpeded. I was getting worried, wondering if we'd be able to get by it before it cut us off.

To cross the river, we had to make it to Chicago Avenue, which was two blocks north of us and then west a half mile. Two engines and a hose wagon slowed and turned north up Dearborn. Three more engines and hose carts turned up Clark Street. Wayne was yelling for Billy to turn, but he kept pace with the steamer. Hose Company 5 stayed right behind us. I could understand running into a fire but driving into one seemed a little crazy.

Obscured by the dense smoke, the flames seemed about five blocks south of us and coming fast. It was hard to tell how far west the fire extended, but I was sure Charlie thought we'd get around it and be in the clear. Unfortunately, that wasn't the case. We passed La Salle and then Wells, and the fire was right there. Finally, we slowed and turned up Franklin. The hundred-foot-high wall of flames was four blocks behind us and was moving our way fast. The wind was blowing embers past us, and one landed on Joe's back and smoldered. Before I said anything, Wayne slapped it off. Joe turned around and punched him. "What the hell you smack me for?"

"You were on fire, you jackass!" Wayne said.

As we neared Superior, a wagon full of children sat there in the road with a man and woman flagging us down. The woman was screaming for help and pointed up at a building on the right side of the street. It was a two-story building that had "Children's Home" written over the door. I looked up at the second-floor windows and counted six young children looking down at us and waving.

Nicholas yelled at the man and woman to get those kids to safety and that we'd get the ones upstairs. We jumped off the wagons as Nicholas told Charlie and Billy to pull the wagons into the alley on the north side of the building, that it would buy us some time and protect the horses from the heat and smoke. Then he looked at us. "Go get me some children!"

We ran up the stairs and searched the first couple of rooms but found no one. Smoke was coming through an open window in one room and filling the upstairs. I ran over and shut the window. As I looked out, I could feel the heat penetrating the window and saw that half the block south of us was in flames. It was moving quick, and I knew we had little time.

We found the six children in the last room down the hall. They were sitting between the beds, curled up with their arms wrapped around their knees, and crying. I stooped below the smoke and reached out to a little girl, about five years old, and said, "Come on, sweetie. I'm gonna get you out of here." She gave me her hand, and I pulled her into my arms then grabbed the child next to her. Joe and Wayne got the other four.

We ran them downstairs, and outside, we handed them to the other guys. David took the little girl and boy from me. As he walked away, the girl screamed over his shoulder and pointed upstairs. "My brudder! My brudder!"

I looked at Nicholas. "I'm gonna go find him. I can't just leave a child up there without trying."

Nicholas patted me on the back and said, "I know."

A bolt of lightning shot over our heads and was followed by a loud clap of thunder. Then it rained.

I grabbed my air pack from the wagon, and Joe and Wayne followed me to the door. I looked inside, and it was full of smoke. I told them to wait for me there. I knew at that point I was on my own and had to work fast. Without the waist strap, the tank was flimsy and rested awkwardly on my back. I had to hold one of the belt ends to stabilize it as I ran up the stairs. The smoke was thick, and I could see flames through the front windows and knew the fire was right outside, if not already in the building. As I ran up the stairs, I realized I had become just like them, running into danger, unafraid.

When I reached the top of the stairs, it was hotter than hell. The fire had breached the front two rooms to my left. I hurried down the hall and searched each room but found no one. I even checked under the beds and knew that, if anyone was up there, there's no way they could survive the smoke and heat.

I went out into the hall, and flames were coming out of the front three rooms and moving across the ceiling. That's the first law they should enact, put doors on all rooms. I dropped to my knees as the fire rolled over my head and across the ceiling. I knew it would only be a minute or two and the whole upstairs would flash; everything ignites at once. I made my way to the stairs and went down as fast as I could and tripped on the bottom step. I lifted my head and glanced over my shoulder and saw flames in all the rooms behind me. I looked up the stairs, and the entire top floor was engulfed, and flames were spreading over my head.

I turned and saw the light coming through the back door and crawled as fast as I could toward it. Just as I reached the door, everything flashed. I opened my eyes and refocused, then climbed through the door and collapsed on the porch. I felt Joe and Wayne grab me and carry me away from the building and lay me in the grass. As they pulled off my tank, I heard someone say, "It's cut. His damn waist strap is cut!"

ACT 50

As I rolled over, my whole body hurt so bad, I just wanted to die. I tried opening my eyes, but the room was so bright that I had to close them then slowly reopen them so they could adjust. Standing across the room with his back to me was a man in a white coat.

"Doc Martyn?" I said.

"You're awake," the man said and walked over to me. He was a round fella with gray hair and looked to be about sixty. "I'm Dr. Duncan. How are you feeling?"

I looked around, and on my right was a heart monitor and on my left an IV pole with a bag of saline hanging from it. The room was quiet and spotless. "I don't suppose I'm in 1871, am I?"

Duncan laughed. "No, you're in 302."

"What hospital?"

"Mercy Medical Center. Do you remember what happened?" he asked as he put his cold stethoscope against my chest. "Take a few deep breaths for me?" After that, he shined a light in my eyes and told me to follow it, then had me wiggle my toes and squeeze his hand.

"No. Why? what happened?"

"You and your partner were inside a house that was struck by lightning."

"Is that why I hurt so much?"

"More than likely. When that much electricity goes through your body it causes your muscles to violently contract. Soreness is a common complaint. Sometimes they can contract hard enough to break bones, you're one lucky guy." Duncan said. "Your mother went to get some coffee. She should be back soon."

"I shouldn't be here," I said.

"You'd be surprised how many people survive lightning strikes," Duncan said as he filled out his report.

"This isn't right. I was saving children in an orphanage, not in a house!"

Duncan smiled. "I'll be back around noon to check on you. Try and get some rest." On his way out the door, he almost bumped into my mother. He said something to her, and she looked in and saw I was awake. She rushed in and hugged me. I was happy to see her, and we both cried. Even though I was comfortable in her arms, I felt lost.

"How are you feeling?" She asked.

"I don't know, Mom. It's like I went somewhere and came back. It's like I don't belong here."

She looked puzzled, then there was a knock at the door and it opened. It was Mike and Don. "We heard you were awake," Mike said.

"You okay, bud?" Don asked.

"Sore as hell, but for the most part, yeah. What happened?"

"After the house got struck, I woke up near the living room wall. Dude, you were a badass and went after the fire. After the smoke lifted, you followed the hose right past me on your way out. Every time you yelled for me, I yelled back but it was like you couldn't see or hear me. I followed you, and you collapsed on the porch."

"You're mistaking," I said. "They never got the roof opened!"

Don jerked his head back. "What the hell are you talking about? They opened it up before they were ordered off the roof!"

"A funny thing," Mike said. "After we got you in the yard and rolled you over, your waist belt to your air-pack was cut. We've beat ourselves up trying to figure that one out."

I sat up and looked at Don. "Your grandfather was a firefighter during the Great Chicago Fire, right?"

"You know he was. Remember? He was a glorified window washer."

I looked at Mike. "That fire, it killed three thousand people, right?"

Mike raised his brows.

Don laughed. "Dude, I think your brain got fried. It was only three hundred."

I asked my mother for her phone and searched Google. I typed in "map of Chicago, 1871." It took a few seconds, then I hit on "map of Chicago, showing the burnt district." I looked at the map and then enlarged it.

"They did it!" I said. "They stopped the fire on the east side of the river. It never made it across the north branch."

Everyone looked at me like I was crazy. As I looked at the map, the fire had been stopped on the east side of Jefferson, just like I remembered. The Saturday night burn had stopped it from spreading north. It happened as Nicholas planned. I smiled as I thought about him and the crew. No one will ever know how many lives they saved that day. I looked at my mother and the guys. They were just staring at me.

"Don, I just want to apologize for calling your grandfather a window washer. In fact, they were the bravest firefighters that ever lived!"

"Shit! Now I know your brain got fried," Don said. "But thanks. That's pretty cool of you to say."

They stayed for about a half hour then left so I could get rest. As I thought about Lindsay and the crew, more tears rolled down my face. If it were only a dream, why did it seem so damn real?

The next morning, a nurse woke me and took my vitals. I looked at the clock, and it was seven o'clock. My head was pounding. I guess I had a morphine hangover.

"How are you doing?" she asked.

"Other than my head killing me, good."

"I'll see about getting you some Tylenol," she said. Then another lady walked in pushing a cart with breakfast. She uncovered my plate and put it on the table next to my bed. It had scrambled eggs, bacon, and toast. The portions were small, and all I could think about was Gladys's biscuits and gravy. While I ate, my mother came in and sat in the chair next to me.

They kept me another day and released me at noon. On the way home, my mother said she had gotten the job at the hospital and said her first day would be on October 16. I was happy for her, but I just sat there quietly and stared out the window, thinking about Lindsay.

"Are you feeling okay?"

I nodded. "I'm sorry I'm not very good company, but something incredible happened to me."

"What do you mean?"

"If I told you, you wouldn't believe me."

"Now why would you say that? You've never lied to me before."

I turned from the window. "Mom, everyone thinks I was hit by lightning three nights ago, but I wasn't. I've been in Chicago for the past two weeks."

"What?" she said and laughed. When she looked at me, her smile changed to concern. "No, dear, you've been in an induced coma since the night of the fire."

"What if I told you I was in Chicago and I helped fight the fire of 1871?"

She pulled the truck to the curb and stopped. She held my face and looked into my eyes. "Do we need to go back to the hospital?"

"No," I said as the tears worked their way from my eyes and rolled down my face. "Listen, I know this sounds crazy, but the day before the house got struck by lightning, I made fun of Don's grandfather from the 1870s and how they let Chicago burn. Before going to bed that night, I researched the fire and read stories all night. At that time, over three thousand people were killed and the whole city had burned. I looked at the map the other day, and only a portion of the city was destroyed. I was working with Engine Company 8, Nicholas DuBach was my captain, and there was Joe, Wayne, Dale, Billy, Daniel, and Charlie. But the best thing of all, I met a girl. Oh, Mom! You would have loved her. She's the most beautiful girl I have ever seen!"

My mother reached down and started the truck. "You know, you've been through a lot these past few days, and they had you on some pretty powerful medications. Sometimes when the body is in that deep of sleep, people sometimes have some unbelievable dreams that seem real. With you reading about that fire, I'm sure that's all it was, a vivid dream."

That made sense, but then I thought about something Mike had said. "If it had just been a dream, how did my waist strap get cut? Dale cut it in 1871 because they didn't understand how to unbuckle it!" Then I looked at my hand, and that's when my stomach flip-flopped. I had a fresh scar on it. "Mom, you gotta listen. I know it sounds farfetched but look at my hand. That happened when Joe and I became blood brothers!"

She glanced over at my hand then took a second look. "How did that happen?"

"I just told you. Joe and I cut our hands so we could be blood brothers."

She stared out the front window. Her face was blank. I could tell she was trying to make sense of it and knew that, if it would have happened within the last couple of weeks, she would have known about it. I think I may have just gotten her attention.

ACT 51

We pulled into the driveway, and my mother reached down and shut off the engine, then looked at me. "Okay, the hand has me stumped, but you have to realize what you're saying is impossible. It's like me saying I went back and helped invent this pickup. As far as the fire goes, it had always killed three hundred people. We learned about that when I was in grade school."

"You couldn't have known about three thousand people dying because it didn't happen. We changed history. Just think about it," I said as I surfed the phone. "Look! The Peshtigo fire in Wisconsin burned on the same day, October 8, 1871. It killed 2,500 people! Why isn't that remembered as the great fire if only three hundred died in Chicago? That's because in the rewriting of history, that part didn't get changed!"

My mother shook her head. "No, the reason they call Chicago the great fire is because of the damage it caused to the city. It wiped out over four miles of the business district."

"Come on, Mom. Think about it. If two ships sank on the same day, one was the size of the Titanic that killed five, and the other, a steamboat that killed 500, which would get the most coverage? Would it be the Titanic, because it was a larger ship and cost more? Or the steamboat where one hundred times more lives were lost?"

My mother just sat there and looked out the window in deep thought. "No, absolutely not! You pose a good argument, and I want to believe you, but no."

We went inside and I went straight to the computer. My mother walked to the kitchen. "Would you like some coffee?"

"Sure," I said. A few minutes later, she walked up behind me and massaged my shoulders. "So, tell me about this girl you met."

"Oh, Mom, she's the most beautiful girl I have ever seen. She's an actress at a theater called McVicker's, and she sings." I typed in "McVicker's theatre 1871" and then clicked on the Wikipedia link. It was right there, a picture of McVicker's with the Green Room sitting next door. "There! That's where she worked. See the place next door? It's a bar Joe and I went to a few times and had whiskey."

She just stood there and stared at the picture with a smile.

I continued searching the web then found a story about Nicholas. I sat back in the chair as my eyes watered. It said Nicholas died in 1901 from pneumonia. It showed a picture of his tombstone, and it was shaped like a tree with a fireman's hat on top. Underneath Nicholas's name was Frank's. Little Frank died in 1948 at seventy-five.

My mother looked over my shoulder and saw the article. "Who's that?"

"That's Nicholas, Nicholas DuBach. He was my captain, and he loved to train," I said and smiled. "If you weren't a man before you joined the company, you would be by the time he got done with you."

Then the tears began rolling as I thought of Joe and Wayne. The short time I was there, we really bonded. I continued reading the article, and it told how Nicholas fought the Great Fire and how brave he was. If they only knew, I thought. I searched for the other guys and couldn't find anything about Joe, but I got a hit on Dale Van Nornam. It said he died at fifty-six when his heart failed. He was survived by his wife, Dawn, and a son, Beau.

Another story I read was about the Chicago White Stockings. It said that in the 1870s, after the fire, the Stockings were nicknamed the Cubs by a writer for the Chicago Tribune. I smiled because Charlie was studying to become a writer. Then in the early 1900s, the Stockings were bought by a writer from Cincinnati, and he changed their name from the White Stockings to the Chicago Cubs, the new owner's name was Charlie. Nah, it couldn't be!

Then I found a story that said David Kenyon and a fireman name George Reid invented the first fire pole in 1878. I laughed. "Eat your heart out, Boston!"

As I read on, it said on October 3, 1884, while acting as battalion chief, David Kenyon was fatally injured while responding to a fire on Clark Street. His buggy collided with Engine 32. As I stared at his death certificate, my joy turned to tears.

My mom looked at me. "You're really serious about this?"

"Yes, Mom, I was there. I knew all these guys." I pulled up a map of Chicago. "See, look where the fire burnt. Right there on the corner of Jefferson and Van Buren was a beautiful house we blew up to stop the fire. We created a fire break by using black powder."

I kept searching the web and pulled up pictures of the fire, before and after. The Chicago Water Tower was one of only a handful of buildings that survived. I smiled as I remembered the night Lindsay and I carved our names on the wall. It was such a tall building, but looking at this picture, it seemed tiny compared to the buildings behind it.

My mom looked at the pictures, and I explained what they were. She smiled when I told her about the night Lindsay and I carved our names on the wall. I thought about Lindsay and wondered what she was doing. Then reality sank in. She's probably been dead for a hundred years, and I would never see her again. I had close to nine thousand dollars in the bank. I thought about the jar Lindsay and I buried and said, "That's it!"

"What?"

"We're off till the middle of October. Let's take a trip!"

"A trip . . . and go where?"

"To Chicago. That way, I can prove I'm telling the truth and that this wasn't just a dream."

She smiled and gave me a hug. "If it makes you feel better, I'm game!"

"Can I use the truck? I need to do something."

"Are you feeling okay to drive?"

"Yeah. I feel fine."

She tossed me the keys, and I went to the jeweler in town. It was a small shop, but he had everything you could imagine.

ACT 52

The next morning, we packed and left for Chicago. That night, we stayed at a casino in West Wendover, Nevada. After eating, we played the slots. I spent ten dollars and won nothing. My mother played five dollars and won a hundred. Go figure.

The next day, we traveled through Utah and into Wyoming. Talk about being in the middle of nowhere, rolling hills and dead grass as far as the eye could see. We stopped at a place called Little America in Wyoming and had ice cream cones. It was a large truck stop with a fancy motel.

I drove from there, and every so often, we saw herds of what looked like antelope. My mother searched the internet and discovered that they were pronghorn, the second fastest land animal on the planet. That night we stayed in Cheyenne.

The following night, we stayed in Clive, Iowa, a suburb of Des Moines. Before leaving for Chicago, we went across the street to a place called the Cracker Barrel to eat breakfast. We had seen their billboards advertising home-cooked meals, so we thought we'd give them a try.

After about fifty miles, my mother had to pee. I guess the coffee went right through her, so we stopped at a truck stop called Loves in Newton, Iowa. I couldn't believe that in the middle of nowhere, surrounded by miles of rolling hills and cornfields was a huge race track. It was the Iowa Speedway where NASCAR raced.

"I could live in a place like this. Nothing around except a race track!" I told my mother. She smiled.

About an hour later, we passed by the Iowa 80, the world's largest truck stop. My mother stared at it as we went by. I swear she must have a fascination with truck stops.

"We should have stopped," she said.

"Don't you feel uncomfortable around a bunch of truckers staring at you?"

"No. It makes me feel safe!"

"How does that make you feel safe?"

"With all those eyes on me, what could happen?"

She sure had an odd way of looking at things, but it made me laugh. A few miles later, we crossed the Mississippi River and were in Illinois. She was so excited; she took pictures of everything. That was the first time I'd seen her happy and having so much fun since my father died.

"So, what are we gonna do when we get there?" she asked.

"Well, while you were driving, I was looking on the web and found a hotel a few blocks from the water tower called the Sofitel. I made reservations on the twenty-ninth floor."

"No way! You want me to sleep on the twenty-ninth floor?"

"Unless you prefer the lobby?"

"Hahaha," she laughed. "You're funny."

When we got to Chicago, I was in shock. I recognized nothing. There were people everywhere, cars honking. It was noisy. When we got to the hotel, I thought my mom was going to pass out. She looked around the lobby with her mouth wide open. The lobby was unbelievable with couches and flowers all over. I felt like I did when Lindsay took me to the Crosby Opera House for dinner.

While I unpacked my clothes, my mom stood at the window and took pictures of the city below. She was mesmerized. I lay on my bed, and the mattress swallowed me. I felt my whole-body melt. I lay there thinking of what tomorrow had in store for me. The first thing I wanted to do was take my mother to the water tower and show her where I wrote our names on the wall, then she would have no other choice but to believe me. After that, we could go to Lincoln Park and then the zoo.

The next morning, we stopped at the front desk on our way out. I asked the lady for directions to the Chicago Water Tower. She gave me a map with different points of interest on it and said the tower was located at Michigan and Chicago streets.

"Are there two water towers? Because the one I'm looking for is at Chicago and Pine Street," I said.

She laughed. "No, we only have one. It was at Pine and Chicago streets over a hundred years ago, but after the fire, they changed Pine Street to Michigan. You've heard of the fire they had back in the 1800s, haven't you?"

I looked at my mom and smiled.

We drove to Michigan and Chicago, and sure enough, the old water tower was still there. As we walked around it, I told my mother everything that happened that night, and how much in love we were. We walked around to the back, and I was getting excited, as I picked up my pace and told her how I'd carved our names in the limestone while Lindsay kept watch.

When we turned the corner, I said, "Right here!" and pointed to the spot, but our names weren't there. My heart skipped a beat as I looked around for our names, but I couldn't find them. I could only imagine what my mom was thinking.

"It's been over a hundred years. I really didn't expect that they would still be there. After all, a hundred years of weather and the fact they probably clean it every so often," I said, trying to explain the reasons they weren't there. I didn't know if it was an effort to keep my hopes alive, or to keep from looking like a total fool.

We left and drove around the city. I was trying to get my bearings, but everything was different and unrecognizable. I pulled over to the curb and asked some folks on the sidewalk if they knew where Lincoln Park was. The man and woman just looked at me, and he said something in a different language. I guess they were tourists too.

My mom sat there quietly for a few minutes and then said, "Go north on Michigan, and it'll run us into North Lake Shore Drive then west on Fullerton. Phone GPS, a great invention!"

I looked around and couldn't believe how different everything was. I was doubting that I was ever there but remembered what my grandfather said. "If my father saw how things have changed over the years, he'd roll over in his grave." That helped cheer me.

We made it to the zoo, and trust me, if I were dead, I'd be rolling over. The place was enormous and full of animals, everything you'd see in a zoo, from polar bears to giraffes, unlike the zoo I remembered. The trees were tall and plush; everything was green and groomed. That was the paradise Pastor Starcevic spoke of at my wedding.

After we left there, we found the location of Engine Company 8. It was still in the same spot, but the area was so different. They had changed Twenty-Second Street to Cermak Road. As I looked around, I wanted to cry. How could they do that to a city I loved so much?

We had somewhat of a fun day in Chicago. Well, I know my mother did, but my being there in the 1870s was becoming like my mother said, just a vivid dream. I knew my mom was trying everything she could to support me, but I knew she just wanted me to figure it out on my own.

"Well," I said and took a deep breath. "I have one last chance to prove that my dream was not a dream."

"I'm hungry. How about we get a hot dog first?" she asked, as she stared at a man on the corner selling hot dogs from one of those pushcarts. We got out of the pickup and walked over there. I had pickles, tomatoes, and mayo on mine. It was probably the best hot dog I'd ever eaten.

"So, what's this last-ditch plan of yours?"

"Well, before the fire, I wrote you a letter and put it in a glass jar and then buried the jar in a wood box. I put four horseshoes on the box, so it could be found with a metal detector."

"So that's why you brought a shovel and metal detector?"

"Yep!"

"So… where did you bury it?"

"Straight down Twelfth Street, at the lake."

"This is getting fun," she said. "It's like were going on a treasure hunt."

I glanced at her and smiled. I looked at the map on my phone but couldn't find Twelfth Street. I Googled the map of 1871 and figured out that Twelfth was now called Roosevelt, and it went straight to a park along the lakefront. "That's gotta be it!" I said.

We headed that way and found a parking lot at a yacht club. I looked around, trying to see something familiar, but nothing was the same. The row of trees we passed through to get to the lake were gone; the sandy beach was, since then, green grass, and there were walking and bike trails along the shoreline. North of the club, the land curved, forming a cove. It wasn't like I remembered, but there were several trees over there. Most were medium in size, which meant they weren't that old, but in the middle were two huge trees. That's when I got the sensation I've been there before.

"Come on," I said as I quickly walked that way. Since I'd gotten that excitement back, I walked so fast I was almost running. I stood between the trees and looked around, then smiled at my mother. "This is it!" I said. I felt it in my gut.

The sun was setting behind the buildings, casting us in its shadows. I took my detector out and scanned the area with the wand but didn't hear anything. I turned up the sensitivity and tried again. That time I heard a beep. I kept scanning the area and heard another a few inches away. "That's odd. Something the size of a horseshoe should be sending my needle to the moon, especially four of them," I said. Am I in the right place, or ain't I?

I looked around. The only other place that remotely looked like the spot, the trees were too close to the lake. I sat down to think.

"What do you think?" my mom said as she sat down beside me.

I shook my head, mostly out of frustration. "I don't know, Mom."

ACT 53

I sat there for a minute, thinking when I had a weird sensation of something brushing against me. When I turned, I didn't see anything but got a whiff of roses, the same scent Lindsay wore. It was only there for a second, but it made my skin crawl. "Did you smell that?"

"Smell what?"

"Nothing," I said, looking around. After I unfolded my camping shovel, I rescanned the area and dug over the spot where I heard the beep. While I dug, my mother kept an eye out for people. I felt like I was making a criminal out of her. After digging about a foot, I hit something hard and reached down to uncover it with my hand. It looked like a curved stick but rusted. I ran it under the wand, and it was metal.

"Well, it looks like it could have been a horseshoe," my mother said and then laughed.

I glanced at her. She just didn't understand how much that meant to me. As I rescanned the area, the detector beeped two more times. Each beep was a few inches apart. In each area, we uncovered more rusted metal, and when we put them together, they formed somewhat of a horseshoe.

My heart was thumping. "This is it! It has to be!" I said as I dug faster, trying to get to the box below. After digging about three feet and making a mess, I found nothing. I scanned the hole but got no other hits. "I don't understand. Why would only one horseshoe be there and not the box?"

"Honey, maybe it isn't a horseshoe. Maybe it's debris they covered when making the park," she said as she hugged me.

I sat there as my hopes faded, and I cried. I wanted so much for this to be real, but I think I was finally proving to myself that it wasn't.

The next morning, we packed. As we got in the pickup, I said, "You know, since all this turned out to be nothing more than a dream, there is one thing I can do."

"What's that, dear?"

"I'd like to stop at Saint Boniface Cemetery. That's where Nicholas is buried. Before leaving home, I went to the jeweler and had something made for him. I'd like to pay him respect."

We left the hotel and went to the Saint Boniface. It was a beautiful Catholic cemetery at the corner of North Clark and Lawrence. We walked around, and after a few minutes, I saw the tombstone with a fire helmet on it. When I got to it, I got down on my knees in front of it. I had tears rolling down my face, thinking that, only a few days ago, he was alive and energetic.

"Even though it's turning out to be a dream, you were one hell of a captain, and I'll admire you for the rest of my life," I told Nicholas. "And Frank, I never really got to know you. You were just a newborn and had a loud cry."

I brought two twelve-inch flags and crisscrossed them in front of the tombstone. I opened the box I brought and pulled out a ribbon. It was red, white, and blue and had a Maltese Cross medallion on it. It read, "To an unknown hero that the fine folks of Chicago will be forever indebted to." I stood on my tiptoes and reached up to hang it on the helmet when a man asked, "Can I help you?"

I turned, and there stood a gray-haired man and one walking up, holding flowers. The man in front of me looked to be in his fifties and was wearing a sweatshirt that read, "Don't let the gray hair fool you, we can still kick ass." He was a Coast Guard veteran, and if I weren't so startled, I would have laughed.

"I was just putting this on Nicholas's helmet," I said.

"And you are?" he asked

I had to think quick and said, "My great-great-great-grandfather was a member of Engine Company 8 and fought the great fire with Nicholas. I was just paying respects to the men who served with him."

"I'm Chris DuBach. Nicholas was my third great-grandfather, and this is my son, Nicholas," he said as his son walked up.

I looked and almost swallowed my gum. He was the spitting image of Nicholas, down to the dark hair, lazy eyes, and scruffy beard. I shook their hands and couldn't take my eyes off Nicholas.

"What was your grandfather's name?" Chris asked.

"Kirk. John Kirk."

Chris rubbed his chin for a few seconds and said, "Yes, I think I recall hearing that name. Well, it's been a pleasure meeting you. What did you say your name was?"

"John Kirk. I was also named after my grandfather." I shook their hands again, and Nicholas laid flowers at the base of the tombstone behind the flags.

My mother and I walked back to the truck. It made me feel good inside, as if Nicholas was living on through his grandson. That made me happy.

After we got home, I was pretty much bummed out at not finding anything. As I lay on the couch, watching cartoons, something popped into my head. If I hadn't gone back to 1871, then how was it that David Kenyon and George Reid invented the first fire pole and not Boston? Or was I dreaming that too? But Mike told me that before the accident. It just didn't make sense. My mind was going in all directions. Maybe I was going crazy.

A short time later, I was awakened by a knock at the door. My mother was in the kitchen, talking on the phone.

"I'll get it," she said as she walked to the door. She told the person on the phone that she'd call them back before opening the door. She stood there talking for a minute and then told me to get up, that we had company.

I stood up while she let them in. It was four elderly people: two men and two women. The two that walked in first were old, I mean really old. The other man and woman looked to be in their sixties. The younger man carried in a cardboard box and set it on the table. It had "F. W. Woolworth Company" printed on it.

"Would you like some coffee or tea?" my mom asked.

"Why yes. It's been a long journey. If you don't mind, I'll have tea," the eldest woman said with a shaky voice. I got up, so they could sit, but the older lady just stood there with her eyes fixed on me so much, it was making me feel awkward. My mother noticed it also and stopped on her way to the kitchen.

The lady walked toward me; her eyes trained on me the whole time. The people that came with her watched intently as she lifted her wrinkled hands and held my face. She stared directly into my eyes, and then she gasped for a breath. "Oh my God, it is you!"

I looked at her shaky hands on my face and said, "Okay. Now that we know it's me, who might you be?"

"I'm Sissy, your great-great-granddaughter, and this is my brother, Tim," she said as tears rolled out of her eyes, and she pointed at the older man.

"Huh?" I said and looked over at my mother. Talk about being stumped. "What do you mean you're my great-great-granddaughter?" I asked and chuckled.

"It's true! John Junior is my grandfather. His mother's name was Lindsay, and you were Lindsay's husband," Sissy said.

I didn't know what to say or how to react. My mother stood in the doorway of the kitchen with her hand over her mouth.

"We brought you something you've been searching for," Tim said and put his hand on the box. It was old, and the creases in the flaps were worn and taped. It looked like it had been sitting somewhere for a long time. "Go ahead. Open it."

ACT 54

I looked at Tim, then slowly pulled the tape off. It had been on it for so long, that part of the box stuck to it. As soon as I saw what was inside, I immediately cried. My mother rushed over and put her arm around me. "What is it?"

I looked at her. "It's the box Lindsay and I buried 147 years ago on the beach, the one hidden with the horseshoes."

Her mouth dropped open as she watched me lift the wooden box out and set it on the table. Other than a few rotted spots, it was still intact. The nails in the box top had rusted, and when I tried, the top lifted right off. Before looking in, I glanced back at my mother and then at Sissy and Tim. They waited impatiently for me to open it. As I looked in, I trembled. I couldn't believe I was staring at a dirty glass jar; the same jar we had placed there in 1871.

I lifted it out and tried wiping the dirt off, but it was stained. Inside, I could tell there was what appeared to be the letter. I tried twisting the lid, but it was rusted in place and wouldn't turn. I grabbed the brush off the table and hit the lid with the handle, and the lid shattered like an eggshell.

I reached in, and that's when I noticed that there wasn't just one letter but two. "That's funny," I said. "We only put one in the jar." I reached in and pulled out the second one. My mother was so excited as she opened the first letter then read it aloud:

"'Mom, I wanted to write you this letter in hopes that someday it will find its way to you. By now, you are probably wondering what has happened to me. I don't know how this is possible, but somehow, while fighting that fire in Pine Valley, something unexplainable happened. I have ended up in Chicago during 1871. I am fine, and I have met the queen of my dreams. You know, the one you had always insisted on me finding. Her name is Lindsay, and she is the most beautiful girl I have ever seen, and by the way, did I say that we were married? I wish there were a way I could talk to you, but I just want you to know that I am happy, and I will always love you. Your son, John Kirk.'"

She gazed at me with tears in her eyes as she opened the envelope wider. The twenty-dollar bill I had put in there fell out. I put it there, hoping someone would accept it as payment to deliver the letter or have it sent to my address. I stared at the second letter. It was somewhat thicker and addressed to Kathy Kirk. I handed it to my mother and she smiled. She opened it and pulled out two newspaper clippings. Her eyes got big. "How can this be?"

After staring at the clippings for a minute, she handed them to me. I smiled. The first clipping was our wedding in Lincoln Park. The second was the crew and me standing in front of the firehouse, the day after the Burlington Fire.

I watched my mother as she unfolded the second letter. A picture fell out and landed in her lap. She picked it up, and we both looked at it. It was a picture of Lindsay holding a small child. The feeling I had was indescribable. I felt proud, excited, and sad at the same time. I cried, my mother cried, and it sounds funny, but my grandchildren three times my age cried. Then my mother read the second letter.

"Dearest Kathy Kirk, I don't know you, but from what John has told me, I feel I do in my heart. I pray that this letter finds you along with John's, so you can be assured that John was happy. However, I am sad to inform you that John perished in the fire of October 8, 1871, here in Chicago. John and his company fought the fire bravely, but in the aftermath, they were unable to find him. Although we were married for only a short time, I had the blessing of birthing his child on June 4, 1872. I know it was John's birthday also, and I named our child John Jr. He is truly our miracle child, and he looks so much like his father, I know you would be proud. With all my love, Lindsay Kirk."

I couldn't stop crying and asked, "How did you find this, and why did you come here today?"

"It was September 24, 1930, when we all gathered on the farmhouse porch, and you and Grandmama told us your story. You told us about the glass jar and said where we could find it. In 1945, us kids got together and drove from Newton to Chicago and retrieved it. It was exactly where you said it would be, between the two trees on the north side of the cove."

I looked at my mother and asked, "Newton, as in Newton, Iowa?"

"Yes," Tim said. "In 1901, after retiring from the Chicago Fire Department, you and Great-grandma moved the family to Newton and bought land, lots of it. You and our grandfathers built a large farmhouse, and we grew lots of corn. That day on the porch before you passed away, the one promise you made all of us make was to never to leave or sell the property. That someday, it would be worth a lot of money."

"I died?"

Tim smiled. "Yes, Grandpapa. That's something that eventually happens to all of us."

"We always thought you were talking about the corn," Sissy said. "But in 1957, the government bought a piece of land so they could build a freeway. We didn't have much choice, but after they were finished, it sure made it a lot easier to get to Des Moines."

"In the early part of 2000, we were approached by land developers who wanted to buy another large section of the property and offered more money than we could ever spend. We knew this is what you were talking about. Not too long after that, they built a race track, a truck stop, and several motels there. Imagine that, wanting to build all that in the middle of nowhere," Tim said.

I looked at my mom, and we both laughed. We didn't know what to think. "So, let me get this straight. You're saying I was in Chicago after the fire?"

"Yes," the elderly man behind Tim said.

"And who are you?" my mother asked.

"I'm Joe, grandson to your son Ringo—"

"I have a son named Ringo?"

"Yes, he was born in 1891. You named your boys John Jr., George, Paul, and Ringo," Sissy said. "It wasn't until the 1960s that we found out why. You named your boys after the Beatles."

My mom laughed and squeezed my shoulders. "That was John's father's favorite group. He played their music all the time, and after he died, John would play Beatles songs because it made him feel closer to his father."

"But as far as your question goes, yes, you returned to Chicago," Tim said. "When you came back to 2018 the first time, you found the jar with the letter from Lindsay. After reading that you had a son, you stopped at nothing to find a way to get back to Lindsay and John. You put two and two together and figured it had to be the lightning. Five and a half years later, you discovered a way to harness electricity and returned to Chicago."

"You're saying I returned to Chicago and lived my life out with Lindsay, and you had this box since the 1940s?"

"That's exactly what we're saying," Joe said.

"Then why didn't you bring the box to me a month ago or even a year ago?"

"It's not quite that simple. This is a time-sensitive issue. We couldn't have brought it to you before your accident or the first time you returned."

"Why not?"

"Because we didn't exist," Tim said.

"Huh?"

"You see, for us to have been born depended on you returning the first time. I know this is complicated, but only after you returned the first time and reunited with Lindsay were our grandfathers born. Otherwise, you would have had only one child, John!" Tim explained.

"If we would have brought you the box two weeks ago, it would have been before the accident, and you wouldn't have known anything about it. You would have just laughed us right off your property," Sissy said.

"So why are you here now?" I asked.

"When you started telling us your story, you said you had lived a life without regret, and if you had to do it all over again, you wouldn't change a thing," Sissy said. "But by the time you finished, you were crying. After a tear landed on my face, I looked up at you and asked what was wrong. You looked down at me and said, 'There is one regret that I do have, and that's that my mother never got to meet her grandchildren.'"

Joe walked up and put his hand on my shoulder. "Over the last forty years, me and three other grandchildren have received degrees in physics and quantum theory from the finest universities in the country, all in preparation for this day. With the information you provided in 1930, we have designed a house that we believe will get you back to 1871."

"I'm going back?" I asked and smiled at my mother. I was ecstatic. "Mom, you know I have to go. I don't belong here. This isn't my time." I looked at my grandkids. "I'm going back?"

"Yes," Sissy said as she hugged me. "Your journey continues, Grandpapa. And this time, you can live your life out without regret because we're taking Grandmama back to Newton, so she can be with all her grandkids."

I looked at my mother as her face lit up and tears rolled down her cheeks. I don't think I've ever seen her so excited.

"There's one thing we want you to always remember, grandpapa. On September 16, 1930, you went to the general store for a newspaper. While you were there, a man walked in, a young fella. But you have to remember this because the man was infected with pneumonia."

Acknowledgements:

Based on true events obtained from the book:

"History of Chicago" by A.T. Andrews

Special thanks to:

The DuBach family.

The Chicago Historical Society for their valuable information and direction.

Shasta Lake Fire Protection District, Shasta Lake, California.

Chicago Fire Department.

References:

Andrews, A.T. History of Chicago, from the Earliest Period to the Present Time. (Chicago: The A.T. Andreas Company, 1886).

"Chicago streetcars," Chicago Tribune, December 13, 2013, http://galleries.apps.chicagotribune.com/chi-131212-history-chicago-streetcars-trolleys-transportation-pictures/.

Frederick Francis Cook, "A Bird's-Eye View of Pre-Fire Chicago," Bygone Days of Chicago, The Great Chicago Fire & the Web of Memory, Chicago Historical Society, 2011, https://www.greatchicagofire.org/birds-eye-view-of-pre-fire-chicago/.

Forgotten Chicago Forum, June 11-August 14, 2014, https://forgottenchicago.com/forum/read.php?1,13249.

Grossman, James R., Ann Durkin Keating, and Janice L. Reiff. The Encyclopedia of Chicago (Chicago: The University of Chicago Press, 2004).

"Heyday of the Horse," American Museum of Natural History, https://www.amnh.org/exhibitions/horse/how-we-shaped-horses-how-horses-shaped-us/work/heyday-of-the-horse/.

Tomas Nonnenmacher, "History of the U.S. Telegraph Industry," EH.net, Economic History Services, https://eh.net/encyclopedia/history-of-the-u-s-telegraph-industry/.

"Railroad Maps: 1828 to 1900," Library of Congress, Congress.gov, Unites States Copyright Office. https://www.loc.gov/collections/railroad-maps-1828-to-1900/?fa=contributor%3Achicago%2C+burlington+%26+quincy+railroad+company&dates=1870-1879.

Steve Tarter, "Extra: Peoria earned its reputation as U.S. whiskey capital between 1837 and 1919," Journal Star, August 25, 2015, http://www.pjstar.com/article/20150825/lifestyle/150829711?template=ampart.

"Theaters of Chicago," Chicagology, https://chicagology.com/theatres/.

Louise Carroll Wade, "Meatpacking," The Electronic Encyclopedia of Chicago, Chicago Historical Society, 2005, http://www.encyclopedia.chicagohistory.org/pages/804.html.

"Western Slang, Lingo, and Phrases—A Writer's Guide to the Old West." Legends of America. https://www.legendsofamerica.com/about-us/.

Contact Information:

By Mail: James E. Merl
PO Box 1302
Chewelah, WA 99109

By Email: jmerl.books@gmail.com
Jmerl53@gmail.com

Follow on Facebook: www.facebook.com/jamesemerl

Currently in the works

For future updates follow us on Facebook @jamesemerl

Made in the USA
Monee, IL
09 January 2020

20119470R00182